By Virtue of Fire
a sequel

Dana Lynne Pitely

HIGH ARCH BOOKS

Publisher's Note:

This is a work of fiction. Names, characters, places and incidents are either the product of the author's imagination or are used factiously, and any resemblance to actual persons, living or dead, business establishments, events, or locales is entirely coincidental or completely and totally on purpose.

Cover by the wonderful and talented Amy Fedele.

ISBN-13: 978-0615849119

DEDICATION

To God and for Abdul.

ACKNOWLEDGMENTS

With boundless thanks to:
God; My parents and family for their support and
encouragement throughout my life; Aesop, Aristotle, Erikson
and Abdul for their contributions to my story; Shabana Kayum,
my patient editor, who helped me find Rose's true calling while
scuttling through my unremitting misuse of the word irony;
Deanna, the hardest working news reporter; Elizabeth Griffis for
her daily supportive emails; Michael Steven Fuchs who
informed me that the best way to sell book one is to write book
two, preferably with zombies; Ryan Joseph's penchant for a
name's meaning; and lastly, and perhaps most importantly, the
slumber of Yellowstone.

Preface

The Belling of the Cat

LONG AGO, the mice had a general council to consider what measures they could take to outwit their common enemy, the Cat. Some said this, and some said that; but at last a young mouse got up and said he had a proposal to make, which he thought would meet the case. "You will all agree," said he, "that our chief danger consists in the sly and treacherous manner in which the enemy approaches us. Now, if we could receive some signal of her approach, we could easily escape from her. I venture, therefore, to propose that a small bell be procured, and attached by a ribbon round the neck of the Cat. By this means we should always know when she was about, and could easily retire while she was in the neighborhood."

This proposal met with general applause, until an old mouse got up and said: "That is all very well, but who is to bell the Cat?" –Aesop

7

火山 1 火山

My thunder comes before the lightning,
My lightning comes before the clouds,
My rain dries all the land it touches,
What am I?

"Man, I don't care what those guys up at YVO are saying, there is definitely something wrong. The hairs on the back of my neck are standing up," Horse says driving down Beartooth Highway. "Can't you feel that?"

"Feel what? It's five fifteen in the morning. You're lucky I can sit up. What's it you want me to be feeling?" Benjamin asks. The Californian lifts his Tully's morning blend to his lips before addressing his brawny Native American colleague. "Dude, those guys are the experts; it's the Yellowstone Volcano Observatory for Christ's sakes. If they don't know, then who does? Stop listening to those Doomsdayers. People are just overreacting."

With perfect posture and his strong, muscular hands at ten and two, the twenty-seven year old shoots a combative scowl to his right. "Overreacting? You have to admit that the predictions and the advanced warnings have been off as of late, like completely off. The Medicine Lake volcano went without any warning, and that was after Lassen Peak. Two volcanos within a hundred and fifty mile radius of each other went without any warning." He finishes his proclamation knowing that it very likely fell on deaf ears. He internally reminds himself that it *is* very early and his friend was probably out *very* late. It does not take a Sioux to smell the yeast still emanating from his pores. "What time did you get in, last night?"

"I didn't close the place down, if that's what you're asking. Dude, you're always so heavy, you really need to learn how to chill. Yeah, sure there are volcanoes and earthquakes and stuff, but things happen for a reason. Or do I need to remind you that if it weren't for Lassen Peak, you wouldn't have met Cheyenne." Benjamin leans slightly forward to get a better look at his friend's face that always seems to lighten at even the slightest mention of Cheyenne. He mockingly slaps his friend's shoulder as soon as the expected expression appears. "Besides, these volcanoes, Lassen Peak and Medicine Lake, they are small potatoes roasted over a camp fire compared to Yellowstone. And they're like five hundred miles away from here."

"Still – a little too close for comfort, considering," Horse says looking out over the hood at the road ahead. "Wait? Small potatoes? Lassen Peak and Medicine Lake? Really?" Horse smirks at his blonde, gel-maned coworker before huffing a weighted, "Dude. That's so uncool."

Benjamin drums on the dashboard, over the glove box. "There is nothing else to say. It happened. It happens. Volcanos, earthquakes, forest fires – stuff happens. And because of Lassen Peak – you got Cheyenne. It's nature, Man."

Horse hears and agrees with his co-captain, but remains insistent. "This is different and you know it. These volcanoes and earthquakes, they are more… prevalent."

"Mother nature is fickle," Benjamin says. "She likes to stir things up every millennium." He sips his coffee and looks out the passenger window at the dense forestry.

"Sorry, Man, you really can't feel that?" Horse repeats his earlier sentiment.

"Again, what am I supposed to be feeling, Kemosabe?" Benjamin replies touching his slightly scruffy face.

"The electricity?" Horse replies as he looks out and up through the windshield of the Range Rover to remind himself of the peculiar presence of the Northern Lights. "If the Northern Lights are here, then something is off. I swear the air feels charged. I wonder if this is due to them." Horse nudges the top

10

of his head up in an effort to give a more mystic edge to his argument.

"Must be that Apache blood," Benjamin says.

"Cally, for the last time, I am not Apache." Horse looks down through his steering wheel to verify his speed.

"Chill. You are totally Apache and totally freakin' out 'bout nothing," the Californian asserts. "We have the best warning system in the world. If something was really happening, we would know all about it. Maybe it's Cheyenne. She's got you feeling all native and stuff – sexually-charged, heightened, animal. It's about time you had a woman in your life."

"Yeah, maybe," Horse says trying to find the meeting ground. He hears Benjamin and believes that his friend is actually making an effort to calm him. He recognizes that he *is* behaving uncharacteristically high-strung and probably needs to be brought down to a more earthy level, and talking about Cheyenne might be the absolutely right way to do it.

Horse straightaway recollects his first picture-perfect moment with Cheyenne – the feel of the air, the smell of the wilderness, and the colors of the ground. He remembers how the two of them were simultaneously captivated by the same bright red cardinal nesting in a very old evergreen. Horse determined that their eternal souls must have gravitated in that moment because, at once, they were both reaching for the other's hand. It was only minutes later when they were told that Medicine Lake had erupted.

"Last night, while talking with her, I was watching the birds flying in their standard V and then a group broke off at a thirty degree angle and it was… you know, odd." Horse scratches at the all too sensitive hairs on the back of his neck. "Seriously, Man, you really can't feel that? And the Northern Lights… The whole thing just doesn't make sense."

"No," Benjamin simply says. He shifts in his seat to face Horse. "Actually, I think I can provide an explanation and prove

11

that it almost does make sense. There was a major solar flare reported a few days ago. I heard that solar flares can impact the Northern Lights and bring them more south, you know, like lighting up the magnetic field. The magnetic field isn't shifting, it is just appearing bigger. The ends are highlighted." Benjamin returns his attentions to the sky and its still present light show. "You know what I think – I think they look like pipe organs."

Horse takes a moment to process this. He really admires and respects his friend's conversational science. Benjamin is a very good environmental scientist; he never lets his facts inundate his understanding. Horse adds to the conversation, "Haven't you ever noticed that there also tends to be earthquakes a few days after solar flares? And, are you sure the solar flares weren't magnetic storms?"

"Actually, no. Is there a difference?" Benjamin laughs knowing that the question would drive his friend mad. "Chill out, man. We're in Yellowstone; it's a scientific Mecca here. We have universities, NASA, USGS, seismologists, volcanologists, genius geologists, like us, all watching… just chill."

"I guess you're right. We're park rangers at the greatest national park in the world," Horse acquiesces. He tries to hide his concern as he turns on the car stereo in an effort to find the mundane in the moment. "It's Tuesday, right? Isn't there a twofer Tuesday on ninety-two point nine?"

Benjamin takes control over the car stereo. "Strange. Dude, what's wrong with your radio?"

"What the Fuh…?" Horse slams on his brakes and commandingly steers around a stampede of pronghorn leaping across the road five miles away from their destination, Tower Roosevelt station. The screeching truck comes to a complete stop before the pair start to feel the vibrations.

"You were saying…" Horse says crossly.

12

"Dude, it's just an earthquake. Calm down," Benjamin says authoritatively. "Par for the course around here although that one was a bit high – twenty says it was a five point two."

"You're on. It was a six point oh, easy," Horse says with an affected calm tone.

"Price Is Right rules?"

"Ruff. Ruff. Bark. Bark." Horse takes a deep breath and just stares at the road. He hesitates only slightly before putting his foot back on the gas pedal. "Something has those pronghorn spooked. A five point two wouldn't do it. Check the information channel."

Benjamin toggles for AM and quickly locates 1600. "Dude, it's just static. I suppose it could be magnetic storms," he says thinking aloud. "Maybe you are right about the air being charged..."

Horse presses more firmly on the gas. "We gotta get."

Three hundred feet ahead of the Range Rover, Horse recognizes the wave movements of an earthquake displacing and warping the road, sending chunks of blacktop into the air as the pressure and force attack the asphalt. The peak amplitude of the waves carry the Range Rover toward the shoulder of the road.

"Hang Ten, Dude," Benjamin jives.

Horse is able to maintain control of the vehicle, yet again, but begins to doubt the safety of staying the course. "So, Cally, genius geologist, should we ride it out or hoof it?"

"Now that was a six point oh," Benjamin says. "Couple more Richter points and we'd be surfing pipe."

"Six point oh? That was a six point eight. It totally carried us. Call in," Horse orders.

"No service. Drive," Benjamin says finally starting to pick up the concern emanating from his friend. His mind begins to reel as he starts to pay closer attention to the busted asphalt in front of the truck's cabin. "These kinds of waves can take down radio towers, can't they? Do you think that maybe..."

"Hang on," Horse says. He guns the engine up over the small embankment and back onto the road. They reach Tower station before the next quake hits, a 5.8, an aftershock. Although the shock waves are still visible on the road, the snow and mud of the season lessen the appearance by aesthetically widening the landscape. Various percussions of rocks, trees and ground can be heard over the static of the radio. Horse parks the vehicle and turns off the engine. "Are you ready?"

A complete split, from base to tip, of a nearby evergreen sends a very loud ripping and popping sound that impacts the ear drum of the Californian. "What the hell was that? Dude, something is seriously off!" Benjamin starts to transition from anxious concern to total panic.

"So the coffee finally reached you? 'Bout Time. We need to check in."

Benjamin moves his left arm to prevent his friend from exiting the vehicle. He accidentally spills hot coffee down his chest, staining his khaki uniform. "Dammit." Without stopping to look at the stain, or consider the pain of burn, he muscularly maintains his hold of Horse. "Listen Dude, I ain't climbing those stairs. We're gonna stay in this car and get out of here."

"California!" Horse breaks his hold and puts a firm hand on his friend's shoulder. "We are trained for this. We're just going to ride these waves. Come on now. Man up. There are a few answers up those stairs and we are going to get them."

"Sorry. Momentary loss of..." Benjamin finds his focus and lets out a laugh. "I'm cool. Burnt, but cool. Damn that coffee was hot."

"So, you're cool? Good, 'cause this, this is much hotter than that coffee," Horse says smirking. "Let's go."

The two park rangers step out of their vehicle and immediately head toward their post. Using their ranger training both independently begin to absorb the reality of their surroundings. They subconsciously begin constructing strategies

14

for their survival. Within two steps from the vehicle, they immediately notice the strong smell of sulfur and something else, something less normal in the air.

"That smell, its burning my throat," says Benjamin.

"There are gas masks in the vehicle, right?" Horse asks with a stern look to his colleague. "That's HCl. Something is definitely up with the volcano. Sulfur dioxide, hydrogen sulfide and hydrogen chloride – they are all telltale signs." Horse immediately retrieves the masks from the back and throws one to Benjamin. Gripping the mask in his right fist, Horse takes the lead and runs up the stairs to the station. He quickly scans the overlook at the landing before flinging open the door to the Tower Roosevelt Station. He looks across the room to the sophisticated computer systems nestled in a rustic setting to find his boss, Lisa. "What the hell is going on?"

"I thought you guys were never going to get here," Lisa exclaims running a heavy hand through her short, wavy hair. She quickly checks the three monitors and enters in new data into the database before turning and responding to Horse. "It's the cauldron. We have recorded ground deformation of seven inches last night alone. Its lake has risen three inches in the past four decades, and seven in the past ten hours. We have received immediate orders for evacuation. The national guard has been called in and should be arriving any minute." She delivers these harsh facts in a breathless voice.

"How are we just learning about this now?" Horse asks.

"We thought the instrumentation was being tampered with and we called Homeland Security to check it out. You know, you remember, the numbers just didn't make sense," Lisa says while shaking her head. "By not trusting our instrumentation, we lost hours, days, weeks, perhaps months, especially if you take into account those strange readings we got last July. I just can't stop thinking about those damned readings. Maybe if we…"

15

"What the hell, how could they not see *this* coming?" Horse asks again.

"We have no historical record of a cauldron eruption. The last time this cauldron erupted was over sixty thousand years ago. We could only predict her behavior based upon other models. I guess that we were wrong in estimating her depth, her reach and her source. Old Faithful… Old Faithful has been silent for the past seven hours. Absolutely silent." Lisa stops to look between her two colleagues. Zipping up her fire retardant coveralls, she says, "This is it guys. We got to get people out of this park. NOW."

The two men follow Lisa's lead and retrieve their coveralls.

"This is crazy," says Benjamin.

The outpost shakes and both Lisa and Benjamin fall to the floor. Horse is able to maintain balance using the beam running down the center of the outpost.

"Pretty violent earthquake swarms. They started about three hours ago, small ones, normal ones. They seem to be running about every fifteen minutes and getting progressively stronger. The last two recorded were six point one and a seven point oh."

"That's twenty bucks, or is it forty?" Horse says.

Lisa looks momentarily confused. "I don't know guys, I heard from that big wig from Cal Tech that we may be experiencing a polar shift, and that is why things are going crazy. Like an immediate polar shift. Like tomorrow, the north pole and the south pole will be switched."

"Dude," Benjamin says as he digests the information. He concurrently turns a shade of pink as he realizes that Horse was really, earnestly trying to tell him something.

"Dude?" Horse complains. "A polar shift? I guess I knew about them. I guess I thought it was a slow process."

"Catching up might be. A very slow and painful process," Lisa says. "The working theory now is that the earth's core is changing; it's shape-shifting. This theory explains the increased

16

activity of the Pacific Rim. It also explains the strange readings of the shrinking Vermont mountains and the slight raise in altitude here. Oh and it also explains the deeper tides in Japan. You know the ones that we were blaming on melting glaciers? The reality is – I think that our sweet, hot Yellowstone might just give the scientific community all the proof we need. That is, if we survive her tale."

"Isn't that just like her," Horse says wisely, with a deep and kind look aimed at his boss.

"Either way, it's certainly getting pretty rough out there. Almost all tectonic movement can be linked to magnetic reversals. Seafloor spreading, sea level changes, mountain growth, earthquakes, and volcanism all seem to speed up whenever the frequency of reversals speeds up," Lisa explains as she watches the two men put on their fire retardant suits. "For now, in order to get through the next few hours, I am just trying to focus on the bright side. I'm just thankful that this is happening now and not during peak season. Could you imagine if this started happening during peak season, like in July? I am glad that the camp sites are closed. Per protocol, we are heading out there first to verify there are no renegade campers."

"The bright side…" Horse laughs at Lisa. "It's November and half the roads are closed."

"Do you really think after these rumbles that there are people still dumb enough to…"

"Of course I do. Listen, it's five forty-five now, there's still time. The guard should be here any minute. They are setting up base at each of the entrances: Northeast, North, East, South, and West," Lisa says with an impressive degree of command coupled with admirable emotional restraint.

"Where are we going?" Horse asks as he finishes snapping his coveralls.

"Tower Falls. And no wise cracks, I'm not in the mood," Lisa tells him. After working together for three years, she can easily

17

predict her teammates' senses of humor, even under these circumstances.

"You mean like this Tower is going to…" Benjamin smirks.

"Crack?" Horse interjects.

"I said NO!" Lisa yells with eyes bouncing between the two and a wry smile appearing on the right side of her mouth. She exhales. "I love ya both, but we gotta go! You guys head down Chittenden and hit Canyon Village, Lake Village, Grant Village and then exit on the South. I'll head West through Norris and Madison."

"Wait, where's Rowen?" Horse asks as they move to leave the station.

"Fishing Bridge. He's organizing the Rec Vehicles. One guy from each station was sent there, and we could not get a hold of you guys. Go there if you have a car-full," Lisa yells back as she runs down the stairs. "Good luck," she adds as she enters her own Range Rover and slams the door.

She is gunning in reverse before Horse and Benjamin reach their truck. Both are breathing heavy, yet remain silent as they follow instructions and stop at Tower Falls camp ground and then at Canyon Village. Both campsites are empty. They make a third stop just past Canyon Village to put on their gas masks. They picked up a couple whiffs of hydrogen sulfide.

"Two and done," Horse says reminding Benjamin the rule that hydrogen sulfide disables the sense of smell.

"HCl is picking up, too," Benjamin replies.

"I think we should go to Fishing Bridge. More drivers could help," Horse recommends, his voice muffled by the plastic of his mask.

"I've a really bad feeling about all of this…a really bad feeling," Benjamin says adjusting the strap of his mask.

"Riding the waves…"

At 6:15 AM the Range Rover pulls into the Fishing Bridge Recreational Vehicle Park. Both Horse and Benjamin furrow their brows as they enter the recreational vehicle parking lot. There is a very large tank parked on the diagonal where there are normally Jeeps and trailers. The odd scene is amplified by the appearance of a camouflaged soldier sitting on top of the tank gripping an automatic assault rifle.

"Ya guys need another driver?" Horse yells through the plastic. "I am guessing you will need to get these vehicles moved and I've got an extra driver."

"You rangers?" the soldier yells bouncing his machine gun from his right hip to his left.

Horse slaps the door of his vehicle that clearly designates the car as property of Yellowstone. "Is the machine gun necessary? Do you need more drivers or not?"

The soldier yells into the tank and then returns to Horse. "Keys are inside each truck. Head East. South is no longer passable. It's toxic. Shoshone Lake is gone."

"Gone?" Horse and Benjamin nervously look to one another. Knowingly, they bump fists before Benjamin jumps out of the truck and runs to the closest vehicle. He yells back, "Riding the waves, Kemosabe."

"See you on the other side," Horse yells back. He looks to the soldier. "You should really put on a mask."

The soldier nods in agreement yet does not move from his position. "You should really watch out for elk."

Horse waits for Benjamin to start his truck before making his return to the road. The two men race down Highway 20 to the East Entrance. Smaller earthquakes seem to follow their vehicles. The two exit the park at 7:00 AM and are immediately stopped by the National Guard.

"Where you guys coming from?" asks a large man wearing fatigues.

"We're rangers from Tower Roosevelt. We were told to go to the South Entrance, but stopped at Fishing Bridge. Your pal 'Tank' told us to head east. Here we are."

19

"The park is closed," the soldier responds.

"Duh. Is it true that Shoshone is gone?" Horse asks.

"Sir, the park is closed."

"Keep up the good work, soldier." Horse salutes and slowly drives past the nine trucks and forty soldiers in plain view. "Man..." he whispers to himself.

At fifty five miles per hour, both Horse and Benjamin drive away from the park. At the first available rest stop Horse pulls in and Benjamin follows. He pulls up next to him and lowers his window. "This is crazy."

"Drop the truck and jump in," Horse commands.

"You sure?"

"I'm sure. It was probably a pretty bad idea for us to split up in the first place. I thought that maybe having an extra truck..."

Benjamin leaves the keys and hops out of the truck. He retrieves the first aid kit and other various cargo, including blankets and flashlights. "So it's not a total waste...Who knows, we may need this stuff... or someone else might."

Horse nods in agreement. "What we need... we need to get as far away from here as possible."

"Do you really think she's gonna go?"

"Yeah."

"Shit."

"Yeah."

"My guess is that we will need to get at least two hundred miles from here to survive the initial..."

Horse interrupts, "The birds..." He turns to look at his friend with eerily calm eyes. "Did you see the birds?"

"What birds?" Benjamin asks. "Dude, drive."

"Drive where?"

"East."

"I have family outside Rapid City, but I gotta get Joke. And Cheyenne...I should probably call Cheyenne..."

"Rapid City? The Badlands?"

20

"Tell her to meet us there. Tell her to just get in her car and drive."

Benjamin asks, "Do you think that maybe she might be safer just staying put?"

"No, Man. She's got to head south and east," Horse says with a believable degree of authority. "Lake effect winds…Jet stream… she's got to move. Dammit." He slams his palms on the steering wheel. "Dammit!"

"What do you want me to do?"

"Call her," Horse says reclaiming calmness. He nudges his chin to point out the cell phone in the change console.

Benjamin finds the number and calls. Cheyenne answers and a brief yet commanding set of instructions are passed from Horse to Cheyenne through Benjamin. "Meet us at Black Hills - my uncle's place. You remember, right? Be careful. Be safe." The connection is unstable. The call is dropped.

"Black Hills? That's about seven hours, right?" Benjamin asks in an attempt at distraction, wanting to soothe the love lines on his friend's forehead.

"I guess," Horse says diverted. He looks at his speedometer before looking at his friend and finding renewed focus. "Yeah, it's about seven hours."

"It's not far enough, is it?"

"Probably not."

"It's over. Isn't it?"

"We are trained for this, remember? We are forest rangers. We are trained for this. If anybody can make it through…," Horse says, shoring up his own courage and possibly that of his friend.

"Let's get Joke and get out of here. We'll rest in the Badlands," Benjamin says.

Horse presses harder on the gas pedal as he locates his bearings. "I think it's around five hundred miles, we'll take highway twenty then ninety."

21

"How are we doing on gas?" Benjamin takes off his mask.

Horse lifts his hand from the steering wheel to see the gauge. "It's full."

"Traffic is going to be really bad, really soon."

Horse increases his speed to eighty-five. "You'd think we would hear bells or air sirens?"

"Yeah."

"We'll get 'em next time," Horse jokes.

"Yeah, next time." Benjamin sees the humor.

***

On a very cold day, in late November, the Yellowstone caldera reaches a critical stage. Enormous volumes of over-pressurized granitic and basaltic magma erupt from a deep caldera fed directly from the earth's core. The first initial blast annihilates 500,000 acres in a super-heated instant. Cities, towns, and villages within those acres are swept away by the super-hot pyroclastic flow. An estimated 25,000 people and countless animals are killed instantly.

By the time the second blast of the caldera occurs twenty-eight hours later, with a force equal, if not larger than the first eruption, the deadly gasses and toxic ash from the first eruption are already billowing across land and sea. Half of the North American continent is covered in ash so toxic that a layer only one millimeter thick is capable of destroying all vegetation that exists below it. With satellite signals blocked, it is left to amateur radio communications to report when the death toll rises to two million due to an unprecedented release of Sulfur dioxide and Hydrochloric gases that cause semi-immediate fatal damage to our respiratory systems.

Deep and intense earthquakes are reported across the northern hemisphere as the earth's core takes its new shape. Tidal waves and tsunamis starting in the northern Hemisphere pound the Hawaiian Islands, Japan, and the Philippines. The destructive

22

and damaging effects are keenly felt in Peru, Chile and Australia.

After the third and final blast, forty-six hours after the initial eruption, a historic fourth caldera is formed, twice the size of the Yellowstone caldera. Even with the eruptions seemingly over, the world can only watch as indeterminate amounts of dense volcanic ash continuously rain down on cities across the US, Canada and Europe, burying plants, people and buildings. The death toll can only increase as the poisonous gases and toxic ash reach large population centers across these regions.

Within three weeks an estimated 400 million cattle and 900 million birds succumb, destroying a significant food source. This coupled with the destruction of virtually all of North America's agriculture heralds the reality of an immediate and lasting food shortage with world-wide implications, including epidemic famine conditions. Transportation services dispatched to those hardest hit are halted across both continents due to a contaminated atmosphere that prevents visibility and destroys engines. The human death toll becomes incalculable.

Blankets of ash trapped in the ionosphere hinders satellite communication indefinitely and also prevents high band radio and digital communications. All nuclear power plants, across North America and Europe must be shut down due to contamination of towers resulting in power outages and grid overload. States of emergencies are called in fifty-five countries across the northern hemisphere. Economies dependent on America and Canada crash within days resulting in a catastrophic economic downturn. International riots ignite, governments collapse, and lawlessness prevails.

Civilization, as we recognize it, is devastatingly crippled…

Δ2Δ

Minerva's Olive

THE GODS, say the heathen mythologists, have each of them their favorite tree. Jupiter preferred the oak, Venus the myrtle, and Phoebus the laurel; Cybele the pine and Hercules the poplar. Minerva, surprised that they should choose barren trees, asked Jupiter the reason. "It is," said he, "to prevent any suspicion that we confer the honor we do them for the sake of their fruit." "Let folly suspect what it pleases," returned Minerva; "I shall not scruple to acknowledge, that I make choice of the olive for the usefulness of its fruit." "O Daughter," replied the father of the gods, "it is with justice that men esteem thee wise; for nothing is truly valuable that is not useful." – Aesop

SEVEN MONTHS EARLIER...

"Did you mean *a priori*-tease or *a priori* –Tees?" Rose shouts to Aris as she tosses the Frisbee in his general direction.

Aris runs and actually makes the seemingly impossible catch. "I said you need to reconsider your priorities," Aris shouts with an affected exhaustion. He returns the Frisbee directly into her hands.

"I thought that was what I was doing? A priori..." Rose points to her right ring finger. "...Tie..." She spins and then lets go of the flying disc. "...ZING..." She watches the Frisbee fly right over his head and into the large tree in the distance. "Prioritizing," she shouts.

Aris lifts his hands in disbelief. "You expect me to run after that, don't you?" He smiles and, of course, accepts the challenge. He yells to Rose as he locates the Frisbee only a few

24

branches up, "I am part cat. I never met a tree I could not climb."

Rose shields her eyes as she leisurely strolls across the impeccably trimmed field to the base of a very large and mature black walnut tree. She locates Aris sitting comfortably in a sturdy bough vertically tossing the Frisbee. "Out on a limb, eh?"

He floats the Frisbee to her and reaches out his hand. "Au Contraire, this is a pretty big bough."

Rose sets the Frisbee down and, exhibiting her own cat skills, mounts the same branch in under fifteen seconds. She tests her balance and walks out a bit further on the branch. Facing him, she straddles the limb. "Cool shades. I don't think I need to say this, but we really should play hooky more often. I'm having such a great day."

"Yeah, me too." He motions for her to sit closer.

She gently smiles as she scoots forward and swings her legs to complete a 180 degree turn. She looks to the ground below her as she dangles her feet. Noticing the sheer size of the tree, she says, "We need to get one of these. Although I suppose it is not really possible to register for a two-hundred-eighty-year-old black walnut tree."

"Probably not," Aris says with a deep smile settling on his face. He waits to hear more of his fiancé's incessant musings as he watches her awkwardly situate herself on the limb before finally nestling into his body. "Definitely *knot*," he says in the moment, fully comprehending the language, the weight and the texture of their relationship. He sighs, expressing his complete contentment.

"There is something about garden parks, public or private, that make you feel, I don't know, blessed somehow," she says taking in the scenery. She spies through the natural windows of leaves and branches at the couples and families enjoying themselves. "Picturesque Gardens," she says followed by a deep

25

inhale and luxurious exhale, nestling deeper into his arms. "I think this is my new favorite place."

Aris moves her hair with his chin and tightens his embrace. "I thought you would like it here. I used to come here often when visiting my grandparents. In fact, this very tree was our family's meeting place," Aris says simply, quietly explaining the significance of this particular location.

"Are you happy?" she asks.

"I am more than happy," he says as he recognizes another perfect moment with his Rose. With a deep inhale, he gently and deftly slips his engagement ring from her right hand and slides it onto her left. "Your dream wedding is just this simple, right? Just the two of us – the two of us with God as our witness."

An emotionally touched Rose closes her eyes to drop a very full tear. "It's like a dream," Rose whispers. She burrows deeper into his embrace and audibly purrs her satisfaction. She gracefully looks up into his perfectly handsome face. "I don't think we need more. Do you, Husband?"

"I suppose not, Wife. But the state on the other hand…We still need to get our license."

Rose acknowledges the simple legislative truth with a wry laugh. "Ah the romance of it all. It's like a kiss and a slap. And a blood draw?" Rose asks passively wondering whether blood tests are still required. She thinks she remembers reading that they were no longer necessary.

"Ah priori–tie–zing," Aris replies leaning his head against the tree and looking up through the branches into the light indigo sky. "We need a license to wed."

"If you say so," Rose says with a distant voice indicating to Aris that she has, for the moment, spiritually left his side.

Aris is very accustomed to her "here one minute, changing the world the next" escapist personality, even on a moment such as this. He has been her best friend and trusted confidant for years. She has shared, to the best of his knowledge, every

26

thought about every curve of road she has traveled. He knows her well enough, deeply enough, to know that she will, in deed, always return to him.

He daydreams himself for an instant as he replays the past decade in his mind and how he arrived on this tree at this very moment. It was her passionate interest in chocolate that started to take her away from him. She had found a new love – and it was this love, a love for a child she never met, that woke him from his slumber. He realized, almost too late, that he had fallen in love, or more precisely, that he had always been in love with his best friend – this wonderful, charismatic, energetic, manic and scary creature he is currently holding in his arms.

Rose, still relatively distant on her own mental departure, lifts her wedded hand to the side of his face. "It's scary how much I love you."

"I know the feeling," he says tightening his hold and capably pulling her back from wherever she is or was – back into his arms and back onto his family's tree. After gently kissing the palm of her left hand, he mocks the overt romance with his sense of humor. "Anyway, now that we are married, you need to quit your job. You hate it," he tells her.

"A kiss and a slap." Rose gently and mockingly pats his face. "You just want me to move in."

"We are married. We should live together. Quit and come home to me."

"You realize that you just married a fiercely independent woman, right?" she says gently smiling and fluttering her eyelashes.

"I do," he replies. "You realize that you just married a fiercely dependable man, right? Stay here, with me."

"Stay here, on this tree? I do like trees," Rose says more than half-serious about staying on this bough forever. "I do, I do, I do."

27

"Have you thought about maybe working for the Cocoa Initiative? You have made some pretty valuable connections in recent weeks," Aris says sincerely, hoping to steer her away from the job she detests, the job that keeps her in Pennsylvania.

"Of course I have, but I have to admit that I'm thinking more about my Garden Gates than I am about chocolate. I know that building a school for Abdul is going to take time and that the task is pretty much out of my hands. I am confident that I've done what I could to start the ball rolling. I also realize that Nicolas and Rebekah are capable of seeing it through... But if you must know where I'm truly at, it's the possibility of an educational Mecca in Ghana and the Ivory Coast serving as the first Garden Gate that provides me the most satisfaction. I am most proud of the Garden Gate."

"Do you mean you are really not interested in the Cocoa Initiative anymore?" Aris asks.

"Of course I am still interested. Abdul is part of my heart now. But I want to grow the garden. If these chocolate companies build these schools – then that section of the garden will be complete. I will need to build another section," Rose says.

Aris listens to his wife and immediately recalls the blueprints of her "Dream Garden" – a garden built by contributions from the world given to the Mesopotamia region – the original location of the Garden of Eden. His beloved believes that the world would be much better served sending 400,000 intellectual gardeners to this region, rather than 400,000 military soldiers. According to her, these intellectual gardeners could sculpt a garden out of the worn-torn area – a garden filled with museums, libraries, medical research facilities, and space exploration posts – a garden representing the accomplishments of mankind contributed by nations all over the world. She also believes, perhaps naively, that the notion of the world's participation in recreating mankind's vision of the Garden of

Eden as a tribute to God would soothe the physical jihad of Muslims by providing the faithful with a spiritual jihad.

Aris does what he can as her husband by holding this shared blueprint in his mind's eye. From there he proceeds somewhat cautiously, bracing himself with a deep inhale, before he asks the seemingly next logical question, "Alright Rose, I'm ready, what's the next gate?"

"Somalia," Rose answers quickly. She reflexively plucks a leaf from the tree in an effort to occupy her hands. "I have a plan for a garden gate in Somalia that involves red wood trees, taking the mud from the Ganges and …"

"Where are you going to take the mud?" Aris asks laughing. "You're thinking of moving mud - to Somalia?" He continues to laugh through his nose but, for the most part, is romantically thrilled that she is actively working to solve an environmental predicament that caught his interest as an environmental scientist. He told her months ago about the dwindling glacier that feeds the Ganges, which will more than likely create a future with insurmountable economic implications for the region and the world.

"I want to dredge the river and move the mud to Somalia," Rose answers briefly. She moves her fingertips along the deep ridges of the limb. "The plan needs more work, more detail. I need to do a couple of things first. The first - I need to go back to school," Rose announces. "I don't know if you know this, but I have actually set aside quite a bit of money – eighteen percent of each paycheck for the past eight years for school. I have, ironically enough, decided to study economics."

"I think you could really use a few classes in economics. Your theory that arrowheads are still worth more than a dollar… Sane people just do not dream of stacks and stacks of arrowheads."

"They don't? What do sane people dream about?" Rose asks.

29

"Last night, I dreamt I was in a pet store. And there was the coolest little creature explaining to me in a really high pitched voice why it was better than a dog."

Rose smiles at his dream wishing she had a similar experience last night. She did not. Since around the time of her engagement, Rose has been seriously haunted by very vivid, devastatingly destructive nightmares. It is a fact that she has intentionally kept from Aris. She considers telling him now but decides to try to keep the conversation about her daydreams rather than her nightmares. She focusses on her ring and continues, "And I still think arrowheads are worth more."

"I know you do," Aris says.

Rose looks up into the tree and immediately recalls the ancient conversation he is referencing and is heartily amused by how long ago it was. "I cannot believe you remember my arrowhead rant – that was years ago. And you didn't know you were in love with me?" she asks fishing for a smile.

"Well I thought, for obvious reasons, that you were bat raving mad back then," Aris jokes with the love of his life. "So, what's the second thing? You said you had two things to accomplish..."

"Landscaping. I guess if I am serious about this theological garden of mine, I should really learn how to garden," Rose says leaning into his left shoulder and kissing his chin. "I was thinking of getting a part-time gig in landscaping while seeking a Masters or Ph.D. in Econ. Economics and landscaping – I think they sound like a good combination."

"For you they do," Aris agrees. He kisses the top of her head and then leans his against the tree. "Economics. If you really want to understand economics – I would start with Aristotle."

"Didn't I just marry him," Rose says as she feels herself fall deeper in love with her best friend. She tells him exactly how she feels. "I am so in love with you right now."

He takes her left hand and kisses the top. "Are you sure it is me you love, and not the philosopher?"

30

"Well…almost sure, pretty sure," Rose says and follows it with a toothy smile.

"The fabulist and the philosopher – we really are a great pair." Aris tightens his embrace and kisses her cheek before he begins to sell the virtues of the area including the good universities. He tops his argument with surprise information. "I have a very good friend here – one that I have known for ten years who has recently opened up a topiary landscaping business just a few miles from here. I can call him and ask if he is looking for help."

"Serendipity! How lucky are we?"

"Indeed. And on that note, we should probably get going. It's actually a bit later than I thought. It's past five and I have a plan in mind of getting you to like this place, your new home, even more."

"Do we have to? I think I could stay right here for hours and hours and hours."

"Yes, my love, I am pretty sure you think that… yet like arrowheads, there are some pretty serious practical issues we must consider," Aris says lightly gripping both of her shoulders as she begins to sit upright.

"You mean that man and woman cannot live on walnuts alone?"

"Aye, for one," he replies. "So how are you at getting down?"

"Excuse me Miss, I speak jive," Rose says giggling as she quickly swings her legs up and over the branch. She easily finds the lower branches and then the ground. "Don't worry, I'll catch you," she says looking up at Aris, who is exhibiting an uneasiness rarely shown.

"If you catch me… who is going to catch us?" Aris asks as he regains his footing. "I do think that having smaller feet helps when climbing trees. I guess that is why you rarely see boats in trees."

31

"Is that why?" Rose says watching him descend. He reaches the ground with both feet before she throws her arms around his neck and wraps her legs around his waist. "Home?"

"Wife?" Aris asks.

"Husband?"

"I need my kiss." Aris powerfully pulls her body into his and finds her lips with exquisite grace. He finishes with a trail of gentle nibbles on both her upper and lower lips. "I love you Rose Panna Isope."

Rose's body goes limp as she lowers her legs to the ground, upheld in his embrace, signaling her desire. "Home," she says breathlessly.

Aris simply takes her hand in his and they start walking.

Δ3Δ

The Mountain in Labor

A MOUNTAIN was once greatly agitated. Loud groans and noises were heard, and crowds of people came from all parts to see what was the matter. While they were assembled in anxious expectation of some terrible calamity, out came a Mouse. – Aesop

Rose passes through the meticulously landscaped park entrance and locates the furthest spot on the lot to park, as is her custom. While still in the driver's seat, she performs a quick check of her pack to verify the presence of her walking essentials: water and music. She locks her vehicle before heading toward the entrance of her favorite hiking path. After compulsively ensuring the laces of her sneakers are double-knotted, she makes her first steps up the steep, woodsy path.

She walks a predetermined distance and breaks at the first marked overlook of the hike, one that is flanked by a natural wooden fence and affords an excellent view of the valley. Rose takes the time to mentally capture and admire the rich and colorful landscape below. From the tree tops she estimates that she has walked about three miles on this path. Taking a moment to stretch her calves, she notices rocks that do not belong to this mountain. *Why would they attempt to landscape something already so naturally beautiful?*

She squats to get a closer look at the alien stones. At first guess she thinks they are river stones. They are rounded, black, and smooth. "River stones? Up here? These could be flint stones, Yabba Dabba Do," she says with a laugh. She grabs a couple and puts them in her pocket. She takes a few more and arranges them in the shape of a happy face. "Someone may guess, yet I think they will know…" She stands and looks out over the scenic landscape. "Natural Landscaping," she says before returning to the path.

There are couples returning from the mountain top, holding hands and for a moment Rose thinks about Aris and tries to remember why he is not with her. She continues to notice the people as they descend the mountain – the families, the couples and the runners with their strides noticeably adjusted to accommodate the terrain and the slope.

"Is it slippery?" she asks one of the runners and looks to her own sneakers. *Yellow paint? I must have picked it up along the way.* She looks back at the log railing for wet paint signs to explain the bright new color on her sneakers. *I didn't see any signs.* "Caution?" She shrugs.

She turns back to the path and continues her climb. While looking through the sun dappled leaves, she notices that the sun is lowering more quickly than it should. "The day is turning into night - like an eclipse. Is there an eclipse today? I didn't know there was going to be an eclipse," she says while walking closer to the edge to witness the strange and confusing phenomenon. "How did I not know that there was supposed to be an eclipse?"

Just as she arrives at the edge of the path, the ground starts to shake. She quickly squats for balance and to feel the ground. "An earthquake," she says in a voice that is actually more excited than scared. "A volcano?" she asks with the same elated voice. "That's so cool," she says.

A throng of people appear at the curve of the path two hundred feet ahead. "It's the volcano," a forty-ish man says holding the hand of his seven-year-old daughter. "It's the volcano. We need to get out of here," he says directly to Rose as he passes her in a fury.

"Dad, I am scared," the child says. She also looks directly at Rose.

"Don't be scared," Rose answers the child calmly as if there is nothing happening. "The volcano is doing what it is supposed to be doing," she says looking at both the father and daughter, who have both curiously stopped their running and are standing completely still, about a foot away from Rose. Rose notices that they are just blankly staring at her with what could only be described as dead eyes. She adds, "It was sleeping and now it is waking up."

Loud and multiple screams fill the air as more people run down the path, past Rose, past the child and her father. "Run!" a woman screams as she pushes the father and child down the mountain slope. "Run for your lives," she yells to anyone who can hear her.

Rose looks down at her shoes. "I am wearing sneakers," she announces. She looks behind her to see if there is room for her to join the stream of people running. Confused by the appearance of numbers on the runners' chest, she asks, "Is this a race? Or is the volcano erupting?"

"Just run!" a man says. "The truth is chasing us down this mountain. Run!"

"The truth?" Rose asks unable to move. "What do you mean the truth is chasing us?" Rose looks up the mountain trail just as an enormous heat blast warms her face. "Did the mountain erupt?" she asks an older woman as she passes.

"Rose, you are the last. You need to get things in order - your priorities. You are the last," the woman says. She bears a remarkable resemblance to her grandmother who passed several years earlier. "You are last, my love. You cannot have another."

An air siren blares in the background.

Rose wakes up in her bed, next to her husband. "It was just a dream," she says into the air, pushing her hair from her face. "Wow, and what a dream it was," she says with a hard exhale. She wipes the sweat from her sternum and peels the covers from her body. "I suppose it doesn't get any hotter than volcanoes," she whispers to God. "I'll use less comforter tomorrow night."

She rolls to her right hip to look at her husband's face. He remains still, completely relaxed in a deep sleep. She reaches her hand out to gently stroke his perfectly arched eyebrow. His nose and lips twitch in reaction.

"Again?" Aris says with a smile. "Insatiable."

"Hey, I love you," Rose whispers.

"I was just having the nicest dream," Aris says finding her hand and lifting it to his lips. "I dreamed I married my dream girl." he admits.

"Again? Am I supposed to be jealous?" Rose jokes with a gentle whisper.

"I love you too, Rose," he mumbles as he falls back asleep.

She joins him a few minutes later.

Δ4Δ

Happiness depends upon ourselves. –Aristotle

Aris watches his Rose sleep. He wants to wake her because he misses her. Yet he remains still and finds contentment watching her eyes shift and listening to her breathe through her dream. He starts to shift on his elbow and this simple action steals her from her dream state.

"You ever notice how different people look with their eyes closed," she says feeling his stare. She covers her face with their comforter and rolls over to the other side. "How long have you been awake?"

"Almost long enough to wake you with my eyes alone," he says. He wraps his arm around her ribs and pulls her closer to him. "I was beginning to think you were never going to wake up. Or that I was going to have to resort to other means."

Rose turns to him and nestles the top of her head into his chest. "I am a really good sleeper. Sleeping is one of my God-given talents. Need someone to sleep through a hurricane – I'm your girl. It is my third decade and I am pretty sure I slept through my first two. Sometimes I am even a good dreamer," she says with an undetectable sorrow.

He happily squeezes his sleeper. "Well, I'm thinking breakfast. We have a lot of ground to cover. Cake for my pretty little landscaper?" he asks.

"Cake and coffee."

Unabashedly nude, he walks from their room and returns minutes later with two coffees and one plate with two forks. "So what do you think? Do you think that Diane is going to be surprised when you give her notice?"

37

Rose remembers their half-agreed upon arrangements to have her quit her job. "It is not exactly in your nature to rush things. The facts are not all in. The cost of living here is not cheap."

"Au contraire, ma femme," he replies. "The cost of living here is very cheap. In fact, it is pretty much free."

"I don't understand."

"This house belongs to my grandmother. She is only asking for utilities. She wants to sell the place, yet the market is down right now so she was looking for a house sitter. We are staying in this three bedroom brownstone for the cost of the electricity."

"I was actually wondering how you could afford this place. I was going to ask, but…I figured you would eventually tell me… I don't know, I guess I thought you were borrowing money from your folks."

Aris is both amused and upset at her assessment. "Thorn, I hope you realize that I was just kidding when I told you that I chose an expensive education because my parents named me Aristotle, and that it was just payback time. My parents are very generous; however, I do not and will not live beyond my means. I wish you had asked me about it…"

"Testy, testy, testy. I heard that most married couples fight about five things – money, religion, sex, children and… I forget what the other thing is. I did not mean to imply…what I mean is… this is a really nice house and I am pretty sure that you could not afford it on your salary."

Aris takes a sip of his coffee. "Fair enough. By the way, I think the other thing is family." He takes a bite of cake and offers a forkful to Rose. "My grandmother has given us one year to stay here and save for a home. This is her engagement present to us."

"I guess now it is a wedding present." She takes the cake, smiles and then kisses him gently on the lips.

Aris lifts his hand to cradle her neck and prolong the kiss. "A wedding present for my bride," Aris says languorously. "I don't know if I need to mention this or not, but I really like having cake for breakfast. So decadent and it makes your lips taste like icing."

Rose dips her finger into the icing and brings it to his lips. "So this place is free? Sweet. Like frosting."

"For a year," he says before sucking from his wife's finger. "I have an idea, instead of getting out of bed, maybe we should…" Aris backs up his suggestion by trying to take her coffee mug.

"Hold on. Wait a second - it is not exactly fair for me to take advantage of this gift and freeload," she says tightening her grip on her mug. "I think it would be dishonorable for me, I mean us, not to take full advantage of her generosity. I should continue to work and stay here on the weekends. The sacrifice could be great for our future and would definitely show due respect to your grandmother. It's only twelve months."

"Maybe that other thing that married couples fight about is work," Aris says, huffing in both physical and mental frustration. "Rose, you hate your job."

"Aris, the truth is, almost everyone hates their job. And besides, I don't exactly hate my job. I hate the hours, I hate the travel, and I suppose you could definitely say I hate the industry. The job itself is not so bad. I like my boss." She delivers a piece of cake to him.

"You can't go to school unless you quit."

"If Erik is not hiring, what am I going to do?"

"You can start that underground radio station," Aris says reminding her of the Amateur radio he presented to her as a wedding gift last night, both as an inside joke and a sincere push toward a technical hobby.

"Radio? That's not going to bring in money. And I would never get out of the house."

"I kind of like the idea of you never leaving here." He starts to lift the comforter to reveal her legs.

39

Rose starts to respond to his interest by shifting her hips down. "Receiving signals?"

Aris teases by withdrawing his interest and moves to cover her legs. "Once you have your *license*, you can wake someone else with your rants and let me have a little rest."

Rose's face flushes. "Yeah, and I am so sure that you want a wife who never leaves the bedroom and who rants into a metal box. She sounds dreamy." She pictures a Hefner-esque version of herself. "Listen, this gift your grandmother gave us –we should not waste it on want. We should fill our silo and prepare for the winter."

"Come to think of it, I actually really like the sound of a wife who never leaves the bedroom," Aris teases as he tries to tug at the comforter covering her breasts.

"Aris!" Rose pleads with a giggle. "You really should know what you want by now. A wife who never leaves the bedroom or..."

"Huh, what do I want? What do I want?" Aris eyes the form under the covers. "What do I want?"

"Well, I know that I want to *not* take advantage of your grandmother," Rose says with a tone of anger. "This is serious."

His expression changes and the spicy smile leaves his face. "You are being very practical."

"Are you pouting? Did I actually win this argument and you are going to pout. I have never won an argument with you, have I?"

"No you haven't. And you are not going to win this one either. Remember when you told me about José, the pediatric cardiologist from Cuba. He gave you a picture of what love was. Remind me...what did he say?"

Rose looks down into the white linens as she recalls the memorable conversation she had with the gentleman at a coffee shop. "He said that love is like a beautiful field filled with grains and animals and in the center is this giant tree with a full

40

canopy. Underneath this giant tree is a reflecting pool of pure, delicious water…"

"Pure, delicious, water… Go on."

"He said that the secret to long lasting love is remembrance that there is a pool of pure, delicious water and that a partner can take water from the pool when they need it. Yet, it becomes his or her responsibility to bring the water back. If a partner takes more than they give, the water will disappear and so will the relationship. The water symbolizes the virtues of trust, respect, kindness, sacrifice, generosity, and understanding."

"Virtues. Aristotle said 'educating the mind without educating the heart is no education at all.' Finding a job that inspires you rather than just pays you is good home economics. He also warns that working for money does not fulfill need, it only creates want. I want you to find something that makes you happy. I want you to find your…"

"Don't you dare say 'bliss,'" Rose says.

Aris floats back down to her pillow. "Warning me against taboo chocolate products and hippie-esque sayings that have no basis among educated people. I do so love your rules." Aris looks at his wife's face and is happy to concede. He repeats the best of his logic, "Working for money does not fulfill need, it only creates want."

"Ah my Aristotle," Rose says dreamily as she falls to his pillow to meet him. "Maybe I did fall in love with the philosopher. Speaking of filling needs and wants, will you please kiss me now?"

Aris notices the way her strong, wavy, strawberry blonde hair completely covers his pillow. "Will you quit your job?"

"Are you winning the argument now?" Rose adjusts her body to a full reclining position and puts her hands behind her head.

"I got you where I want you."

"How much are utilities – electricity, internet, trash, and etcetera?"

"Parking included for the both of us - four hundred dollars a month."

"I can easily afford two hundred a month for a year. Can I just give you the money right now?"

"Are you going to quit your job?"

"Are you going to kiss me?"

"Are you going to finish your cake?" Aris asks eyeing the frosting.

Rose feeds him the last bite with her fingers. "Are you going to kiss me now?"

"Landscaping, eh?"

"Landscaping."

"Sounds like really hard work," he says trying to remove the comforter from her body. "Have you ever done landscaping before?"

"I have done a little. I have a bit of rock wall experience and basic garden maintenance experience. I think you're right though. It is a pretty labor intensive job. Yet, I feel I am physically up for the task," she says with a suggestive smile.

Aris lifts his own comforter and simply lifts his eyebrows. "What would you want… from a job as a landscaper?"

"I would want to learn about landscape architecture and planning budgets. I would also learn about the actual cost of running a landscaping business – i.e., machinery, labor, storage, and business partnerships. I suppose that a landscaper probably has arrangements with the mulch guy and the rock guy. How much do those relationships cost? Can I pay the rock guy with rocks?"

"Hmmm Economics." Aris kisses the top of her right shoulder. Resting high on his right elbow, he pulls her body toward him. "Call me Teacher!"

"Alright, Teacher," Rose jokingly complies from the pillow.

"Aristotle thinks that there are four varieties of economic turfs: exchange, barter, retail trade and usury. To start he defines

42

'True Wealth' as the available stock of useful things. If the world were in perfect balance, I suppose you could pay the rock guy in rocks." He kisses her shoulder again and starts to gently trace the top of the comforter with his index finger, making sure to lightly graze her very sensitive skin. "Exchange occurs because what the participants want is different from what they have to offer. Need plus demand is what goes into determining proportionate reciprocity."

Rose watches his finger on her skin. "Sexy."

"Uh huh," Aris whispers into her ear. "I think God inherently understood proportionate reciprocity when he created man and woman. However, I think we are entering into your field." He lifts the comforter and looks down the length of her body. "Our exchange is mutually satisfactory."

Rose hugs her body over the comforter to shorten the distance of his sight. "Wait. What happens if the partners in the exchange are not equal?"

Aris drops his body and head onto the bed in frustration, and turns to watch his wife's mind work through the dark browns in her eyes. He can see her make the connections like no other woman he has ever met. "Uh oh," he says with a laugh.

Rose rolls on top of him completely wrapped in bed linens and steers the conversation back to its start. "What do I lose in this exchange? What happens if I quit my job and we run into financial problems? The responsibility would be mine – tame and blame."

Aris reaches up to tuck her hair behind her ear. "La femme," he says. He lands both his hands on the fold of her hips.

"Right now, I feel I am your equal. If I am unemployed, I would be a less valuable member of our household. I would be useless," Rose continues determinedly.

He repeats his action of placing her hair behind her ear and again finds her hips. "I think that Aristotle suggested that a contract be drawn up. I believe his argument was that the two

43

parties involved in the exchange of goods must be satisfied that both utilities and costs are equalized before the exchange takes place."

"Huh," Rose harrumphs. "A past boyfriend's mother told me a story about her wedding anniversary. Apparently she and her husband spent a day of their honeymoon writing down what they wanted from life and they have returned to that list every year on their anniversary to check off items accomplished, revise previous notions, or remind each other of the necessary work in order to check off another item on the list. Sounds like the best form of marital contract to me." Rose leans forward to kiss her husband on the forehead. "I think we need a contract like this for our marriage and something similar for this financial adjustment you are requesting."

"I think I am suggesting rather than requesting."

"Are we negotiating?" She squeezes his hips with her thighs. "Am I going to need a lawyer?"

"What do you want?" He tries to find a way in through the wrapping.

"More coffee." Rose lifts her left leg and gently lands on her right hip. She rolls out of bed and takes all of the covers with her. She grabs both mugs and leaves their bedroom.

"That is so cold," a naked Aris yells to her just as she starts descending the stairs.

She laughs. "I am soooo hot. No worries; I will bring back water. And husband, I castled," she says.

"I already moved my bishop," he responds. He glances through the bathroom door at the small crystal chess board given to her as an engagement present. Rose once told him that her perfect mate would be happy to play bathroom chess with her. He smiles at the memory. "Perfect," he murmurs. He takes great joy in listening to the sounds of Rose in the kitchen. She is singing and laughing and talking to herself. He sits up in his marriage bed as he hears her climb the stairs.

Rose returns with two mugs in her left hand and a glass of water in her right. "Can I earn money on your interest?" she asks baring all.

"Depends, what do you got?"

"Coffee, tea…" She lifts the water glass to her mouth and then asks demurely, "What is the value of my exchange?"

"Priceless."

Δ5Δ

**"What is a friend? A single soul dwelling in two bodies." –
Aristotle**

For himself and for his bride, Aris enters the main office of Evergreen Palaces, Erik's topiary business located minutes from the beltway.

"May I help you?" a petite and fit woman in her forties addresses him immediately.

"I'm looking for Erik. He and I have an appointment. I'm Aris. Can you tell him I am here?"

"You're Danika's brother?" Julie asks.

"I am," Aris responds. "Have you met Danika?"

"No, I have only heard of her. She is often used as a cautionary tale," Julie responds honestly.

Aris smiles in amusement. "That's my sister, alright."

"Erik!" Julie yells to the break room. "Danika's brother is here."

Erik emerges. "Aristotle Irwin, good to see you, Man." He extends his left hand and squeezes Aris's left shoulder with his right.

"Erik, it's been a long time. Two years?"

"Has it been that long, really?" Erik asks. "Seems like yesterday," he says with a sarcastic tone.

"It is close to two years. It might be more like eighteen months," Aris says making a mental note that his friend looks the exact same as he did at their last meeting – the exact same haircut, the exact same amount of facial hair, the exact same shirt and pants. "You look good."

"So you are engaged to that girl who, and I quote, 'scared the living bejesus out of you,'" Erik says loud enough for Julie, who loves to hear stories about people she does not know.

46

"I am," Aris responds proudly. "You're going to like her Erik."

"She's got to be better than Naomi," Erik says.

"Rose did not like her either," Aris admits. "I think you might have met her once, years ago. Anyway, she is interested in landscaping."

"Well, I could use the help. I just had two people, Evan and Marilyn, run off to Colorado to teach skiing to over-privileged white kids."

"Sounds serious." Aris laughs. "Wait? Skiing in May?"

"Crazy kids," Erik says while looking at Julie. He turns back to Aris. "So, you're taking me to lunch, right?"

"Yeah, ya ready?" Aris asks.

"Julie, I'll be gone for an hour or so. You want us to bring you anything back?" Erik asks.

"I'm good," Julie responds. "I'll keep watch."

"Thanks," Erik says. "I'm thinking blooming onion."

"Outback?" Aris responds.

"Perfect," Erik says inadvertently checking his pocket for his wallet. "You driving?"

Aris nods. "I am pretty sure I will never get into another car with you behind the wheel. You drive like... like Danika."

"Man, that's harsh. How is the bitch, anyway?"

"She's good. She has a new guy in her life. He's pretty," Aris says.

"Good. Pretty boys are a good match for her," Erik says. "I am glad she's doing well."

Aris looks to the profile of his friend as they approach the car. He has always liked Erik, from the first moment they met. Danika brought him to his graduation party. He is the first and only one of Danika's gentleman callers that Aris could stomach. They became fast friends and have remained so even after a pretty ugly break-up that involved gross lies and deceptions all

47

perpetrated by Danika. "Yeah, Danika… Mina says hi, by the way."

"Mina and I are Facebook friends," Erik reports as he comfortably eases into the passenger seat.

"Huh, I had no idea," Aris says. "She is like friends with everybody…"

Aris and Erik arrive at the Outback Steak House just after the lunch rush. They are seated immediately and the waitress takes their orders and brings them their beverages.

"So tell me about her," Erik starts.

"She's not like anyone else," Aris answers honestly. "She has a ridiculous amount of energy – both physically and mentally."

"High maintenance?" Erik asks.

"Like you would not believe… hmmm…How would I describe her?" Aris says staring off into the rafters of the restaurant. "How would I describe her?" he repeats. "I can safely say that she is probably a genius, yet is more embarrassed by it than proud of it. She's got a great sense of humor. She tries to be honest, you know, and tell the truth. Yet her definition of truth is probably a book in and of itself. She's loyal and hardworking."

"Is she attractive?" Erik asks.

"She's gorgeous," Aris says straightforwardly.

"Then what is she doing with you?" Erik asks dryly.

"I have no idea," Aris answers honestly. "Luck of the Irish is her answer."

"So tell me, why does a gorgeous, energetic genius want to work in landscaping?" Erik asks with the serious tone of a possible employer.

Aris sighs loudly, wondering just how much he should relate to his friend on her behalf. "I think that you should ask her that question, and then you would probably be able to understand who she is. However, for the purposes of hiring her, you will not find anyone better."

48

"Doesn't she have a job now?" Erik asks. "I mean, is she unemployed?"

"She works in pharmaceuticals – clinical trials. She hates the industry. She compares it to Washington and says that they really need a bath."

"What?" Erik says.

"Washing-ton," Aris says trying to capture a sampling of his Rose for his audience. "She breaks down words and forms new definitions. She thinks both Washington DC and Big Pharma are dirty and need a serious bath."

"Washing ton," Erik repeats the same cadence. "That's funny."

"Actually, most of the time it is; other times it is just really annoying," he admits. "I love her though - more than anything. She is interested in learning about landscaping and landscape architecture. I want to give her what she wants – so I'm here, asking."

"We need people, and you know that I do not want to surround myself with…"

"Erik, you are going to like her. I'd bet our friendship on it," Aris says.

"Say no more. I'd like to meet her. Why don't you bring her by the house tonight. It's pizza night. I could just order another one for you guys. Cheese?" Erik says.

"Not tonight, she has already left to go home this morning. She is going to put in her two weeks' notice tomorrow. And it would be great if she could have this job to help curb her fears about being unemployed," Aris says. "The thought of her just standing around without a job… seriously frightening." He laughs as he pictures her as a pin ball in a pin ball machine. "I wish I could describe her energy level – it's closer to hummingbird than human."

"I will give her a try. If it doesn't work out…"

"That's all I could ask for," Aris says. "Thanks, Erik."

49

The waitress delivers their appetizer. Erik immediately dives into his second favorite food. Still chewing, he says, "So now you're getting married…"

"I am," Aris responds with a satisfied smile.

"Seems like we are at that age. Everyone I know is pretty much getting hitched. And I can't even get a date," Erik says. "Well there is this one girl who stopped in to buy a gift for her aunt's something or other. Aubrey."

Erik relates the story about his initial encounter with Aubrey and how he was immediately attracted to the young woman. He explains to Aris the humorous way she presented herself. She entered his greenhouse and bee-lined to him, the man who was holding a hose. Erik smiles recounting how she just wanted to know whether topiary was a practical gift idea, and that she was asking the guy with the hose because she feared that those working the front would be offended by her questions. "I told her that topiary is not like Bonsaii, and I really took my time telling her. She was so pretty and it was so cool talking to her. She liked my jokes. She actually laughed. I thought something was happening between the two of us, so I gave her my card. You should have seen her face when she realized that I was the owner. She was so cute trying to apologize. Anyway, I haven't heard from her. I guess she wasn't interested…"

"Did you say something like – 'I check my email often'?" Aris asks dipping a chunk from his half of the onion.

"I am not sure if I remember what I said. She had pretty eyes – they were grey with a dark blue circle around them," Erik says looking away.

"So, you already know the color of her eyes?" Aris asks.

"Yeah," Erik admits.

"I guess it is safe to say that you're in trouble. And you did not get her contact information?"

"No," he says dejectedly.

"Did you get any information?"

50

"She's a student at Georgetown," Erik admits.

"Well then, you can start looking there. Type Aubrey and Georgetown into a search engine. Maybe you will get lucky. It's not like students these days are overly protective of their identity."

"Even if I do find her – what am I going to say?"

"I don't know. I suppose you could just send her an email to let her know you know the color of her eyes. Perhaps she will swoon," Aris says.

"Or run to the cops," Erik says half-entertaining the thought.

"I guess I have found that when I have a deep connection with someone – they usually feel it, too. You could just send her an email saying that you were the guy at the Evergreen Palace and that you were hoping that she was going to use the card you gave her but got tired of waiting for her to come to her senses…"

"That might work for you, Man. Look at you. You look like Josh Hartnett," Erik points out the obvious. "And I – well I look more like Tweedle Dum with dark hair."

"Nonsense, you look much more like Tweedle Dee," Aris says trying to humor is friend's self-deprecation. He smiles as he remembers the long past conversations he has had with Erik when he was dating Danika. They always have had very similar senses of humor. He had forgotten this aspect of his friend and is presently very happy to be having this lunchtime reunion.

"Nah, Tweedle Dee has that thing on his cheek," Erik says finishing the last of his side of the onion.

Aris laughs. "I heard he got that thing lasered."

"The vanity market is really booming these days," Erik responds.

The waitress brings them their entrees, and the lighthearted conversation moves very easily through the rest of their meal – from Aubrey to women to Rose and then back to Aubrey.

51

"Listen, if she made that much of an impression. You should do what you can. Find her," Aris advises.

"I suppose you are right. I should try, at least." Erik says. Thinking out loud, he continues, "You know if I really think about it. She may have given me her last name. I actually sent the item she chose to her aunt. I may be able to start there and work backward."

"There's the stalking spirit," Aris says and follows it with an affected creepy laugh.

"I suppose that *is* a bit unprofessional," Erik says stopping himself from any further thoughts on the matter.

"Nah, it's romantic – like the start of one of those cheesy romance novels," Aris eggs on his friend.

"You could have said that it sounds like the backstory to a really cool nouveau X-box Donkey Kong."

"Where Tweedle Dum captures the princess?"

"You know that is not such a bad idea – those guys liked to play games – a dark, twisted Tweedle Dee and Tweedle Dum game could be cool," Erik surmises. "Maybe something like 'The Rabbit Hole' or 'Alice in Chains.'"

"Are you still programming?"

"Actually, I still get to do a bit of programming. My web site is all me. And my web business is growing super-fast. I might be able to retire in ten years."

"It's awesome that your hobby has turned into such a great business venture," Aris says commending his friend's success. "I have been trying to interest Rose in a hobby. I gave her a radio system. She needs a technical hobby to occupy her."

"Why do you say that?"

"Again, you are going to have to meet her. I think you will understand what I mean. You almost have to trick her to ground her," Aris says.

"Trick her?"

52

"Yeah," Aris says unapologetically as he pushes his empty plate to the left for the waitress.

"Trick her? Really?" Erik is slightly upset upon hearing this. He is not a fan of manipulation in any form. It was most decidedly the fundamental reason he and Aris's sister broke up.

Aris immediately picks up on his displeasure. "I will tell you more about it later. For now, I should really get you back to work," Aris says placing his credit card in the black check book and quickly handing it to the waitress.

Trying to give Aris the benefit of the doubt, Erik asks, "Do you mean that sometimes she's a little too smart for her own good."

Aris listens to the phrase, and seemingly contemplates it for the first time. "Actually, I have never understood that phrase until this very moment. I would have to say that yeah – sometimes she is more than a little too smart…She's scary."

Erik smiles as he says, "I do believe that is exactly how you described her years ago."

When Aris retrieves his card and receipt from the waitress, the two quickly make their escape from the restaurant and find their way back to Evergreen Palaces. "Rose is gone until Friday. If you want to get together tonight around some pizza and the X-box…" Aris says.

"How does eight o'clock sound? My place?"

"I'll bring beer?"

"Cool. Thanks for lunch. See ya at eight."

Ian

A young boy squats down to dust off his white sneakers that are now completely covered in black soot. Ian's worry becomes apparent on his face. "My mom is going to kill me," he says to Kyle who is standing a few feet away. He and his best friend, Kyle, have been digging into the culm for the past three hours. They are building a fort, a fort they plan to call Gotham.

Kyle stops his digging to listen. His stance on the sharp slope is both wide and stable. He readjusts his grip on the small, rusted shovel that he found between two of the smaller mounds of coal remnants. It was this finding, a finding of an old coal shovel that sparked the idea to build a fort. He looks at his friend's shoes and shrugs. "My mom just washes my sneakers. It's not a big deal, you're worried about nothing."

Nearly a year ago, Kyle named himself big brother to Ian, right after his own big brother left for boot camp. He decided then that it was his turn to play big brother, and because he did not have a little brother of his own, he chose Ian, the smallest in his class; the smallest, but the smartest.

Ian watches the small pebbles of rock and coal dust avalanche down the mound. "Do you think this is stable enough?" he asks his friend, exhibiting his keen sense of observation.

"We just have to dig a little deeper. It's like clay. My brother showed me how to do this," Kyle says. "You'll see, just keep digging."

Ian hears the call and stands with renewed energy. Before he grabs his own makeshift tool, he scans the enormous mounds of coal and rock and dust that stretch to the horizon. The mound that they are currently digging into is at least ten stories high and as wide as two football fields. The twenty or more culm dumps are the defining feature of his hometown, Carbondale,

54

Pennsylvania. He and Kyle play there every day during the summer, but he usually is wearing his other sneakers.

"We can paint the bat signal on its door," Ian says as he starts to envision their bat cave complete with its own electronic station – a place for his XBOX 360. He quickly finds his design error. "Actually, maybe we should just paint the door to match the culm – like camouflage."

Kyle quickly agrees and picks up the energy of his friend. They continue to work at hollowing their entrance for another two hours before making their plan to return the following morning with even better tools. "We have tons of shovels and stuff at home," Kyle says looking at the small shovel in his hands with its rusted spade and unusual bent neck. "But we should keep this a secret. We probably shouldn't tell our folks. Swear."

Ian agrees with Kyle initially, but quickly changes his mind. "My mom is going to know, no matter what. She is going to look at these sneaks and know."

Kyle just shrugs his shoulders. "Tell her that my mom washes my sneakers."

The boys race each other back to their respective homes. Ian's mom greets him with a smile, a hug and a lecture. "Ian. I told you that you cannot play in the culms until you are old enough to do your own laundry."

"Then teach me," the brave boy says. "Kyle told me I can wash my sneakers. I can, right? We want to go back there tomorrow. We have a plan," he says with a look of determination that can only be met with a smile by his mother.

"What are you boys up to now?" Dawn asks as she looks over his scrawny four feet, five inch body, completely covered in dirt and soot.

"It's a secret. I swore," Ian reports.

Dawn smiles knowing that her son cannot keep secrets for longer than a day. "Alright. Let's get you out of these clothes

55

and into the shower. We are having mac and cheese for dinner. Mac and cheese and hotdogs," Dawn reports stripping her son in the kitchen. "I'll teach you how to do laundry next time."

Nine hours later, Dawn is awakened by dreadful screams in her son's room. She bursts through the door to find him struggling under his sheets. "Ian, honey. Wake up. You are dreaming. Wake up."

Drenched in sweat, Ian opens his eyes and starts to cry. "My fort. My fort caught on fire. The whole thing – the whole mountain, the whole mountain caught on fire. And Kyle, Kyle too..."

"It was just a dream, Sweetie. It was a just a very bad dream," Dawn says. She brushes his damp hair with her hand and kisses his forehead. "It was just a dream."

Δ6Δ

The Camel

*WHEN MAN first saw the Camel, he was so frightened at his
vast size that he ran away. After a time, perceiving the
meekness and gentleness of the beast's temper, he summoned
courage enough to approach him. Soon afterwards, observing
that he was an animal altogether deficient in spirit, he assumed
such boldness as to put a bridle in his mouth, and to let a child
drive him. ~ Aesop*

A tired and emotional Rose enters her childhood bedroom
and closes the door. She leans her back against it and forces out
a complete, unburdening sigh. "It's all moving too fast," she
says to her ceiling, "way too fast."

She just spent the last four hours with her parents discussing
her plans and her options. The conversation went well; it is
agreed that she will quit her current job, move to Maryland and
enroll into a Master's program in Economics, preferably at
Georgetown. "How does that sound? Biology, Theology and
Economics – a renaissance woman!" she says to the ceiling. *It's
almost too easy*, she thinks.

Rose looks around her Van Gogh inspired room at the various
knick-knacks from her youth, mostly small frames of her
childhood heroes. She picks up one of her favorites, a copper
framed postcard of Maria Tallchief, the ballerina. She presses
the frame against her heart. *No limits.* Rose sets down the frame
before turning off her lights. After undressing in the moonlight,
she climbs into her twin bed that is nestled in the right corner of
her small, sparse room.

After two hours of tossing and turning, Rose shifts her focus
to the red digits of her alarm clock. She plays a game with

herself; one that she created as a pre-teen. She counts to sixty in between minute changes – trying to get a feel for how to count a perfect second. She actually has done it several times but usually falls two or three seconds short of her goal. She does this in an effort to quiet her mind.

It is true, that in the past, Rose was usually able to fall asleep pretty quickly. However, since the nightmares started, even finding the courage to close her eyes has been a formidable undertaking. Her newly-wed activities have helped in this area, but not tonight. Tonight, she is alone.

To cover, Rose rearranges her pillows to fake her husband's presence in her bed and tries to nuzzle into her creation. She begins to hear her husband's words echoing in the back of her mind, as if they are being whispered into her ear. "You need to reconsider your priorities," he says while throwing a Frisbee in her mind's eye. The picture is very clear. She coos as she considers the romance of the past few days; she misses him dearly at this particular moment. To honor the feeling, she reflects upon his words. *I need to reconsider my priorities,* she thinks.

Even after such a whirlwind weekend, Rose can easily and earnestly list her top five priorities: God, her marriage, Aris, herself, and her family. In an attempt to improve upon this list, she considers moving her family's position up next to marriage; she thinks it sounds better. She reconsiders. It may sound better, but as a newlywed, she feels that her priorities can allow for a bit of selfishness. Her family is both new and growing and she is sure they will take their rightful place, in time.

Rose's mind returns to the park and to the tree. She searches her past romantic memories deeper and recalls the morning when Aris made a surprise appearance and a surprise proposal. She remembers how he said, on that morning, that he was ready to lead her. *Follow his lead and prioritize,* she ruminates.

"My top five," she says looking at her wedded hand. *I love you.* Satisfied that she has at least begun to follow her husband's directive, she slips deeper into her bed and rolls onto her left hip. Rose looks to her clock and counts to fifty-nine. *I think I can sleep now.* She closes her eyes.

Minutes later, she drifts off into a dream. In a slightly peculiar setting, an abstractedly aware Rose tells her kind and receptive manager, Diane, that she is quitting the pharmaceutical industry to work as a landscaper. Before receiving her boss's reaction, the dream quickly devolves into a nightmare; a nightmare where her office is immediately engulfed by hot flames. Both Rose and Diane get lost in the smoke. Rose is able to find the stairwell that will supposedly take her to safety, but it is soon overtaken by a searing, deep black and bright orange lava flow.

Rose wakes, panting and sweating. She quickly puts the dream, and the heat, behind her by turning toward the wall and pushing her heavy covers away from her. Just as the weighted comforter falls to the ground, she falls into another variation of the same dream.

Rose quits her job. Diane responds with a disappointed tone, "You think that there are more people preventing good medicine than practicing, don't you?"

"Yes. I do. It's about money, not medicine," Rose answers. "Maybe I should try to find a job within the FDA – fix what's broken."

"That's my girl," a voice says from the corner.

"Your girl," Rose says with a tone of irritation. "I am not your girl."

"Whose girl are you, then," a dark misshapen man says from the corner. "Who do you belong to?"

"I'm married to Aristotle," Rose says loudly in the direction of the man.

"Are you?" he replies. "Or are you just playing?"

59

"We are married," Rose says lifting her left hand to show her ring.

"Good, then someone is going to take care of you now, feed you, clothe you, change you," the eerily low voice utters in a very unsettling tone. "You're trapped. You can't get out. You're going to burn." And with those words, fire engulfs the room.

This time Rose wakes herself up with a panicked inhale, a residual attempt to obtain oxygen from clear pockets in the smoke filled room of her nightmare. She initially laughs off the dream. *Silly,* she reasons. Yet her mind keeps on returning to the dark figure in the corner of Diane's office, a character stolen straight from the cover of an H.P. Lovecraft novel.

Frustrated and tired, she sits up and puts her feet on the ground and her head in her hands. "Are these dreams trying to tell me something? Are my priorities wrong?" she asks the air. "God, just tell me what you want me to do? I swear I'll listen. Just tell me." Rose almost starts to cry due to exhaustion. "Am I making a mistake?" Deep down, Rose knows that this is the right decision for both her short term and long term goals. "I want to build You gardens." *Why are You doing this to me?* she thinks. She continues her prayer, "Is it because I haven't told him? I don't think he'll understand… well, not completely…"

With her eyes heavy with exhaustion, she stands and, out of habit, searches her floor for a towel. Realizing that it has been close to five months since she stayed in this room, she concocts a new plan and walks to her sock drawer. Even an emotionally laden Rose takes much amusement in discovering that the sock drawer of her youth is very similar to the sock drawer of her fledgling adulthood. She smiles as she is able to choose the absolutely perfect single soft, fuzzy sock from a mass of single socks to sop up her sweat. "Where do they go?" she asks. She steps in front of her window fan to finish the job. Looking down at her moonlit sternum, still beading with sweat, she continues to dab. "I will tell him, in my own time. It's just that I am pretty sure that he'll think that I'm crazy. I still want to… I still need to hide my crazy from him. Just for a little longer," she says with a smirk.

Tossing her colorful striped sock into the far corner, where her basket used to be, Rose remembers the priorities she has just set. "I have to tell him, don't I? Married partners do not keep secrets. Well, not important ones, right?" she says to her sky-swirled painted ceiling. "Do you think that the reason we get along so well is because I know that I can't hide my crazy from You? Tell You what; I will make it a priority. I will tell him. I just need to come up with some sort of candy coating for that pill…"

Rose climbs back into bed and picks up and untwists her comforter. Rather than continuing the battle with her comforter, she folds it down and places it at the foot of the bed. As she returns to find her pillow she recognizes that she accidentally put her pillow-Aris on the wrong side. He is supposed to be on the left. *That explains it*, she thinks. She makes the adjustment, pulls up the top sheet over her shoulders and is finally able to fall into a dreamless sleep.

***

Her alarm sounds one hour later. Rose hits the snooze button and utters, "Sleep. Sleep is a priority. God, sleep?" She quickly rises and showers.

Dressed in a khaki suit with her hair in a tight bun, Rose steps into the kitchen. She takes a moment to notice the soft yellow sunlight streaming in through the eastern window before uttering, "Morning." She nods to both her parents as she helps herself to coffee.

"You look very tired," Grace says.

"I didn't sleep very well. Nightmares." Rose lifts her coffee to her lips and meditates on whether she should ask the question she wants to ask. She takes a thoughtful sip and then speaks, "I

61

was wondering, do you guys ever have nightmares? Is it a genetic thing?"

"I have dreams where I lose one of my children in a crowd," Grace admits. "The sheer panic... It wakes me up every time."

Joseph reflects upon his daughter's question for a few moments before answering, "In most of my dreams I am struggling to get somewhere that I cannot quite reach." Satisfied with his response he shrugs his shoulders and returns to his sports page.

"I guess I have had a few of those," Rose admits to her father. She shifts to her mother. "I am pretty sure that I have never had a lost child dream. Do you think it is strange that I'm having nightmare after nightmare, night after night. I am beginning to think that... well... never mind..."

"Black, right?" Grace thoughtfully hands her daughter a sensible and necessary travel mug. She lowers her head to catch her daughter's eyes. "You've always had such powerful dreams. I remember when you were a kid, you used to wake up all the time screaming. It used to take me hours to get you back to sleep. Do you remember?" Grace reminisces about her daughter's youth, while admiring the woman in front of her. "Back then, I remember thinking that your nightmares were caused by you trying to keep a secret. You were always terrible at keeping secrets."

"Huh," Rose says lifting her day's lifeline elixir to her mouth. "Secrets? Really?" Rose takes her mother's observation to heart and instantaneously learns something new about herself. "Actually, that's kinda interesting and explains a lot..."

"You should also keep in mind that you are taking a big step today – quitting your job. That's a pretty big deal for you. Whether you would like to admit it or not," Grace says. She looks at her daughter's face, which is at the moment expressing exhaustion, confusion and fear, but mostly exhaustion. Grace decides that it is probably best to offer some reassuring

62

guidance. "You're going to be fine, Honey. I think school is a really good idea for you. If you guys run into money problems… that's what we are here for. We can help."

Joseph momentarily looks up from his paper with a notable expression of disagreement.

"Thanks, Mom, but I'm sure we'll be fine," Rose says as she casually notices her father. She looks around the kitchen while processing the suggestion provided by her mother. She takes comfort in the fact that she did just tell her parents about the nightmares. It's only a matter of time until she finds the courage to tell Aris. "About these nightmares…What bothers me, is that there is nothing really bothering me. Everything is going great right now. I have never been happier," Rose admits looking directly into her mother's face. "I guess I would think that these dreams were normal if things were going badly. Yet, seriously Mom, I have never been happier. So why am I having these nightmares now? It must mean something, right?"

"Maybe it's just sleeping in a strange bed," Grace says.

"Maybe. Thanks, Mom," Rose says. She successfully hides her disappointment as she realizes that she and her mother are not quite on the same page. *Telling Aris is going to be harder than I thought,* she thinks. "Well, I should really get going. I have a job to quit, a storage unit to rent, and an apartment to pack. I won't be here for dinner tonight. I really need to get started on that apartment. How about Thursday night? I should pretty much be done by then."

"Did you want help?" Joseph asks. "I can bring pizza."

Rose smiles. "If you don't mind. That'd be nice. I could really use the help. Josephine is dropping by tomorrow, but…"

Grace and Joseph immediately volunteer to help their daughter pack. They jointly suggest Angelo's pizza with an arrival time around 6:30. Rose excitedly accepts their offer with hugs all around. "Good morning, Mom. Good morning, Dad. Thanks for everything. Have a great day. See ya tonight." She lifts her coffee mug in salute, grabs her purse and keys, and heads out the door.

Δ7Δ

The Kites and the Swans

THE KITES of olden times, as well as the Swans, had the privilege of song. But having heard the neigh of the horse, they were so enchanted with the sound, that they tried to imitate it; and, in trying to neigh, they forgot how to sing. – Aesop

Rose knocks on the familiar-styled door of her new neighbors. While awaiting an answer, she amuses herself with smelling the deep and vibrant roses growing on the decorative trellis adorning their front yard. The door opens just as Rose's nose takes its second inhale. Physically frozen, Rose turns her head to greet her neighbor, Abner Griffis.

"Hello, Miss. Can I help you?" A well-groomed seventy-nine year old man wearing pressed khakis and a crisp white golf shirt stands in his doorway.

"Abner Griffis?" Rose asks, scanning the man and smiling at his blue corduroy slippers. They remind her of her own grandfather.

"Yes." Abner looks at Rose inquisitively.

"Sir, my name is Rose Isope. I live five doors down. This package was accidentally delivered to us. I suppose the carrier just transposed the three and the five." She hands a small box to Abner. "I cannot help but to notice that it is from ICOM. My husband just bought me a radio system."

Abner smiles. "A fellow Amateur Radio enthusiast."

Rose returns his smile. "I haven't exactly started... I am just learning Morse code for now. I have been practicing for a few months."

"You have to start somewhere and the best place to start is with the code," Abner says, nodding as he takes the package from Rose. "Thank you. I have been waiting for this. I was going to call about it today. My hobby is homebrewing."

Rose looks puzzled. "Homebrewing, sir?"

"I am a classic Ham. I've been building my own system."

Abner's wife appears behind him. "Abner?" she calls.

"Clara, this is Rose. She is bringing me a package that was accidentally delivered to her. She is interested in amateur radio," Abner says craning his neck to the right to look at his wife.

Clara nods and remains silent.

"Nice to meet you." Rose smiles a very toothy, innocent smile and leans her entire body to look at Clara.

"I didn't think that kids your age were interested in Amateur Radio," says Abner.

"I am older than I look, sir," Rose says defiantly, following it with a gentle smile. "I am thirty-three."

"Like I said, I didn't think kids your age were interested in Amateur Radio. So what did your husband get you and why?"

"Oh Abner, you just met this young girl. Go easy on the questions," says Clara, lightly slapping her husband on the shoulder. "You will have to forgive my husband; he has always been very direct, perhaps too direct. Would you like to come in, Dear? We were just about to have iced tea on the Veranda."

Rose looks down the road toward her house. "I don't mind directness. I'm a big fan of efficiency. And to answer your question, my husband won't be home for another two hours, so if it is not too much trouble, I would love a glass of iced tea. I would like to learn about homebrewing and tea seems like a good place to start." Turning her attention back to Abner, she says, "And Sir, to answer *your* question, my husband bought me an MFJ QRP radio. I guess it's a low power radio – just five watts."

"You guess or you know?" Abner asks abruptly.

66

"I have really only read the box that the radio came in, Sir. I really have no idea what I am looking at? I have heard it is a good starter radio."

"Any radio is a good starter radio." Abner squelches.

With a simple slap followed by a gentle tug, Clara starts to lead the conversation toward the Veranda. "We just had this built and we are trying to spend as much time in it as possible. The tea is unsweetened. Would you need sugar, dear?"

"No ma'am, I prefer my tea unsweetened," Rose responds as she walks through the French doors into her neighbor's courtyard. "This is beautiful. The grape vines are fantastic. I thought you said you just had this built?"

"We have had the grape vines for years, growing vertically along the back of our garden. We just moved them overhead with the help of a very clever landscape architect. I feel like I am visiting an ancient Greek palace when I sit back here." Clara looks delighted as she sits comfortably in her well-made wicker chair with sea foam and coral striped cushions. She looks up into beautiful, crisp white wooden framework adorned in Concord grape vines.

"Your husband – he is into radio?" Abner asks with an almost palpable softness, yet still abrupt.

Rose smiles as she tries to stop herself from laughing at his manner and mode of speech. "No, not that I know of ... he keeps lots of secrets from me." Rose almost winks at Abner then reconsiders. "We are both just learning Morse code."

"Then, why did he buy you a radio? Seems a frivolous purchase," Abner says.

"Sir, he thinks I need a hobby; he thinks I need a technical hobby. He also thinks that this hobby blends well with my other interests. I am a theologian. He thinks that someone who is intellectually fascinated with old-style communication should be interested in the new old-style communication."

Abner smirks. "And your husband's name?"

67

"Aristotle Irwin," Rose responds.

"Gwyneth's grandson?" Clara asks.

"Yes Ma'am."

The pair lights up. "Why didn't you say so? We have been playing bridge with the Irwin's for twenty years. You are his new bride? I didn't know you two got married already." Clara is almost giddy as she gently claps her hands together a few times.

"Well, Ma'am. We are married in God's eyes. We have not had a social ceremony yet. We are still making plans." Rose hopes her answer is sufficient and that an awkward conversation about wedding plans does not unfold.

"You just met the young lady. Go easy on the questions," Abner says, winking at Rose. "Frank's new grand-daughter-in-law wants to be Ham. He's going to be so pleased."

Rose lifts her glass of tea. "To Frank and Gwyneth."

"So how far have you gotten regarding your station," Abner asks with a renewed interest.

"Not far at all. As I have said, the radio is pretty much still in the box. I think I heard Aris mention that I need an antenna."

"QRP radio you said. We'll have to put up a dipole for you," Abner says. "I think I have all we would need in my radio storage shed." He points to the nearly two story white storage shed built as an addition in the back of the courtyard. "I got aluminum wire and coaxial cable." He looks from the striking architectural feature multi-tasking as a shed to his backyard's garden gate. "I am a retired architect. I pretty much built this entire development and pretty much own most of the land surrounding the area. I have chosen this unit because the hill that is right beyond this fence is the highest elevation in the area." Abner stands and walks approximately eighteen feet to the gate. After a few seconds with what is apparently a complicated latch, he opens the garden gate and points to a giant antenna. This antenna has three YAGI arrays - A tribander," he yells.

Rose meets him at the gate. "A tribander, sir?"

68

"A tribander – well that is just a familiar term for an antenna that allows access to more frequencies than any other. My antenna has a boom with a twenty-meter, a fifteen-meter, and ten-meter elements attached. How much do you know about how antenna's work?"

"I guess the short answer is not much. I guess I know that an antenna has to be made of a good conducting metal – copper, silver or aluminum. I am pretty sure that I have no idea why they have a particular form to function." Rose answers.

"You need an Elmer," Abner says.

"An Elmer?"

"In the Amateur Radio circuit, an Elmer is someone who teaches you about radio," Abner quickly answers.

"Could you be my Elmer?" Rose asks with straightforward eye contact. Rose watches Abner relock the gate and the two return to Clara.

"I will help you set up your system. Your husband Aristotle and I will build you an antenna and you can start listening. But you need to do the work to get your first license – your novice license. I need to know that you have at least that much initiative. After you get your novice license, I would be more than happy to be your Elmer," Abner says. With a smile at his wife he adds, "I am going to have to tell the guys about this."

"Abner belongs to a Ham radio club called Ionosphere," Clara says as she offers a refill.

Rose declines. "No thanks. I have had a good deal of trouble sleeping as of late. I am trying to minimize my caffeine intake." Turning to Abner, she asks, "The ionosphere?"

Abner takes a deep breath before standing. He leaves the room only to return a couple minutes later with two text books: *Ionosphere: The High-Latitude Ionosphere and its Effects on Radio Propagation*, and a giant paperback entitled *The 2011 AARL Handbook*. "I started my interest in amateur radio as a Boy Scout. My continued interest is mostly the Ionosphere. In

69

particular, the effects of the sun on the Ionosphere. You can say that I am interested in the top and the home base of the hobby."

Rose notices that Clara is becoming a bit restless. Listening to Clara's body language, she adequately adjusts her own. "Clara and Abner, thank you for your hospitality," she says, "but I should really get going. My husband will be home soon, and I would like to feed him at some point." She stands as she accepts the two rather large and heavy text books from Abner. She reviews their binding before continuing, "Rather than borrowing what looks to be a very pricey text book, I will do a bit of online research about the Ionosphere, first. No offense, but even the cover art of this textbook frightens me." Rose huffs a giggle and then quickly expresses seriousness as she returns the text to the table. "The ARRL Handbook on the other hand... I was going to borrow the handbook from the library. They only had the 2009 version available. I'd love to borrow this book. I promise I will take good care of it." Hugging the handbook, she asks, "Do you think that maybe we could get together this Saturday and make plans to build my antenna? I would really like to start listening."

Abner looks at his wife before answering, "I am sure we can arrange something. Here Miss, here is my card." He pulls out a business card from his wallet. "Call me later in the week, Thursday perhaps, and we will try to figure out something."

"Thanks. I cannot believe how serendipitous this all is... starting with radio equipment being accidentally delivered to my house. Every once in a while... I don't know, I think that Aris likes to keep me guessing." Rose smiles as she looks at her feet. "He didn't plan this, did he?"

Abner smiles and lowers his head and taps his right foot. "Serendipitous, indeed."

"Please tell Gwyneth I said 'Hello' and to visit soon. I do miss our weekly Bridge evenings," Clara says as she gently escorts Rose to her front door. "It is so nice to meet you. Frank

70

and Gwyneth must be so proud to have such a bright and charming young grand-daughter-in-law."

"Thanks for the compliment. I have only met them once. I hope I made as equally a good impression on them as I have appeared to make on you," Rose says. She humbly lowers her head as she presses through the front door. "Thank you for inviting me into your beautiful home."

"Start studying for your novice test. It's just thirty-five questions, multiple-choice. Easy as pie," Abner says.

"Sir, have you ever made a pie?" Rose glances at Clara before continuing, "Making a good crust and rolling pie dough is not exactly easy. I think they should replace it with its as easy as box cake mix, or box brownies."

"Pillsbury makes these pre-made crusts that are pretty good. And easy," Abner returns. "I love apple pie. And if I want a slice I have to make it myself."

"Is that so? Thanks for your help with all of this and have a great evening." Rose hugs the handbook a bit tighter as she descends the few steps that return her to the sidewalk. She turns around to offer an additional nod to her gracious hosts before they close the door. With a light heart and a gentle skip, Rose quickly heads down the sidewalk to her fortunate abode.

Δ8Δ

Excellence is never an accident. It is always the result of high intention, sincere effort, and intelligent execution; it represents the wise choice of many alternatives -- choice, not chance, determines your destiny. – Aristotle

In the kitchen, Rose tends to the tuna while taking great delight in rejecting the advances of her particularly randy husband. Staving off his advances, she tells him about the particulars of her relatively interesting day. She tells him about her visit with their neighbors, the very cute Griffises. When she informs him of her promotion, he does not react well to this news.

"Please tell me you are not that naïve."

"I am not naïve. I'm flattered. I'm flattered that they want to keep me so much that they are willing to increase my salary by twenty three percent and let me work from home sixty percent of the time." Rose has no intention of taking their offer. She just wants to see how far she can push.

Aris stops his movement to look at her. He notices the spirals in her hair and the golden flecks in her eyes. With a very strong, even tone, he says, unequivocally, "They're lying."

Rose continues to push by remaining silent, pretending to focus her efforts on the tuna steak she bought specifically for her husband as part of an "I really, really missed you" dinner. "Maybe they are," she says in an effort to continue her ruse.

"Rose, why are you even considering their offer?" he asks as he tries to squelch his tone of frustration. "Is it money? I know money is not that important to you. Why are you concerned about it now – now that you have doubled your income by

72

simply marrying me?" He lifts the small fryer and flips the vegetables. "I can take care of you."

Up until this moment, Rose had every intention of letting him in on her little joke. Yet she cannot help but hear the voice of her week long recurring nightmare wrapped up in his flippant comment. "Why do you want to fight?" she snaps.

"You know why."

"I do?" she asks. She clenches her jaw and awaits his reply.

"I like making up, especially when we…Come on Rose, I haven't seen you naked in almost an entire week," Aris says as he feels a renewal of his initial reaction to coming home and seeing his wife in their kitchen four hours earlier than expected. The suggestion of acting on that reaction was, much to his chagrin, put on the back burner because she already started to cook this "special" dinner.

"What are you, eighteen?" she says with a smirk. "Listen, I don't want to be dependent on you. I'm actually having some pretty serious nightmares about it. Without the ability to take care of myself, I'm pretty sure you are not going to like me as much. I'm worried that I will lose my value."

"Your value? You're invaluable," he says. Thinking that all she is worried about is money, he responds, "All we really have to do is adjust our spending. Stay in rather than go out. Eat oatmeal rather than cereal; tuna fish instead of tuna steak. These subtle changes add up, I promise."

"Yeah, yeah, you also said that we could save money on clothes too, if we just stopped wearing them," she says with a relaxing laugh, falling into his embrace. "Okay, fine, I will give up my job and my clothes."

"That's the most sensible thing you have said all day," he says as he reaches under her pink summer sweater to unhook her bra. He then begins to move his hands toward the intended targets. He leans in to whisper in her ear. "Come on, please," he begs.

73

With one hand, Rose magically re-hooks her bra. She turns and dishes out a slight slap on his shoulder. "Patience, handsome," she says. She follows that up with a maternal pat on his left cheek to cool him down even further. "Patience is a virtue." She turns off the grill and reaches across the counter for her favorite spice, coarse garlic salt. *And on that note*, Rose thinks. She takes a deep breath. "So, Aristotle, my patient purveyor of virtues, I think I stumbled upon another potential career this past week. It works with my degree in Theology and will work with my degree in Economics... Do you remember that comic book I was working on years ago, the book where I was breeding virtues?"

"Let's see, do I remember?" Aris says looking into his wife's hair as he instinctually moves closer to smell her skin. He seductively moves her hair behind her ear. "I distinctly remember you telling me years ago that patience wasn't a virtue. It supposedly fell under the umbrella of temperance. Patience wasn't a virtue and temperance was..." Aris leans to his right to look at her profile. "Rose, are you sure dinner can't wait?" he says nearly whining. He accompanies his tone with a very apparent nod to the stairway and an obvious use of Rose's kryptonite, his perfectly-arched eyebrows.

Rose replies raising her own eyebrows and states, "Two words. Cold fish."

Aris sighs loudly, affectedly, jokingly. He even stomps for effect and to make her smile. He finally concedes to her conversation. "So yeah, okay, fine. Of course I remember your virtues...You kept them in that white spiral notebook," he says in a full and affected pout followed by one last stomp.

Rose gently kisses a sensitive trigger spot on his neck to let him know that his angling is understood, but tabled. "Yep. That's the one. In it, Patience is a virtue, and she married Impetuous," she says with a smile as she turns to locate the white notebook hidden, in plain sight, under her laptop. She

74

hands the notebook to her husband. "I found this while packing. It's odd, or maybe serendipitous...It was this comic book that initially sparked my interest in economics nine years ago. I had almost forgotten about it."

Aris moves from the stove to the other side of the island to flip through the cardboard pages of her comic book. Bound in a heavy card-stock spiral notebook, it features short stories that depict the personifications of virtues and their opposites. He familiarizes himself with the memento of their past, sighing and snickering at certain pages. "Actually, there are some pretty good couples in here," Aris says. In her book, Rose paired off her virtues and chronicled their falling in love, getting married and having children.

"My favorite is still Simplicity, the costumer and Intricate, the female Kabuki actress who had to pretend she was a man pretending to be a woman," Aris says laughing as his eyes review the thirty stills, the last of which features the couple's baby, Creativity.

"I think that one is my favorite, too. The dialogue of their courtship is very good. Simplicity is really funny," Rose says as she watches her husband flip through the pages. She returns to arranging dinner on their plates. "And Baby Creativity – masterful. Water to drink?"

"Yes, please. Baby Creativity – the baby with reflective skin. Just like that guy in Terminator Two," he says, repeating her simple explanation of Creativity's skin from years ago.

Rose nods. "Reflective skin for reflection," she says as if it were obvious. Rose picks up both of their plates and carries them to the table.

Aris follows her lead. He brings along the notebook and sets it down next to his plate. "And Charity and Greed bred to create Baby Generosity."

"Yep, they met when Greed was trying to get a tax write-off for his old computers to help purchase new ones and Charity was collecting his old computers for the local high school. It was love at first sight," Rose reports with a self-satisfied, yet child-like grin on her face. "Getting some of these pairs to fall in love in twelve stills was difficult. Greed and Charity – they were pretty easy."

Rose watches her husband pour over her comic for a few minutes before getting to the heart of the conversation she wants to have. She has spent the past week suffering under more serious and demanding nightmares. These subconscious stirrings are both increasing in frequency and in destruction, and she has found that she can no longer ignore their message. In an attempt to balance her mind's horrific scenes with what her mother said was a possible cause for her nightmares, keeping secrets, she has been quite occupied for the past five days. After nearly a week of nighttime solitude, she has decided that the only way to tell her *secret* was to attribute both value and meaning, sense and story to these night shadows. They must be happening for a reason and that reason is – she has to tell people. She has determined that this lost-and-found notebook will give her a way.

She makes her first pass. "So I spent the better part of this week doing what you asked of me on our wedding day. You asked me to reconsider my priorities. I guess now is the time to tell you that I think I want to make *this* a priority. I think I found a place for them."

"A place?" Aris looks confused.

My garden, she thinks. "I have decided to write a novel. In it, an ad hoc government forms after the volcanic eruption of the Yellowstone cauldron. A new government for a new calendar era –Anno Domini, A.D. becomes After Yellowstone, A.Y." Rose pauses for a brief second as she watches him process what she is saying.

"Huh," Aris responds.

76

"I am going to use these personified virtues and build my government around them. It will be sorta fable-like – but probably closer to a tale than a fable." Rose looks at her husband who is obviously listening, yet is mostly focusing on the pages in front of him. "And Aris, I'd like to keep my name. Okay? Irwin Aesop? I think my name is also top priority for me. I'm an Aesop. I don't want to lose that."

"Irwin Aesop, with an A?" he says. He reaches across the table and grabs her wedded hand. He thumbs the top of her diamond. "Sounds good to me."

"I love you," Rose says deeply touched by the simple gesture. She inhales deeply to stop tears from forming. "Now that that's been said…" Rose switches gears and mentally runs through her plan, strategically outlined this morning while driving back to Maryland. She crosses items off her mental checklist. She told him about the nightmares she is having about losing her independence. She told him about the book. She is now ready to take them both to the next level. "So yeah, I was inspired by this comic book, but this 'novel idea' came to me in a dream. On Tuesday night, I had this *really* intense dream that the Yellowstone caldera actually erupted. The fallout was incredible; nations just fell apart. In my dream I was told that the world will need a new government. I had that dream, and the day after…I find this comic book."

Aris looks directly into his wife's eyes and simply smiles in support of the idea. He gently lifts the comic and says, "I really like that Justice, the lion tamer and Injury, the acrobat paired up."

"Baby Progress," she says with a smile. *He is with me, for now.* She internally congratulates herself on her delicate pacing in letting her husband in on her Yellowstone plan. "So what do you think? Walking, talking and breeding virtues teaching the world building-block principles is similar to Aesop's Scorpions

77

and Frogs teaching morals, right? It's not a completely crazy idea, right?"

"No, Honey, it's not a crazy idea. People meet, fall in love, get married and make babies all the time. We met, fell in love, got married and…"

"Babies are cute," Rose says quickly, tearing her eyes away, "especially babies with reflective skin." She understands that he wants to have *the* baby conversation. She also knows that he knows that she is not ready. She winks. "The more you rush me, my nefarious one…"

Aris huffs at her dodge and quickly finds Nefarious in her comic. He pinches the page and smiles. "Writing your own book of fables based upon virtues? I am assuming you are going to do this as a children's book. If so, maybe you should learn how to draw first," Aris says. He displays her comic to her similar to how one would read a children's storybook to a group. "Look, every single one of them has mitten hands."

"That's not true, Regret has hooks," Rose says touching the edges of her place setting. "And besides, there is drawing from a well and drawing a well. One is more valuable than the other. But I do want this government to be both animated and colorful. You know, alive. Plato's forms, Aristotle's virtues, and Aesop's morals, I can actually see them. I can actually see all of them – walking and talking."

"You are such a nerd," he says. A gentle smile sits on his face before he returns his attentions to her notebook to review the last of the couples. When he reaches the end of the book, he closes it, turns it around and slides it back to his Rose. "My wife wants to build a virtuous government? Hmm." He takes a bite of his perfectly seared tuna and tries to stifle his laughter. He fails. After a good hearty laugh, and while still bearing a big grin, he says, "So you are going to build a virtuous government while laboring as a landscaper, studying for your amateur radio

78

license, and obtaining a Master's in Economics. If you were anyone else, I'd say you were taking on a bit too much."

Rose nervously grabs at her heels in response to his compliment. She returns with her own. "What did Aristotle say – working for money does not fulfill need?"

"Something like that," Aris says. He takes the last bite of his tuna and chews. "So, my beautiful wife, do you want to tell me more about Abner?" Aris says trying to conceal his curiosity about how his crafted intrigue played out.

Rose displays her patentable Mona Lisa smile and immediately begins to chatterbox about her conversation with Abner, answering every question Aris asks. The conversation moves from the neighbors to her week away from her new home.

Just glad to have her back, and knowing her all too well, Aris happily carries the conversation back to her book idea. "So, a virtuous government?" he asks replaying his stifled giggle. "And what does a virtuous government look like?"

"A Physiocracy," she answers quickly, "a government of nature. I know that even merely suggesting a Physiocracy makes this a work of fiction, fantasy." She grips the corner of the placemat as she tries to stop herself from changing the subject to her theological garden. Yet, she cannot stop. "A Physiocracy seems infinitely more suitable for the Middle East."

Aris recognizes the on ramp. He has to stop her. "Did you say fantasy? My current fantasy is that my wife no longer wishes to wear clothes," Aris says with a wry smile.

"Nefarious." Rose returns a coquettish smile. "My fantasy is that my husband will help me understand a few more concepts of economics."

"Let's make a deal. I will tell you what I know about economics for an item of clothing."

"Seriously?" Rose quickly agrees to his deal.

79

Employing his most successful tactics for getting his ridiculously nerdy wife into his bed, Aris proceeds to enlighten his bride with the principles of economics while taking an article of clothing for each explained concept. For her shirt, he gives her Adam Smith; for her shoes and earrings, David Ricardo and Ricardian Economics. He is more than pleased with himself after he gets his bride in just her underwear and bra with an explanation of how the recent government intervention into the auto and banking industry was an example of Keynesian Economics.

A nearly naked Rose sits comfortably in her living room after dinner and Aris's lessons. "Hmm. The virtues of economics. Thanks Aris, you are a good teacher," she says, moving to straddle him. "You know how much I like arrowheads, but this stuff is really starting to make sense to me. I might even be able to draw a couple from this conversation. How about Value and Scarcity. They meet in Haiti, after the earthquake."

"Value and Scarcity?" He takes in the sight of his wife in her pale pink lingerie. "You're not really considering keeping your pharma job, are you?"

"After spending a week without you – no way," Rose says with a satisfied smile. "So Nefarious, are you tired of being patient?" She jumps to standing and moves into a running man pose. "I run when chased."

Aris immediately jumps to his feet and does his best to make her swoon. "I think Value and Scarcity sound like compliments rather than opposites. Something is valuable because it is scarce, right?"

Rose's heart melts. "I have really missed you this week, too. I couldn't sleep. It's nice being able to share even my un-shareable thoughts – the thoughts I keep secret."

Aris walks toward her. He puts his hands on the curve of her hips. The simple action immediately reminds him of his earlier

80

intentions and his deeper intentions. "I missed you too, so much. I don't think you will ever know just how much you add to my life. Things certainly are way too quiet around here without you."

Rose rises to the balls of her feet, tugs at his ear and kisses him.

Aris pulls her closer. "So, I was wondering…Do you happen to know who is the mother of invention?"

"I think Necessity bred with Genius," Rose says.

"Come on, Wife, let's make love," Aris says.

She clutches the collar of her husband's shirt and tugs. "What do you think about a blog? I could start a blog and get these characters out there."

"A blog? Wait, what about radio?"

"I think I can do both," Rose says pulling on his belt loops. "Yeah, a blog, something like – the Volcano's Virtues. It'll be hot." Rose turns and skips toward the stairs. "Ya coming?"

He looks up the stairs to see that his wife is already on top, patiently waiting. "Grâce à votre seule presence," he says taking the first few steps, and then stopping to take a perfect still of his gorgeous wife, his radio intrigue no longer taking residence in his mind.

"What?" Rose asks.

"By virtue of your mere presence…" Aris translates.

"By virtue? Nefarious." She giggles and runs into their bedroom.

"La Femme."

81

Δ9Δ

The Seaside Travelers

*SOME TRAVELERS, journeying along the seashore, climbed
to the summit of a tall cliff, and from thence looking over the
sea, saw in the distance what they thought was a large ship, and
waited in the hope of seeing it enter the harbor. But as the object
on which they looked was driven by the wind nearer to shore,
they found that it could at the most be a small boat, and not a
ship. When, however, it reached the beach, they discovered that
it was only a large fagot of sticks, and one of them said to his
companions: We have waited for no purpose, for after all there
is nothing to see but a load of wood. – Aesop*

"Topiary is the art of living sculpture," Erik begins as he
walks with Rose through his greenhouse of woodsy animals.
"These are pretty much my pride and joy. The squirrel and the
deer are the most favored of the lot. Although I have sold a few
bunnies and a couple of bears – the squirrel and the deer seem to
attract the most attention from paying gardeners. I am not sure
why. I really like the bears. Anyway, the word derives from
the Latin word for an ornamental gardener, *topiarius*, a creator
of *topia* or 'places.' This place, this greenhouse – I call it my
'Woodlands.'"

Rose looks at her tall, comfortably well-nourished and soft-
spoken boss with a sense of wonderment after taking in the sites
of his 'Woodlands,' complete with rabbits, squirrels, deer, bears,
gnomes and even a few Smurfs with mushroom houses. "These
are truly incredible. You made all of these?"

"I did," Erik says with a satisfied tone. "They almost look
alive don't they? As if they could walk right up out of here."

"They do," Rose says in total agreement. She tries to peer a
bit closer at the deer that seems to have shifted positions in her

periphery. Rose strongly huffs through her nose to mimic the sound of the deer and then patiently waits for a response.

Erik cocks his head to the right with an overture of judgment at her attempt to communicate with a yew. "These are about five years old – and therefore carry the highest price tag. They are well trained and would only require a serious maintenance trim about once a year. However, I trim them about once a season. I almost shed a tear every time I sell one of these guys." Patting the deer's head, he walks over to Rose and points to the elephant. "I have been working on him for nine years. I am not sure if I could ever sell him. I had a giraffe too. I regret letting her go."

Rose walks to a picture framed in the space behind the elephant. It is of Erik standing on a ladder, trimming the neck of the giraffe. "How tall was the giraffe?"

"The ladder was a hundred fifty feet." Erik opens the back door of the galley green house and then immediately opens the door to the next.

Rose looks behind her to the seemingly endless halls of greenhouses connected very much like train cars. She decides that each greenhouse is about forty feet long. "How many greenhouses do you have?"

Erik ignores her question. "These are my more traditional topiary pieces. Cones, spirals, pom-poms, Indian heads, and, of course, the poodles." Erik barks and then howls.

"Do you have wolves?" Rose asks, disrupting his process.

"These creations are about three years old and you are going to start to learn on these." Erik scans the room and rotates a few of the large clay pots for a more complete assessment of the plants' health. "Although I get a few independent gardeners here – my main clients are actually landscapers. In the spring, we are called out for trimmings about two days a week. We are also called out on consults one to two times a week. The rest of the time is spent training the plants and creating new ones – wire

83

designs." Erik leads her out of the greenhouse and they enter into a cool, white and sparsely decorated concrete structure located in front of the train-like greenhouses. "This is our online business. Here we use wires to create topiary that are stuffed with moss and then covered using small leaved ivy. The cages can be fully covered in a matter of months. I think that the true topiary artist might find these creations a bit like cheating – I find it fascinating – a topiary plant assembly line. Here we can create almost any shape – house numbers, monograms, monkeys swinging on a trapeze bar. There is really no limit."

Rose looks around the room and notes large coaxial cable entering in from the top windows, as if it were a basement design. "Are we in an above ground basement?"

"I also find that making the cages helps me see the lines better – helps me be a better natural topiary artist." Erik waves hello to a man sitting at his desk twisting wire into a small-mouth bass on a lure. "Prince Harry Lake outside of Bethesda has commissioned the fish topiaries to frame their multiple community beach signs. On the days we are not called out – this is where we are. This part of the biz is quickly becoming our bread and butter."

The seated employee pulls out a bagel from a toaster located on his work bench. "It's a joke. Bread and Butter. I prefer bagels."

"How many people work here?" Rose asks as she notices the number of empty desks.

"I have a staff of twelve – well, you make thirteen. How is your luck?"

"As you know, my husband is Irish," Rose says. "Thirteen has never been unlucky for me."

"I am going to pass you over to Julie. Julie is our resident green thumb. She is going to explain the varieties of plants we work with as well as how to care for them. This is the most important part of the job. I want you to be able to recognize if a plant needs nitrogen or magnesium. I want you to be able to recognize a plant that has been recently trimmed versus being trimmed weeks ago or month ago, for that matter. You will be tested on this information by at least two of us – maybe more. Understand? You will be tested," Erik says seriously. "We cannot afford to lose plants, and like any nursery, diligence is required. It takes a village and all that. Any questions?"

"I have my paperwork for tax purposes. Is there someone you would like for me…"

"Ship Shape!" Erik interrupts and smiles at his joke. "Forgive me. I cannot resist a good topiary joke." He takes her papers and vanishes, leaving Rose alone with Julie.

"Hi, Julie." Rose reaches her hand out to the athletic looking woman about ten years her senior, standing in a cool closet surrounded by soil, manure, and burlap.

"Rose. I heard you were starting today. Welcome." Julie's bright, clear blue eyes sparkle as she takes Rose's hand into her suede and rubber dark green glove. "Gosh those are some mighty soft hands."

"You are wearing gloves, how can you tell?" Slightly self-conscious for being so forward in her introduction, Rose averts her attention to her palms. "Do not let my soft exterior fool you – I have naturally clammy hands and therefore they remain soft even under the harshest of conditions."

"Pretty big talk for such a little girl," Julie says as she hides her smile. "So did Erik scare the hell out of you explaining that you must be a plant physiologist by the end of the workday?"

"Well, sorta, I guess. Actually, I took a class in both Botany and Plant Physiology as an undergrad – monocots and dicots. I was tested. I think I passed."

"Good. Actually, that will probably speed things up quite a bit. Let's walk over to the printer. I created a cheat sheet for this walk – for study purposes." The two women walk over to the printer and Rose watches Julie pick up four very large and

85

colorful pages from the extremely robust printer nestled in the corner of the concrete building. "This is the information you need to know, and I mean like the palm of your clammy hand, by the end of this week or you *will* lose your job here."

"Understood." Rose confidently takes the papers from her hand and worries for a moment that her ridiculously sweaty palms will make the pages illegible.

"First, I am going to show you the healthy plants and then I will take you to greenhouse four – the ICU – to show you the signs of plants that are very sick," Julie says. Looking over to the work desks, she yells, "Do you need anything before I go?"

"Hi, Rose. I am Jim 'Hot Wire' Wilson!" the bass maker yells across the room.

"I am sorry. I thought Erik introduced the two of you. Rose, meet Jim. Jim, meet Rose."

Rose meekly waves in his direction. "Hot wire, eh? I am not going to touch that."

"I am all black baby!" Jim says, trying to gently haze the newbie.

"He's all black?" Rose questions herself and then gives a wave to Jim as they leave the concrete building. The two women enter a new greenhouse.

"These are the plants to be trimmed into traditionals."

"Not split level? Or Ranch style? ... What? No greenhouse jokes?" Rose looks past Julie down the galley at innumerable potted variations of evergreens that completely fill the greenhouse, stacked from floor to ceiling. Rose makes a mental note of the deep green hue assaulting her vision. "This really is a green house."

"This is not your house," the woman says, piercing Rose's right ear and recalling her attention back to the task at hand. "The front half will be shaped into cones. A good rule of thumb is to not have to trim more than one third of the plant to make the topiary. As you can see – these already look pretty much like cones. The second half will be trimmed into spirals." Julie walks halfway down the galley and removes a wide rope from her latex gardener's belt and ties the top of the rope to the top of the shrub. "These have already been shaped into a cone shape. Now, you just drape the rope similar to how you would place garland on a Christmas tree."

"Is that why you have Christmas lights here?" Rose asks looking at the pink and blue lighting surrounding the trees.

Julie takes out her very large, polished pruning shears and without touching the plant explains, "Trim the twig ends where they touch the rope. Shape the spiral so that the shrub curves away from the rope. The shrub above the string should curve upward and downward below the string. Understand?"

Rose walks around the plant to obtain a better vantage. "I would imagine that first cut is always the hardest."

"The plant pretty much tells you when it is ready to be trimmed."

Rose huffs through her nose again to communicate. "I don't speak plant."

Julie starts walking toward the industrial sink in the back left corner. "This is one of the most necessary lessons about keeping a plant healthy – clean your shears!" Julie points to the five clear plastic spray bottles located in the shelf above the sink with black lines annotated with a B and W. "Before you can cut a single branch on any tree you must first clean your trimmers or hedgers with a solution that is one part bleach and nine parts water."

"Got it. BW. One part bleach and nine parts water."

"The pink is mine." Julie grabs the bottle and starts thoroughly spraying down her pruning shears. She fixes her make-up and adjusts her earrings in the reflection of the enormous blades. "Do not touch any plant with shears that have not been cleaned. And now on to the ICU."

87

They enter the galley of the greenhouse marked 'IV' – the ICU. "The big three are plant scale insects, fungi and human error – and yes we have a few plants suffering of all three. We try to diagnose them, separate them to prevent cross-contamination, and then treat them to the best of our knowledge and ability. I just want to teach you to recognize the signs so that you can bring the plants to my attention, when necessary."

Rose walks toward the plants and squats to get a closer look. She peers into the branches of an evergreen that has been over-run by scale insects. She touches the end of the branch to lift it for a closer look. The insects jump from the branch to her arm and form lines as they race up her arm toward her neck and face, chomping and biting. Rose braces herself.

Rose!

"Rose!"

Rose opens her eyes to find her husband complaining about her nail penetrating grip on his arm. "Rose, you are dreaming."

Catching her breath and laughing at herself, she says, "Remind me to not read about scale insects before bed."

"Okay, Rose, don't read about scale insects before bed. You were having a nightmare about scale insects? That's a new one." He gently twists his hand around this most recent wound made by his dream girl. "Nervous about your first day?" he asks with a chuckle.

"I guess I am," Rose says somewhat confused. "I just dreamed about my first day. I am happy to report that it was going fine up until the scale insects."

"Well, it's almost time for the alarm. Now that I am awake, I wonder what we can do for the next twenty minutes…"

"Is Julie a redhead?" Rose asks snuggling into her husband's chest as he moves her hair from his face.

"No, she's a blonde."

Rose kisses the hairs on top of his sternum. "I dreamed I met her."

88

Aris smooths her hair.

"Did I hurt you?" Rose asks lifting her eyes and chin to meet him.

"I'm glad you keep your nails short," Aris responds.

"It was a strange dream. Must be first day jitters," Rose says.

"I think I have a cure."

Δ10Δ

The Birdcatcher, the Partridge, and the Cock

A BIRDCATCHER was about to sit down to a dinner of herbs when a friend unexpectedly came in. The bird-trap was quite empty, as he had caught nothing, and he had to kill a pied Partridge, which he had tamed for a decoy. The bird entreated earnestly for his life: "What would you do without me when next you spread your nets? Who would chirp you to sleep, or call for you the covey of answering birds?" The Birdcatcher spared his life, and determined to pick out a fine young Cock just attaining to his comb. But the Cock expostulated in piteous tones from his perch: "If you kill me, who will announce to you the appearance of the dawn? Who will wake you to your daily tasks or tell you when it is time to visit the bird-trap in the morning?" He replied, "What you say is true. You are a capital bird at telling the time of day. But my friend and I must have our dinners." – Aesop

Days after her training ends, Rose finds herself standing on the second to last rung of a forty-eight-foot ladder. She carefully and confidently reaches for her long-bladed hedge clippers to trim the right side of a topiary representation of a Big Top tent set atop a very full blue spruce. "I think it might be too soon for me. Are you sure I'm ready for this?" She waits for an answer and hears none.

Mustering courage from within, she continues to delicately sculpt the branch in front of her. As pieces of the hearty branch fall, she begins to uncover an intricate nest filled with tiny colorful birds chirping at an extremely high frequency. "Hi, little ones," Rose says with a look of wonder. Amazed by their colors, she leans closer to get a better view of the tiny, vibrant beings. "Hi," she says in a maternal tone, "you are so colorful."

90

Unfortunately, her voice ostensibly rouses their mother – an enormous black fowl.

The vulture-like creature swoops down from above and delivers an excruciating squawk. Alarmed and justifiably frightened by the sight of the huge menacing bird with a hauntingly grotesque beak, Rose shifts her weight and accidentally tips the ladder. With both hands, she tries to regain her balance on the stilts of the ladder and in so doing, drops the hedge clippers. She watches it fall, snapping every branch it encounters, before smashing into pieces upon the boulders below. "Sorry," she yells, seemingly more troubled by the breaking of a tool than her precarious situation at the top of the ladder. "I can buy you a new one when I get home."

"You must find the balance," says a deep voice rising to her ears from the ground below. "It is the only way."

Rose takes a breath and notices that the ladder has finally stopped swaying. "The balance," she utters. Moments later, the surreal, consummately angry vulture attacks again. It sends its creepy, scarred claws into her hair. She desperately reaches for the tree's outstretched arms to stop her from falling. She is able to grab hold of a single branch, one that is sturdy enough to hold her. With her eyes, she follows the branch with its intensely green foliage to its trunk only to discover that it is not attached to the tree. She falls. Turning in the air, she screams centimeters before the ground.

Her body jerks awake. "Geesh…"

"Fire?" Aris asks sleepily, with a soft chuckle.

"No. Birds," Rose says and turns into her husband's embrace. Both return to sleep, but Rose continues to have nightmare after nightmare throughout the rest of the night. At 7:15 AM, the squawk of the alarm wakes them. "Big bad birds," Rose says as she toggles the snooze and then turns to rest her head on his shoulder.

91

Aris pulls her tightly to his body. "What do you want to do today?" he says into her ear.

Rose spends a few seconds enjoying his embrace as she processes his question. She remembers the plan she made after her second nightmare of the night, the nightmare she decided was inspired by Scarcity. "Can we go to the library? I need to take Value and Scarcity to the stock market. And if you can believe this, there is actually a book on the stock market that has both myth and rational in the title…" For a brief moment she wonders whether she should say something about last night's second and third nightmare. *He gives me so much, and takes so little,* she thinks. She decides he deserves some quiet time and therefore she does not tell him about the horrors that did not wake him.

"Don't move. I will be right back," she says as she scurries out of the room. Ten minutes later Rose returns with a plate of French toast drenched in butter syrup, a fork and two cups of dark roast, black. "We are out of oranges and bananas. Guess we have to venture to the market." Rose giggles at her wordplay as she crawls onto their bed and hands the plate to her husband. "French toast to apologize for last night's dream. Sorry I woke you."

"Aren't you having any?" he asks as he cuts his first piece.

"I ate mine while making yours." She watches him put his favorite breakfast food into his beautiful mouth. She kisses him just to taste the syrup. "We don't have to go to the library. An internet search might be all I really need." She kisses him again.

Aris understands her pass yet pays her no never mind. "It is supposed to be a beautiful day today. Unlike you, I have to spend my days in an office. I could really use the vitamin D."

"Warm enough to go swimming?"

Aris perks up. "Ninety one."

"Will this make my mere-man happy?" she asks with a simple, light smile.

92

Aris charges at his Rose and even manages to flip the syrup covered plate onto the sheets. She doesn't mind.

***

An hour and half later the two emerge from their townhouse wearing comfortable clothes over their swim suits. After a quick trip to the library for Rose's book, they arrive at the pool early and manage to snag two of the coveted fabric lawn chairs with working umbrellas. Aris wastes very little time before finding and using the diving board.

He returns to Rose thirty minutes later. "The water is great. Why aren't you partaking?"

"I am not hot enough," Rose says simply as she takes her dry towel to pat down her glistening husband. She hands him her sunscreen. "I will scratch your back if you scratch mine." He starts to lean in to kiss her. She pulls away and warns, "Kids. Behave."

Aris acknowledges and still manages to land a cool kiss on her cheek. He takes a seat at the foot of her recliner and motions for her to turn so he can put the lotion on her back. "You're lucky you tan," he comments.

Rose reaches into her bag and pulls out her pricey "50+" sunscreen she bought specifically for her husband. "Don't worry. I got you covered." As promised, Rose returns the favor before relaxing into her chair. She watches Aris read from the Sci-Fi book he picked up at the library. "Aris, where did the stock market begin?"

"Didn't you just get a book on this?" Aris laughs at her. "France – twelfth century. Courratiers de change were the first brokers – they managed farming debts for banks." Aris gives in quickly mostly because he actually knows the answer. He looks at the page number of his paperback and tucks it away. "Alright, Rose, so, why the interest in stock market?"

"It started in France? I would have guessed that it started in Africa – Egypt, or possibly on some picturesque marble stairway

93

in Greece. France? Really? Huh." Rose furrows her brow and shakes her head as she reprocesses her mental scenes about the advent of the stock market from Africa to France. "And to answer your question – there is accounting, there is economics and then there is the market. I just want a small understanding of these things and how they inter-relate before starting school."

Aris smiles. "Your mom is totally right about you. You really are like a dog with a bone. So have you named the child of Value and Scarcity? If not, I have a suggestion." He pauses for a few seconds before asking, "Do you know what ayni is?" He leans forward to grab the towel under his feet to put behind his head.

"Spell?"

"A-Y-N-I. It is not exactly a virtue, per se. But it is based on trust and duty. Ayni is a type of natural economic exchange in native communities somewhere in the Andes. I was reading about it in a National Geographic on my flight to Atlanta. In the Andes - a person might help another member when needed, like when building a house or harvesting a crop. The person who got the help will then be ethically obligated to participate in other ayni work helping someone else. In other words, I will scratch your back…The article was very interesting. And I thought that Ayni would totally fit in with your Virtual world."

"Ayni, huh." Rose looks at her husband in a way that almost captures her sincere appreciation for all that he does. "You are starting to look really hot to me. Want to swim?"

Aris nods and is immediately out of his chair and jogging toward the diving board. He slows at the sound of the life guard's whistle directed at him. Rose applauds his flip before slowly entering the pool from the ladder at the five-foot mark.

Rose continues to actively try to keep her morning resolution and her secret nightmares to herself as she entertains herself with an exaggerated doggie paddle to the corner bullnose of the deep end. She watches her husband swim to the ladder, only to

94

just dive back in. Very much wanting to get out of her own head, she begins to look for something, anything to occupy her reeling mind. She finds her husband. *He swims like a fish*, she thinks as he approaches her. *It's not about me.* "Interesting factoid - do you know the difference between schooling and shoaling?"

"What?" Aris says bringing his eyebrows together and running his hand through his wet hair. He takes his place next to her on the wall.

It's not about me, she repeats to herself. "A group of fish that stay together for social reasons are shoaling. And if the group is swimming in the same direction, or in a coordinated manner, they are schooling," she says floating away from him onto her back. "About one quarter of fishes shoal all their lives, and about one half shoal for part of their lives," Rose tells him and then returns to her place on the wall. "Interesting, right? I mean, philosophically."

"You are such a nerd. How do you know that?"

"Fisheries – to tell you the truth there were some really cute boys in that class." Rose tells Aris for the first time of her summer spent taking fishery classes in an effort to earn a minor in the subject. She amuses her audience with anecdotes about how easy it is to fish with a cathode and anode. The two play and swim for another thirty minutes before the chatter of Rose's teeth sparks real talks about costly dental visits. The pair returns to their posts.

On the walk back to their chairs, far enough behind Aris that he cannot hear her, Rose begins to chastise herself. "Dammit," she quietly utters, "why do you always make it about you? Dammit." She reaches the chairs, grabs her towel and hurriedly excuses herself to use the loo. After a few long minutes of condemning herself in the restroom's vanity mirror, she returns to her chair recommitted to the idea that the rest of the day will be about him.

Aris sets aside his novel and reaches for her hand. "Okay?"

"Yes. It's gorgeous out here." Rose lies back and reaches for his hand. "There is a really cute little three-year-old with the prettiest eyes who I met in the bathroom. Her name is Cara Mia." Rose exhales. *He gives and gives and gives and I take.* She wants to make up for it somehow, in some way. She decides in that moment that she must try to change. "Aris, I know you really want kids…"

"I want to experience everything with you," Aris says with his eyes still closed.

"I love you so much, but…" she says with her newly-formed furrow deepening. She digs her nails into her hands to try to stop her stupid mind and keep her resolve. She wants to tell him that the world is not good enough. She wants to tell him that the future is more than uncertain. She wants to tell him about last night's third nightmare with its horrifying images of scarce, ash covered landscapes and hideous vultures pulling at skins and organs of dead humans. *No*, she thinks. She breathes and looks over her husband's beautiful dark hair and his stunning porcelain skin and begs her mind to reassess her resolve, just for him. "How about Greenland? I think I may be able to raise children in Greenland…"

He opens his eyes. "I know you love me. I also know that you're scared."

Rose holds his eyes and says nothing.

"Greenland? Isn't it cold there?" Aris says with his left eye squinting in the sunlight and his right cheek squished against the fabric.

"Yeah, but it's a dry cold," Rose says with a wry laugh. *There he goes, giving again.* She feels herself fall even deeper in love with this beautiful, generous man. While feeling weightless, a genuine and sincere smile appears on her face as she recognizes that she actually was speaking the truth. She really would have children if they could live in Greenland. *If Greenland, then there are probably a few other places too,* she

96

thinks. She adjusts her sunglasses and deepens her incline. She lightens even more. "Did you know that the narwhal is a uniquely specialized Arctic predator? The narwhal can find food at depths of up to a mile under dense pack ice. They are able to feed in the benthic zone - the lowest level of a body of water."

"No. I didn't know that. I suppose that would be something our kids would know, that is, if we live in Greenland." Aris lowers his eyes and watches the drips of water hit the concrete below his wife's lounge chair. "Rose, we need to get our marriage license…"

"Like a kiss and a slap," Rose says.

"Rose, I'm serious."

"I know," she says. Rose bows her head and then looks to the eastern sky. *I wonder if Greenland can survive Yellowstone*, she thinks. She returns her attentions to him. "In Greenland, they have whale, instead of steak. Whale steak. It is a red meat, but it has thick fish oil in it. Steak sounds good to me, maybe I need iron. Steak on the grill for dinner? Steak and salad?"

"Steak is not in our budget. How about jalapeno turkey burgers with pickled beets?"

"Birds for dinner…" She huffs at the near irony. "Did I ever tell you about the black birds in Greenland, the ones who shared their dinner with the Greenlandic sledge dogs? I am pretty sure they were ravens. I wonder where those black birds came from and where they went…"

Realizing she has begun to babble, Aris asks after her, "Do you want to talk about the dream you had last night?"

"The balance. I am supposed to find the balance. I will." She solidifies the thought as she reaches out to hold on to his ring and pinky fingers – for balance. She takes a breath and steals the energy she needs to redirect the dream. She closes her eyes. She paints a new image for her mind's eye. She replaces the hideous vultures with the beautiful large, black ravens from her vacation to Greenland. She pairs them with the beautiful, colorful baby

97

birds from the tree top of the night's first dream. She keeps them together against the stunning, but stark ice and snow covered blue-grey mountains of her favorite country. She puts her husband next to her. Content and happy with her day dream, she nestles into her chair and smiles. "Beets and big bad birds for dinner. Priceless."

For a full ten minutes, probably approaching some sort of record, Aris watches his Rose fight to keep her eyes closed and her mouth shut. He spends those minutes trying to decipher whether the thoughts going on behind her eyelids are good thoughts or bad thoughts. Her facial expressions offer little help. She is twisting her mouth to the right and left, over and over. Amused and hoping to relate, he utters, "Do you know what I think? I think I have changed my mind again. Ayni will have to be the love child of Value and someone else because Value and Scarcity are totally related. And Rose, Honey, if you think you are going crazy – don't worry. Just know that you are taking me right along with you." He sniggers at these contributions and moves his eyes from her adorable face to the water spot below her that has taken the shape of something like a rooster.

Rose opens her eyes to look and immediately notices the arch of his eyebrows. "You should have seen her, Aris. She was beautiful. Her blonde hair was in cute little pigtails, and her eyes were so blue," she says of the little girl that was in the bathroom. "We would have beautiful children, wouldn't we?"

Aris turns to her and shields his eyes from the sun with his other hand. "Rose, relax. It's beautiful out here. And we have loads of time."

Rose thumbs the back of her wedding ring. "Aris…" she looks into his eyes and breathes deeply. "I think we both shoal and school."

"You are such a nerd."

Δ11Δ

It is not enough to win a war; it is more important to organize the peace. – Aristotle

Over the past six hours, every radio and television station across the country and the world has featured its own report of a harrowing surprise eruption of Mount Lassen, the southernmost active volcano in the Cascade Range. The volcano surprised even the most noted volcanologists with both her magnitude and ferocity.

In contrast, Rose Isope is in her kitchen trying to shield her mind from the news feed. This eruption does not come as a surprise to her. She almost knew it was going to happen; one could even say that she predicted that it was going to happen. She had a dream about Lassen Peak – a dream where her grandmother told her, warned her that she was last. *The last*. Rose decides that she cannot think about the eruption, or her dream. She cannot and she will not. She only has to think about her Hollandaise sauce.

Aris sits at the island to watch Rose stir. He tries to obey her forceful, tearful command to *not* talk about the obvious when they first heard the news this morning. He continues to bite his tongue because it is very obvious from her body language that she is still very unwilling to talk about it. She has even gone so far as to avoid direct eye contact with him. He notes that it is odd behavior, even for her. Yet, he sits still in an attempt to be there for his wife when she is ready.

In the quiet meantime, he tries to empathize with what his wife must be thinking and feeling as these ominous events unfold. Although his rational mind has convinced him that the

99

relationship between this event and his wife's dreams is merely coincidental, he cannot help but to draw parallels. Nearly giving up on remaining silent, he tries a different conversation. "When are they supposed to get here?"

Rose looks at the microwave clock. "In about twenty minutes."

"I think you seriously scored a few brownie points with my grandmother. Apparently they had nothing but nice things to say about you. She said they described you as delightful." Aris lifts his coffee mug to his lips. "I dare say they may have changed her opinion of you." He takes a sip.

"What is that supposed to mean?" Rose says as she turns from the stove and grimaces. "She didn't like me? I thought she did."

"Well, again, I think they thought I was more serious about Nora."

"I see. And you have not done anything since to persuade them otherwise," Rose says matter-of-factly. "The drama. I can't believe you actually want drama in your family life. Most people have to work on keeping the peace."

Aris laughs off the affected vitriol taking place in their kitchen. "I knew you would understand. Besides, my sister's response was and is the only one that mattered, and her response I remember. Mina said, and I quote, 'It's about time you figured that out. I was beginning to think you enjoyed being an idiot.'"

"I've always liked Mina," Rose says smiling.

"She feels the same way about you," Aris says as he takes his empty mug to the sink. "She liked you from day one."

"I can't believe I am cooking for 'family' again." Rose shakes her head while still stirring her greatly admired lemony Hollandaise. She reflects on the impromptu visit they had from his mother, Maeve, a few nights ago. She "popped" by to inquire about the couple's wedding plans. However, the inquiry was short-lived. Maeve was much more interested in making the plans herself.

"Thanks, this does mean a lot of me," Aris says as he moves toward her and wraps his arms around her shoulders. "I am sure that this meal's conversation will be much more enjoyable than last week's. By the way, my mom called me yesterday."

"She did?" Rose says happy to have any sort of distraction. Even a distraction involving an overbearing mother-in-law is preferable to the lava singeing her dendrites.

"Yeah, she actually called to apologize. Apparently Mina set her straight."

"I have always liked Mina," Rose repeats. "But isn't the apology due to me?"

"With my mom – you will have to learn to choose your battles. Anyway, enough about her… So, eggs Florentine benedict, home-fried potatoes, apple strudel Danish, and sliced strawberries."

"You do not think I need a breakfast meat, do you? I could make turkey sausage links."

"They only take a minute or two, right?" Aris walks to the freezer and pulls out the thin box from the freezer drawer to read the instructions. "Yep, brown and serve." He grabs the small fryer from the island rack. "I'll do it." He moves in next to her and places the fryer on the element.

"We've got a few minutes yet. Wanna help me set the table?" She takes the sausage from the counter and sets the box back in the freezer.

"Place mats or table cloth? Company gets the table cloth?" Aris asks trying to remember her peculiar hosting rules.

"Brunch rules are different," Rose informs her trainable husband. "I don't have a white table cloth. So let's use those tan woven placemats." She places the morning's fresh-picked roses on the table and immediately heads to the dining room to retrieve her white china, four dinner plates and four bread plates.

101

Her husband finishes the table with four wine glasses and four juice glasses at her request.

Rose puts the Danish on a platter and sets it on the center of the table, between the roses, just as the doorbell rings. "They're here." She skips to the door and speedily opens it. "Good morning, Abner. Good morning, Clara." She steps aside and motions for their entry.

Aris enters into view to greet his grandparents' best friends. "Good Morning Mr. and Mrs. Griffis. Pleasure to see you again," he says.

"Why it's Aristotle, how much you have grown. I have not seen you in years. Not since your sister's wedding. It's been what, six years?" Clara asks as she rushes to greet her best friend's grandson. "How handsome you are."

Aris just smiles. "Good to see you, too." He offers a gentle hug before extending his right hand to Abner. "Good to see you again, Sir. Thank you for helping me with this project. I might have been able to do it myself, but…"

"No problem at all, Son. It's good to be useful at my age."

"It's good to be useful at any age," Rose interjects.

"The table looks beautiful, Dear," Clara says as she passes from the foyer into the great room.

"I hope you both brought your appetite. I'll be serving brunch in about ten minutes. In the meantime, can I get you anything to drink? Coffee, perhaps? I have orange juice, water and unsweetened iced tea."

"Water, please. It's really warm out there. I hear it is supposed to reach ninety-six degrees," Abner comments. "It's important to stay hydrated."

"Yes sir," Rose says nodding. She retrieves the glass pitcher of ice water with cucumbers from the refrigerator. Aris meets her with the wine glasses from the table. Rose pours and Aris delivers. Once refreshed, the gentlemen immediately head to the backyard.

102

"Can I help you with anything, Dear?" Clara asks.

Rose looks around and sees the fryer awaiting the sausage and the toaster waiting for the English muffins. She quickly washes her hands and turns to Clara to answer her question while drying. "I think I've got this under control. You could help by taking a seat and just talking to me. How has your morning been thus far?" Rose replaces the dish towel on the oven's towel rack and then steps to retrieve the breakfast sausage from the freezer. She turns on the fryer before plugging in the Krups egg cooker and setting the time.

"You do seem a bit busy for conversation," Clara notes.

Rose reassesses and meekly agrees. "Would you like to put the English muffins in the toaster?"

"I'd love to." Clara stands and locates the platter of pre-forked split muffins.

The two women work diligently to get the brunch to the table. Nearly finished with all the preparations, Rose says to her gracious assistant, "About that conversation…"

"I thank you for this. It's nice to meet new neighbors. My grandchildren live pretty far away. This is really a nice thing for you to do," Clara says with a gentle smile.

"It's my pleasure. I actually like hosting," Rose admits. "I also like cooking. I kinda need a little distraction right now, so I am quite happy to be doing this." She hands a pitcher of orange juice to Clara. "Do you mind?"

Clara graciously accepts the new task and fills the juice glasses. "The Danish looks wonderful. Where did you buy them?"

"Actually, I made them. Danish is one of my secret talents. Years ago, I heard it was good for a woman to know how to bake. Danish is now the only thing I bake, other than the occasional bread with pasta," Rose gloats. "I thought it would be funny that if I ever had that conversation again… the conversation of whether or not I bake – I could answer, 'yes, but only Danish.'"

Clara has a hard time understanding what she just heard and silently returns with a half empty pitcher. "They look delicious."

"Thanks," Rose says with delight as she tops the last of the English muffins with a poached egg. Taking them two by two, Rose quickly carries all four plates to the table. She then skips to the patio to call in the gentlemen. "Soups on!" She races back to the kitchen and stands next to Clara and nearly whispers, "Thanks, Clara, for all of your help."

The men quickly enter and Aris meets and kisses Rose on the forehead. "It looks great. I am sorry. I was supposed to cook those sausages, wasn't I?"

"I had help." Rose nods at Clara.

The four stand behind their respective chairs for a moment before taking their seats. After the table appears more settled, Rose lifts her wine glass filled with iced water. "To God." The table follows suit.

"Rose's version of grace. Efficient," Aris comments.

Clara and Abner look at each other as if to mark a moment they will talk about later. "This is all so very delicious," Clara says moments after a small sample of everything. "Abner, she made the Danish."

"I am surprised there are a few left. She started last night a bit too early. I had three before bed," Aris explains. He gazes at Rose as he continues, "She is pretty amazing."

Rose blushes as she looks at her husband. "Ah shucks."

The two couples share polite conversation throughout the remainder of the meal. Abner mostly concentrates his conversation on Aris. As they talk about his work and the EPA, Rose and Clara share their own smaller conversation about the neighborhood ladies and their clubs, which include a garden club, a book club and a recipe exchange. Clara is active in all three. Although Rose is not unhappy in her conversation with

Clara, she wishes she could listen more actively to the conversation between Aris and Abner.

When all the Danish are gone, Abner announces that it is important that they start work immediately on the antenna. He wishes to be done before the meteorologically predicted and inevitable thunderstorm mid-to-late afternoon. It becomes immediately apparent to Rose that she is not welcome in the construction of her antenna.

Aris quickly helps Rose clear the table as both Abner and Clara take a few moments to note the small changes in the décor since their friends left. He whispers, "This is men's work, my love." He kisses her on the cheek before meeting Abner in the foyer. "We should go get the wires."

Rose watches both Aris and Abner leave through the front door on a mission to retrieve the necessary wires for the antenna: coaxial cable and simple aluminum wire to create a twenty-meter dipole antenna. As she watches the two walk past her front window and out of sight she turns to Clara. "Can I get you a cup of coffee, or tea, perhaps?"

Clara tilts her head. "I would love a cup of coffee. I noticed your Keurig. I am a fan of the Donut Shop. A wonderful little contraption – the Keurig. My husband does not particularly like coffee. It upsets his stomach. Having a fresh cup of coffee whenever I want is a godsend."

Rose opens her cabinet to reveal her selection of mugs and, upon Clara's choosing, she brews her companion a perfect cup. The two women take their coffee to the shaded portion of the patio table and sit.

"Gwyneth explained that the two of you are living here only temporarily. Is that true?" Clara asks conversationally.

"It is true that we are staying here for one year to save for a house. It is a wedding gift from Mr. and Mrs. Irwin," Rose replies. "I think she is hoping that she will be able sell it in a better housing market a year from now. I suppose we could stay

105

on – and actually pay rent. I really like this house. It's comfortable and classic, albeit a bit beyond our means."

Clara lowers her eyes in modesty. "I do hope you enjoy your time here. It is good to see younger people in the neighborhood. There are a couple of young couples on this street, a few more on Vine."

"We really like the pool. Aris pretty much spends every weekend there." Rose smiles as she thinks about him on the diving board, how child-like and gratified he appears. "The pool makes him very happy."

Aris enters the house. "Honey, I am home," he calls.

Rose smiles and yells, "We are out here awaiting the show. Entertain us. Can I get you gentlemen another glass of water before you begin?"

"Not necessary. Get the ladder, son," Abner says authoritatively.

Aris smirks in Rose's direction, yet follows the order. He sets the ladder up in the far left corner of the yard. The plan is to place the boom of the dipole running up through the rose trellis and run the coaxial cable from the library up through the boom. Aluminum wire will stretch from the top corner of the second story roof to the trellis and then cut across the courtyard to the inside corner. It will still be a bit of an eyesore, however Rose is confident that her mind can bend the reality of the antenna and still see her natural, meticulously landscaped backyard. Aris yells from the top of the ladder, "Ba da bing… ba da boom."

Rose laughs out loud. "That's the spirit." Rose recognizes at that moment just how in love she is with her husband. She sends a hand signal to let him know. He smiles and nods.

"You seem happy, Dear."

"I am so happy," Rose says, her eyes smiling. And in that moment, the word happy eclipses the distant fear of her fiery visions in the back of her mind.

106

"Gwyneth says that you have only been dating a short while," Clara says.

"The two of you seem to be a bit chatty." Rose smiles and hopes that she muted her sarcasm well enough to not be disrespectful. "Did she tell you that we have been friends for close to a decade? And that we have both considered each other our best friend for more than half of those years?" Rose asks.

"Oh Dear, I feel I stepped over the line," Clara says.

"Maybe a little," Rose says, truthfully. She is quickly reminded of the earlier conversation she had with her husband. A smile appears on her face as she recognizes that this conversation is much more pleasant than the similar one she had with Maeve. "It is up to Aris to set the record straight about this perceived whirlwind relationship. I trust he will do so in his time." Rose looks down at her feet through the glass of her patio table. "However, again, I always appreciate candor. Do not make yourself uncomfortable. Needless to say, I love him and I am confident that his love for me will be apparent to his family soon enough."

Rose shifts in her chair to signal the end of what could easily be considered an uncomfortable conversation. "Want to tell me about how you met Abner?" she inquires.

"Boston," Clara responds. "We met at a fraternity social mixer. Neither one of us wanted to be there. He was handsome, quiet and determined. He reminded me of my grandfather. He wasn't at all silly like most of our classmates. I told him so. He asked me out for the following Saturday. We were engaged six months later."

"Economy of method," Rose says.

"That was how things worked back then."

"I am not sure if things are much different now – about things working, that is. I guess that if you ask couples in a successful relationship… Never mind, I don't know." Rose gulps the last of her coffee as she considers her last statement. Although she

107

knew immediately that Aris was the one, it took him nine years to figure it out. She laughs at herself and returns to the conversation with Clara. "I think we need water."

Clara agrees. Rose enters the house and returns with a tray from her grandmother's hutch, topped with the glass pitcher and glasses for all four of them. "It is important to stay hydrated," she yells to the men.

The two men look at each other and recognize the wisdom. Confident that they have found a good stopping point, they set down their tools and walk toward the patio table.

Rose raises the umbrella before pouring from the pitcher. "I will bet Martha Stewart could build a more aesthetically pleasing antenna. I watched this one episode where she happened to have a giant coaxial wire spool in her backyard that she repurposed as a bees wax candle chandelier while her Thanksgiving turkey was cooking… ah that Martha."

Aris laughs. "I don't know what you are talking about – our boom is gorgeous."

Abner says nothing while he stands through the first few sips of his water. Clara takes his hand and he sits.

"Clara was just telling me how the two of you met," Rose announces.

Abner nods.

"He built a few buildings in Boston," Aris adds. "He says he caught a few breaks upon graduating." Rose is amused at the idea that while laboring atop a roof, the men were having similar conversations as two ladies sipping coffee on a patio.

"Aris told me that you used to work in the pharmaceutical industry. That is a very healthy industry – one of the only ones untouched by the recession," Abner says. "Seems foolish to leave it."

"I am on a sabbatical of sorts – but I have half a mind to challenge your use of the word 'healthy,'" Rose says disdainfully, her amusement dissipating. "I do think the health of

108

our nation is an accurate portrayal of the health of our medicine."

"Aristotle also told me that this was a touchy subject with you," Abner says laughing.

Rose blushes and turns to her husband. "You taught him how to tease me in thirty minutes?"

Clara chuckles. "My husband must really like you, Dear."

"Radio needs more fire and a lot less politics," Abner adds. "Your husband also told me that you are interested in end-of-the-world scenarios. You will find good company in some of the higher bands. I know I already told you about my interest in the Ionosphere. It will be very important if your Yellowstone erupts. Volcanic ash in the Ionosphere can be pretty dreadful for communication systems."

"I told him about your Yellowstone dreams," Aris admits with a gently nudging tone. "I thought it pertinent given the recent surprise eruption of Lassen Peak."

Rose hears her husband's tease, but steers the conversation in a different direction. "And here all we talked about was how gossipy the women's clubs were in this neighborhood." She smiles at Clara. "I think women get a bad rap."

Clara laughs a tiny laugh. "I think Frank put him up to the task, Dear."

Aris and Abner look to each other and say nothing.

Rose glares at Aris playfully. "Huh…. The drama," she says before taking a sip of her water. Craning her neck to look at the boom, she wonders aloud, "I still think that Martha Stewart could build a more aesthetically pleasing antenna. I also think the government really should have put her to work while throughout her detention. I will bet she could have made remarkable strides in reforming their organization. I really think that they missed a golden opportunity there. I mean, seriously, how often does a person like Martha Stewart end up in prison?"

Aris laughs. "Did Rose tell you that she was planning on studying economics this year at Georgetown? Martha Stewart working in prison reform while detained captures Rose's notion of economics."

"Economy of method. We need better standards of efficiency if we are ever going to pay down our nation's debt. Do you realize how much money is wasted in our nation's prison systems? And have you ever seen Martha Stewart's junk drawers? Yes, she pretty much did a program about those, too. Even her Band-Aids are alphabetized. Under B – if you must know."

"I almost built a prison," Abner adds. "There is a good deal of interesting issues to take into consideration. I am actually happy that I did not get the contract. Hospitals are far more innovative."

"The great awakening, circa 1840s, is one of my favorite periods of history. I think that was the last time intellectuals were interested in prison reform. Pennsylvania pretty much led the way," Rose interjects.

Abner nods with quiet appreciation of the conversation obviously steered for his benefit. "I remember studying Philadelphia's Cherry Hill Penitentiary. The architect was British...what's his name... John... John Haviland. If I remember correctly, it had a wagon wheel design - called hub and spoke. When that prison was built, it was the largest and most expensive public structure ever constructed. It ended up serving as the model for prisons worldwide. The Haviland design consisted of cell wings radiating in a semi or full circle array from a center tower from where the prison could be kept under constant surveillance. Each cell was lit only by a single lighting source from either a skylight or a window. It was called the Eye of God. It really was quite provocative for the time."

"My middle school had that design – the hub and spoke. Weird. I guess it's a little peculiar that my middle school was inspired by a prison," Rose notes as she remembers a few frightful days in the prison of seventh grade. "The 'Eye of God.' Can I get the two of you to make an antenna forming half circles or full circle arrays?"

"Sorry. They have to be straight."

"Why?" Rose asks.

"You really should already know this, Rose. Because the standing wave is straight as an arrow; it's straight because the electric field is always at a right angle with the magnetic field." Aris softens his tone as he continues, "So sorry my love, no circular antennas for you."

"You will have a really substantial twenty-meter array. The quarter wave will be seventeen point five feet," Abner explains. "A really good antenna for the area. If you need further explanation you will be able to find an adequate course on it in your ARRL Handbook. But your husband is right, I really thought that you'd be further along."

"You can decorate the pole," Clara says in defense of Rose's conversation. "I am not exactly sure how... I'll think about it."

"It's called a boom," Abner corrects his wife.

"Is it?" Clara snaps.

"Ba da bing, Ba da boom," Rose says in an attempt to ameliorate. Only Aris gets her joke. "I am sure I can find something on one of those garden sites – cute little metal bugs that attach to tree limbs? I could talk to Erik about it - a topiary di-pole cover."

"We'll think of something. But, really, it doesn't look so bad. Although I'm sure that Gwyneth will demand that it be removed before she puts the house up. You might not want to even mention it to her, Dear."

"I think she already knows. Aris, you *did* tell her that the Griffises were helping me build an antenna?"

"When you think of an antenna, do you think of something like this or rabbit ears on your television?" Aris asks scanning

111

the table for verbal agreement. "I think ignorance is bliss. Let's just say I told her about the antenna. I just didn't tell her about the boom."

"So all you have to do now is attach the wire to both the outside corner and the inside corner?" Rose draws an imaginary line from the outside of her bedroom to the inside corner of her backyard. "A giant hypotenuse."

"That's it," Aris says.

"Speaking of, we should really get this done. I can almost smell the dropping barometer," Abner says. "I am glad you are the one on the ladder."

"I think we should get Rose to do it. She likes ladders." Aris makes guns with both of his hands and makes the appropriate sounds before blowing out his "guns."

"It is men's work," Rose answers. She smiles cordially and puts her own hand gun in her holster.

Rose and Clara spend the next hour slightly worried about Aris as he performs his task on the top of a very tall ladder. Luckily all goes well and the job is completed before Abner's premonitory nose drives the couple home. Abner and Clara arrive home just in time as the afternoon thunderstorm drenches the town and cools the air of its summer heat.

火山 12 火山

Customer: Waiter Waiter! There is volcanic ash in my soup!
Waiter: Well yes sir, this is a no-fly zone!

Cheyenne looks out at the runway from the large floor-to-ceiling window as she listens to her father report on the status of their flight back to Saskatoon.

"Tomorrow morning, at the earliest, really? I told Meghan I'd be home for her birthday party," Dakota whines.

"Can you believe that's what she is worried about?" Cheyenne says, turning from the window to her father. "Really, Kota. There are people losing their lives, their homes and their land and all you care about is…"

"Oh Shy, you were fifteen once too," her mother says. She sits down next to Dakota and offers her comfort.

Gavin laughs at both of his daughters. "Beauty, it's good to know what your priorities are during these kinds of situations. For instance, I'm starving. Let's go get a good meal and find a few good crossword puzzle books. Oh yeah, I guess I should mention that we're going to be here awhile. Not only is our flight cancelled but I also found out that all hotels and motels in the area are booked. We are sleeping here tonight."

Brooklyn grimaces. "That's just great. Super." She looks at both of her daughters and finds a small bit of grace. "You're right Shy, we should be thankful for what we have. And I am glad I have you girls. And we are safe, here, in the airport for an indefinite time period."

Cheyenne twists her neck to find her mother. "Have we heard anything more about the people at the park? Have they reported casualties or deaths? It's so strange. We were just there yesterday. Isn't anyone else totally spooked? We were walking

113

in that park yesterday. Shouldn't they have been able to tell? I mean predict?"

Gavin steps closer to his daughter and takes the space to the right of her as he stares out the same window, at the same runway. "They are reporting quite a few casualties and quite a few deaths. The good news is…The good news is it could have been much worse."

"What is quite a few, Dad?" the statuesque Eskimo asks quietly.

"They are guessing around five hundred," a solemn Gavin answers.

"Why wasn't there a warning? I mean a substantial warning. I know that they monitor those kinds of things. In my Meteorology class we…."

"They are saying that the source for the Lassen Park volcanos is the subduction of the Gorda plate being driven under the North American plate. However, it now appears as though these volcanos were also being fed by other sources, deeper sources. My guess is that they underestimated the depth of those sources. They also are saying that the small earthquake swarms from last week – remember we felt those when we arrived here – they might have initiated the cascade reaction."

Gavin looks at his daughter who is obviously taking the news to heart. He takes the moment to notice her profile as she stares out the window trying to figure out what airport workers are doing on a grounded runway. He can only smile at their similarities. He really admires the person she is now and the woman she is becoming. "They are saying that, but honey, they really don't know. They are going to have to wait until things quiet down before they take a closer look." Gavin reaches an arm over his daughter's shoulder and gives a firm squeeze. "Volcanoes happen. Without volcanos we really would not have land. There is a blessing in all of this. We just have to look for it. We just have to wait for it."

114

Cheyenne turns to her father. "Thanks, Dad. I know you're trying to make me feel better. And it's working. I guess I'm thankful that we were there yesterday and here today."

"I got a volcano joke. Wanna hear it?"

"A volcano joke? There are probably not too many of those around."

"What did the mama volcano say to the baby volcano? 'Don't erupt while I am talking.'"

"Ugh. Now that's a dad joke."

"Dad, I think I'm hungry, too," Dakota says bounding up on them. "And Mom told me to tell you that she wants a hamburger."

"There is a sports bar and grill on the upper level," Gavin responds.

"I know I could use a drink," Brooklyn reports with a sigh.

"Me, too," Cheyenne says sheepishly, still as uncomfortable drinking in front of her parents as they are of her drinking.

Gavin picks up on his wife's own chagrin from ten feet away. "She's legal," he reminds her.

"Our little girl," Brooklyn says. She checks the seat next to her for her purse. "Let's go get something to eat."

"And then the crosswords," Cheyenne suggests as she walks toward her mom and gives her a hug. "I know it makes you uncomfortable when I drink, so I won't. But Mom, I am twenty-three and a college graduate and in my second year of my Master's. You're going to have to let me grow up eventually."

Brooklyn returns her hug. "Today is different. Today if you want a glass of wine… I always want to celebrate when something dreadful like this happens. These events remind me just how precious life is."

"Can I have a drink too?" Dakota teases. "To celebrate."

"You don't want to grow up too fast, Honey," Gavin replies. "Take some advice from your wise old man. Don't grow up too fast. Stretch out your youth as long as you can. You'll age better.

115

And besides, there is plenty of time to be an adult with adult responsibilities."

"Dad, do you think the planes will be able to fly tomorrow?" Cheyenne asks, stepping up next to him as they make their way to the restaurant.

"I hope so. I suppose it depends on the winds, but we could be here for a while. I suppose if it takes more than two days, we'll rent a car."

"Two days? I don't think so. If we don't fly out tomorrow morning, we're renting a car," Brooklyn announces.

"Can we make a pit stop at Yellowstone?" Dakota asks. "I want to see the bubbling mud again."

The family arrives outside of the small sports bar. Every table is occupied and every eye is glued to the television. It is not tuned to a baseball game, but rather to the news reel showing a helicopter view of forest fires and mudslides.

"Jesus," Gavin says as he looks at the video clip of people wearing gas masks and being treated for burns just outside the park entrance. "Why don't they move? It's possible that it will blow again, right? Shouldn't they be showing people boarding vans and getting the hell away from there?" he says in a voice that could easily be overheard by a few bystanders and table occupiers.

"It's crazy, isn't it?" says an obvious San Francisco Giants fan.

Cheyenne eyes the man in the cap and t-shirt. "Have they given a death count yet?"

"Morbid, much?" asks Dakota.

Cheyenne ignores her sister and awaits an answer.

"Around five hundred. Most died due to gas asphyxiation," the baseball fan reports.

Cheyenne nods to the man and offers a simple smile in response. *Good. Holding steady.*

Still incensed Gavin says, "Shouldn't they be evacuating?"

116

"Drama, Man. They just need more drama," the capped man says as he takes the last swig of his beer.

Cheyenne sniggers at his comment. "Burn."

Brooklyn shoots her daughter a stern look. "Shy!"

Δ13Δ

Learning is not child's play; we cannot learn without pain. ~Aristotle

Rose awakens from a nightmare with a phrase echoing in her head. *Start with Progress.* Unable to fall back asleep, she descends her staircase into a darkened living room. *What is that supposed to mean*, she asks herself and whoever is listening, as she brews herself a cup of Dark Magic. She takes herself and her mug into the study and boots up her computer. "Progress," she says to her initializing screen.

According to Rose, Progress is the child of Justice and Injury. She pulls up her Word document named epictale.doc, which details her virtues and their offspring. Her notes on Progress are comparatively sketchy to some of her other virtues, like Generosity, the love child of Greed and Charity. All she has written on Progress is that she grows up to be a very attractive woman with a defiant streak; she is not the type that likes to be pushed in one direction or another. *Of course she is defiant, she most certainly couldn't be Patient,* Rose thinks to herself as she tries to fully picture Progress. *Okay, God, I am going to try to start - with Progress. So help me.*

Rose falls back into her well-designed, supportive desk chair with her coffee mug in hand. "Aesop? Is Progress a myth?" She puts an arch in her back as she looks to the golden glazed crown molding of her study, a room that makes her feel like she is living in someone else's house. A room that is so decadent that it just reminds her that she is, with her current salary, decades away from being able to afford its like on her own. She sighs. "Progress."

Inspired to take a different direction with her Virtues, Rose immediately pulls on her keyboard and starts writing…

118

"My name is Progress. My parents are Injury and Justice. The first time my parents told me how they met, I was five. My dad stood up in our living room and showed how he used to tame lions using a chair and a whip. He told me about his costume – a sequined wonder, perfectly tailored for his body. He pulled from his pocket the blindfold that he wore, a piece of cloth that he still keeps in his front pocket. He told me that he keeps it in his pocket as a reminder; a reminder of his life before he met my mother, before he learned to see."

Progress stands from her chair and walks to the window of the government office where she is being interviewed for a lead chairman position on the emergency counsel. "My mother, Injury, was an acrobat and a paramedic. Her job was to essentially look after all performers in the traveling carnival. The story my parents tell is that my father was bitten by the lion he was attempting to tame. For its truth - there is a scar and everything. My mother treated his wound. It was love at first sight. They were married six weeks later."

Progress returns from the window with a renewed intensity. She walks to the edge of the enormous desk that takes up nearly half of the room and presses her knuckles on its edge until she hears a few successful pops. She looks directly into the eyes of the interviewer, puzzled. "My question for you is: Why those questions? Who are my parents? And how did they meet? Those are really strange questions. Why is it important for you to know how my parents met? How can that have any possible bearing on this position?"

"You don't know?" the suited interviewer asks.

"What don't I know?" Progress forwards the conversation.

"You were hand selected because of your parents. We have been watching you your entire life, from day one. You were specifically selected because you are Progress, the child of Justice and Injury," the suit says in a tone that pierces the ear drums and vibrates the mind. "Progress, we need you to help us

119

determine how to move our nation and the world forward – out of our past, into our future. You will be part of a team, a team of special people, special beings, like you. If selected, you will be placed on an international counsel that will help usher in a new calendar era. You, with the help of others, will rebuild and reignite our world, the world that has been destroyed by the volcanic eruption of Yellowstone. Progress, you are part of our future; a very significant part of our future."

"Geez, no pressure," Progress says with a cynical smile. "Okay, so I am part of a pre-planned restructuring initiative. One that has been in existence since, well, since my parents copulated? Holy Shhh..." She diverts her eyes and mind back to the window, caught between emotions of amazement and disbelief. Moments later, she returns to her interviewer. "Fine. I will take all this, this conspiracy, this plan.... I will take all of this with the proverbial cotton from the cotton gin, but I have to ask... If I am Progress, then who the heck are you?..."

Rose lifts her coffee to her lips and is quite satisfied with herself and her progress; she takes a cool sip. "Ah, Progress. You really are a good place to start. So, who do you want to meet first? Creativity?" Rose gulps the last of her coffee and returns to the kitchen for another cup. She washes and slices a pear while her coffee brews. *Creativity, the daughter of Simplicity and Intricacy.*

Upon returning to her desk, she reviews the story in her decade old comic, smiling at her own jokes, and recognizing her growth. The jokes are not as funny as they were then. "Aesop?" she asks the air. "What is the difference between Mythos and Ethos? I know they are not Virtues, are they planets? Or is that a question for Aristotle?" Her own creativity tries to fashion a world, both ancient and futuristic, where her virtues could really exist - a planet named Ethos, or perhaps Logos. She laughs at herself and relocates her reeling mind back into the study.

"Creativity, you should be much more fun," she says, pulling her keyboard closer...

"An international initiative to rebuild the world?" the savvy teenager asks, more than a little amused by her interviewer's choice of words. "Sounds like a sweet gig."

The interviewer heartily laughs at her response, makes an attempt to regain composure, and then laughs again. "I have to admit most of our other applicants were momentarily thrown by the request. Apparently that is not the case with you. Make no mistake, this is an enormous undertaking. You do realize what it is you are being asked to do, right?"

"Duh, be creative," Creativity says somewhat annoyed at the condescension. Her skin reflecting quality immediately changes to a soft yellow as she recognizes that her veiled immaturity is shining through. She concedes that even the most mature seventeen year old would find this experience daunting. She momentarily blames the room – it feels so clinical, so governmental. Feeling slightly embarrassed, she remembers the advice of both her parents: be humble and be a better listener.

The past twenty-four hours still register as somewhat surreal to this seventeen year old genius. She remembers hearing from both of her parents, both extremely nervous and anxious, that the official looking, mysteriously hand-delivered letter they were waving in front of her was her destiny. With her curiosity ultimately piqued, she continued to actively listen to them as they attempted to apprise her about their connections to this government and its organization, and how they have secretly worked for this their entire lives. Although she is sure that many teenagers would have a negative reaction to her parents' duplicity, she was ultimately happy to hear of their deception. She found it both intricately simple and simply intricate.

Creativity smiles at the memory, and her pleasure is immediately made visible by her glowing skin, now emitting hues that reflect her feelings of safety and belonging. She carries

121

the feeling and its smile back to the interviewer. "My parents told me I was born for this. I am the daughter of Simplicity and Intricacy. And this scenario...It isn't exactly unthinkable, or outrageous – secret governmental organizations preparing for Armageddon. Heck, it's almost trite, if you really think about it. And besides, it's not like I didn't notice the impact of Yellowstone. Hello? Have you noticed that satellite communication no longer works? My guess is that you don't need to be Creative to point out the obvious. So yeah, it's cool. I was looking for something to do anyway..."

Rose briefly wonders whether or not she should make Creativity older. She leans back in her chair and swivels, staring at the ceiling. She contemplates whether an extremely intelligent seventeen year old could handle this type of responsibility or whether she would be able to work well with others. *Creativity is always best exhibited by the young, and can often be seen as immature,* Rose surmises. "She'll figure out a way."

Rose lowers her gaze to look at the white spiral notebook sitting on the edge of her desk as she contemplates her next move. She extends her arm and almost reaches the book, but decides it is not worth the effort. The notebook needs only to remind her of the cast of characters. *Who's next?* Stretching out by putting her feet and legs on the desk, she deepens her lounge position by adjusting the lever on the side of the chair before finally relocating the keyboard onto her lap. *Am I still making Progress?* Rose looks about the room and notices the World Book Encyclopedia set that matches the one her parent's purchased in her youth. She thinks about the things those books taught her and how future generations may not ever know what a real, bona fide set of encyclopedias looks like. With a deep inhale, she answers aloud, "Ingenuity is next. Ingenuity, the child of Patience and Impetuous..."

The handsome inventor flips through the binder that includes objectives, indemnity contracts and non-disclosure agreements.

122

Legal documents are not exactly new to Ingenuity, but he will always take issue with them. To him, it is essentially unethical to create or sign documents that are seemingly written to confuse clear concepts. "If you were looking for a place to start in making a better world, I would start with legal contracts. They should be written in a language that a child could understand."

The interviewer snorts his rebuttal. "Ingenious?" he asks.

"Yeah, you almost need to be a genius to sign these – a genius or an idiot. Before signing, I would like to know who I will be working with. I would like to meet this 'team' you have assembled." Always stern, Ingenuity stares down his interviewer.

"It doesn't work like that. You cannot meet the team until you sign the documents," the interviewer states clearly.

"In no uncertain terms," Ingenuity says with a wry countenance. "I thank you for your time, but I suppose I am not your man." Ingenuity backs his statement by resolutely standing from his chair and turning to the door.

"Wait," the interviewer says. "Let me ask. Let me ask if you can meet the team, first."

Ingenuity nods politely. "I can wait. Go. Ask."

The interviewer, somewhat stunned by his treatment by a potential employee, immediately, albeit awkwardly excuses himself into the hallway.

While alone in the office, Ingenuity walks to the window and looks over the ash covered city. He massages both of his temples with the wide grip of his right hand. He is very frustrated. He has spent the last nine days, the number of days since the final eruption, trying to invent a way to not only clean up the ash, but turn it into a useful product. He thinks he should be able to do it. He made his initial fortune by making a simple adjustment to a trash compactor. He added an efficient, self-contained heating, pressurizing and chemical processor that compacts a week's worth of trash into a single, useable four-by-eight-inch building

123

brick that can be used in construction of all types. These bricks can be sold and have a decent market value. Thus, he created a machine to make garbage valuable. He also created similar, but larger machines that convert a dumpster's worth of garbage into a durable and flexible sheet-like material that can be used for both roads and bridges. He has spent the past decade priding himself on these accomplishments. Yet this ash problem - the amount of toxic ash from this volcano – is absolutely stupefying. He has been awake nearly fifty-six hours analyzing the data he has collected. He's missing something, but is not sure what. He cools his head on the glass of the window and closes his eyes in exhaustion.

The interviewer returns abruptly. Making rather excessive noises on his way to his desk, slamming doors and filing cabinets, he finally finds his seat. Upon sitting, he immediately transforms back into his customary businesslike manner. He swivels to look at Ingenuity. "I have been given permission to tell you about colleagues that have accepted their positions on the Initiative Round Table. They are Progress, Creativity, Generosity, Persistence, Understanding, Necessity, Value and Efficiency. We are still in talks with a few and there are others we have yet to meet."

Ingenuity bows his head to process what he has heard. "I have a friend, a colleague, Balance. I think it is essential that you speak with her."

"She is scheduled to meet with us later this afternoon, Sir," the interviewer reports. "So, can we count on your expertise?"

"Do your scientists have a firm grasp of the chemical composites of the ash falling this far from the volcano?"

"Of course," the interviewer responds.

"I would like to meet with them, and Efficiency, immediately. I cannot waste any more time..."

"You want to meet with Efficiency. I think that could be arranged," the interviewer smiles knowingly...

124

"Ah, Efficiency." Rose notices the hour, first in her eyelids and then with her eyes – 4:00 AM. She saves her document as AristotlesLogos.doc and shuts down her computer. She is not sure if she has begun to write her book; she knows she has started something, something that could be forged into a story, a myth, or possibly, a fable. She also knows she has fulfilled her dream requirement; she started with Progress. She sighs a sense of satisfaction that she has at least started on a story about both destruction and creation; a story with an ethos, pathos, and logos. "Aesop, what is a fable? I know I should probably already know," she says into the air. She climbs the stairs to rediscover her place next to her husband. *Is that a question for Aristotle?*

"So who did Crazy marry?" a sleep-drunk Aris asks guessing as to her whereabouts. He pulls on her arms to bring her closer to him.

"Logic, my love," Rose answers, kissing the top of his shoulder.

"Makes sense," Aris says with a deep inhale followed by a slow, even exhale.

A deeper answer to his question appears to her and she softly offers, "Baby Sense? Baby Mania?"

"They could have two, right?" Aris asks snuggling into the base of her neck.

"Two?"

"Twins," Aris says in a sigh and immediately falls back to sleep.

125

Δ14Δ

The Lion and the Statue

A MAN AND A LION were discussing the relative strength of men and lions in general. The Man contended that he and his fellows were stronger than lions by reason of their greater intelligence. "Come now with me," he cried, "and I will soon prove that I am right." So he took him into the public gardens and showed him a statue of Hercules overcoming the Lion and tearing his mouth in two.

"That is all very well," said the Lion, "but proves nothing, for it was a man who made the statue." - Aesop

Seated comfortably in the passenger seat of Aris's car, her left hand on his shoulder, her fingers playing with his ear, Rose emphatically states, "I think Erik and I have devised a masterful plan. She will be in love by the end of the night."

"So you're going to be his wingman?" Aris asks.

"Wingman? Hardly, I will be his wing-girl," Rose says bringing her hands up to her shoulders and flaps for full-effect.

"No offense, Rose, but I think you would be terrible at that. You seem to lack…"Aris tries to think of a nice way to say she is somewhat self-absorbed "…subtlety."

"Did you see my selection of cheeses?" Rose says as she looks to the classic picnic basket located in the back seat of Aris's car. "Behold the power of cheese."

"Erik must really like her. I am not sure if I have ever seen him interested in wooing," Aris comments. "Unless… is this your idea?"

"No. He said he wanted to impress her. I thought that a white light lit, menagerie evening garden picnic would do the trick. The fact that it is a double date is merely a diversion." Rose looks back into her picnic basket wondering if they should stop

126

at the grocery store for pickled herring. "We moved the elephant, a couple deer and a bear to the back corner of his mother's garden. We even set up the decorative tarp he bought for his 'Home and Garden' shows. It looks spectacular. Julie and I had a lot of fun setting up this date. The tent, tarp was sorta difficult. It is an artistic design with angles built in. Julie tried to explain it to me... Anyway, it took a couple of hours. It was worth it. I think I may register for one of those."

"You realize in order to register you have to have a wedding, right?" Aris jokes upon their arrival. "Should we park here and walk, or drive up to the house?"

"Well, we would have a reason to excuse ourselves if we had to walk a bit."

"I had no idea you were so manipulative," Aris says, amused. "I married a romantic, who would have thunk?" Aris decides to drive the long, hemlock trimmed driveway toward Erik's childhood home, a farmhouse.

"The secret to being a good wingman," Aris whispers, leaning into her, "is to ensure that things do not appear forced. Your plan seems a bit too forceful. You don't want to scare her off."

Rose leans in and kisses Aris on the cheek. "I thought that the garlic and sundried-tomato cream cheese, cucumber, and bean sprout finger sandwiches mitigated the force. I remember you telling me that you once broke up with a girl because she had bad breath. I also packed mint leaves."

"I am a lucky man," Aris says. He then grabs her hand and squeezes. "Now Rose, this is important...this is the signal to back off, okay?" He squeezes her hand one more time.

Rose smiles and lifts his hand to her mouth. "This is the signal that I understand."

Aris nods in the direction of the front porch. "Look, there's Erik. Wow, he looks a bit... what is that nervous, or angry?"

127

"She is bringing a friend. Why would she do that?" Erik yells as he approaches them.

"Throw you off your game, perhaps?" Rose says.

"What game? You think I got game?" Erik says, making a poor attempt at laughter. It ends up as somewhat of an effeminate squeal. "Aris, what the hell?"

"Don't worry. You still have your parents' croquet set?" Aris suggests.

"You need pairs for that game," Erik states.

"Rose hurt her wrist. You got an ace bandage?" Aris squeezes her hand and kisses her wrist with an obvious wink.

"I hurt my wrist this morning moving the giraffe. Lateral movement really hurts," Rose says easily. "I could not possibly swing a wicket."

"You don't swing wickets," Erik says, cheering up. "Good god, girl. Get some class."

Rose smiles.

"When are they getting here? I'll help you set up," Aris says.

"Thanks, Man. She called me from the car. Yeah, she'll be here in about twenty."

Aris and Erik take off and leave Rose standing with the picnic basket at her feet. She enters the house alone and makes a bee line to the bathroom and discovers an ace bandage in the bottom drawer of the vanity. "Exactly where I would keep it." She takes her time walking to the kitchen as she passes generations of family photos lining both sides of the hallway of a large traditional farmhouse. Rose immediately feels comfortable in this large house. It reminds her of simpler times – historic times – times from books and from movies. It reminds her of a past she has never really experienced herself, yet she can easily picture herself there.

She sets the picnic basket on the kitchen table and looks out over the sink's window. She watches the two men set up the gates in the square field flanked by garden statues of children

128

reading, fishing and catching fire flies. Erik explained earlier that each statue was inspired by him and his two sisters. Rose remembers the story as she admires the tent she spent the afternoon battling. *It looks awesome.*

She walks through the mudroom into the backyard. "You could not ask for better weather. This is going to be a beautiful night," she says.

"Mosquitos," Erik says. "We should pull out the citronella torches now. Rose, would you mind, they are in the broom closet in the mudroom."

Rose immediately returns to the mudroom and retrieves three large citronella tiki torches. *Cool.* She places the torches in a triangle pattern about ten feet from the blankets.

The three are standing on the edge of the blankets admiring their work when they hear a car pulling up the driveway. Erik takes a deep breath and starts a light jog to meet them. Aris extends his hand to Rose while following the same path. Rose grabs his arm instead and leans her head on his shoulder. "He likes her."

The party of five stands on the stones of the driveway for a few minutes for introductions. It is immediately apparent that Aubrey does indeed like Erik. She also seems quite impressed with his house and is adorably nervous. Rose surmises that the blue-eyed Aubrey brought her best friend, Erin because she is anxious for her opinion on her recent find.

"I love your shoes," Rose says to the beautifully maned brunette friend as she casually retreats from the inner circle. "Born?"

"Yes. I have them in three colors – pink, green and yellow," Erin responds.

"I have a very similar pair in red. They are surprisingly comfortable," Rose responds. "Did you guys find the place alright?"

129

"Wow. This is some house. I had no idea that people actually had land so close to D.C. I thought we were lost up until the moment we got here," Erin says in the direction of Erik.

Erik looks at Aubrey and then at Erin. "My family has had this house for over two hundred years. It is almost a headache – if it is not one thing, it's another. However, it is home. I grew up here. The house has taught me lots of handy tricks," he says while gently leading the party to the front porch. "We are actually having a picnic out back. Let me give you all a quick tour."

Erik commands the party as he shows some of the most unique features of this two-hundred year old farm house. He points out the sweet squeaks in the hardwood floorboards, the delicately carved stairway bannister, and lastly explains the plumbing chain. "My parents refuse to update this bathroom. The ones upstairs are much more modern. If ancient plumbing scares you, and maybe it should, feel free to use the ones upstairs."

Aris pulls Rose closer to him and whispers, "He doesn't seem to need a wingman. She is hooked. My boy is growing up. I am so proud." He kisses her on the nose and then the mouth.

Rose bites his earlobe and whispers back to him, "Behave."

"You live here alone?" Erin asks.

"In the summer I do. My two younger sisters are both going to school in D.C. They live with my parents at the ocean during the summer. My parents raised a bunch of free-loaders," Erik jokes.

Fifteen minutes later the party regroups at the aqua tent near the middle-aged oak tree in the corner of the garden. "I think we should play a game of croquet before the sun sets. Agreed?" Erik says as he lifts the wooden rack of clubs. "I am always green. My sisters fight over who gets the red."

"I don't know how to play," Aubrey admits taking a small step closer to Erik. Her arm is touching his dark green golf shirt.

Erin jumps for joy. "My parents had a set at the cottage. I played every night in the summer. It's actually quite easy and does not require much."

"Depends on how you play. Apparently the best do not play to knock out their opponent, rather to set up their next shot," Aris interjects. "It's a friendly game."

Erin laughs. "Not at our house. One year my father even made sand traps."

"You're kidding," Aris says.

"I wish I were... well, now that I think about it, it may have been straw patches for burned grass. Anyway, my family is super competitive." Erin walks to the rack and chooses blue. "I actually think that my parents probably hate each other and use croquet mallets as some sort of warped way to assert dominance... although, they are still married... I don't know."

"Erin, you will be playing with me. Rose hurt her wrist earlier today." Aris looks to Rose, who is standing in the middle of the blankets contemplating how she should bring out the meal. "She is super competitive too," Aris adds, smiling wryly.

Rose watches the two pairs start the course. She feels slight pangs of jealousy as she watches Aris and Erin play, not because of the girl, but because of the game. She has never played and it looks like fun. With nothing else to do, she turns to the task of dinner. She opens the basket and starts to set up a cheese plate with crackers and dried fruit. She places the tray on a makeshift table she created from a section of an old college futon frame she found in the shed. The makeshift table sits about three inches high. She places a large cloth napkin over the tray before standing to retrieve the white wine and glasses from the kitchen. She enjoys the skies as she walks to the house. The peaches and magentas are a perfect complement to the aqua tarp.

Rose is extremely pleased with herself when she is able to carry the corkscrew, five wine glasses and the white wine back to the awning without help. "Aris," she calls as she lifts the wine, "you know how I feel about opening wine. Would you please do the honors?"

Aris makes his shot through the second to last gate and quickly responds to her request. "Hi, gorgeous," he says, hurrying up to her.

"Like this night?" Rose casually points to the sky. "Gorgeous."

Aris kisses her. "Hey, check out the sky!" he yells to the group.

Aris quickly opens the wine and hands the bottle back to Rose. He runs to rejoin the group, still admiring and remarking on the sky, and then makes his final shot. "Victory!" he yells, his arms in the air. He high-fives his partner and then playfully and overwhelmingly gloats in front of Erik by performing a victory lap around the course and mimicking an affected roar of the crowd.

"And you want to marry this guy?" Erik jokes as he walks with Aubrey toward Rose.

"Oh yeah. Ooommm bomp bomp," Rose sings. "Checka-checka-check–ahhh."

Aris smiles in astonishment. "My little beat box. Where did that come from?"

"It's a secret," Rose says, beaming.

Erik walks to the left side of the newly-built storage shed to plug in the white lights that cover the branches of the fruit trees as well as highlight the trim of the aqua tarp. He emerges waiting for accolades.

"Aww… this is beautiful, Erik." Aubrey smiles as she spins to admire the light show. She stops at Erik, leans into him and wraps her arms around his waist. "I am having a nice time."

"Where is my hug?" Erin insists. Aubrey leaves Erik and hugs her friend.

"It is stunning, Erik," Erin says and takes her seat next to Rose. "What's for dinner?"

"Behold the power of cheese." Rose lifts the napkin to reveal an array of cheddars and soft cheeses, dates, apricots and several pepper jams. "I also have veggie finger sandwiches and fried chicken bites with mustard sauce," she says as she points to the basket.

"Thanks, Rose," Erik says graciously.

"No problem, Boss."

"You work for Erik?" Erin asks.

"He was kind enough to give me a job. I am learning how to turn a hemlock into a bunny. Cool, right? He's a good boss."

Aris takes his seat next to Rose and gently strokes her strawberry blonde hair and then takes a nibble from her neck. Ready to swoon, she whispers, "Behave."

Erik stands and runs to the house. Two minutes later, music pours from the living room window. "I do not take requests," he yells as he returns to the party. "Be satisfied with the Beatles, or else."

"A toast," Aris says, lifting his glass. "To mallets and beatles."

"Here, here," Erik says laughing.

The party clinks their glasses and all move slightly closer to the cheese plate to help themselves.

"Hey, did you guys hear about the earthquake-slash-underwater volcano just south of the border in Mexico?" Aubrey asks. "It's pretty awful."

"Love is a burning thing," Aris says. He then starts to sing, "And it makes a fiery ring, Bound by wild desire, I fell into a ring of fire."

"My man," Rose says kissing her husband on the cheek.

Aubrey raises an eyebrow to Erin as the two make note of the strange exuberance emanating from her boyfriend's friends. "I have a friend that lives outside of Lassen Peak," she continues. "She says it is still raining ash there. There have been seven

133

earthquakes in as many days. Kind of scary – horrifying, actually. I guess I am glad I live on this coast."

Aris picks up on the obvious exchange between Aubrey and Erin and recognizes his party foul. He immediately attempts to clear the air. "I'm sorry if our reaction was disrespectful, we didn't mean…"

Rose looks genuinely confused by the situation.

Aris looks at his wife and grabs her hand. "Volcanoes and earthquakes are pretty much a daily conversation at our house. Rose particularly loves volcanos. She has been talking about Yellowstone for years now. She thinks that if the ring of fire is the coasts of Mexico, America, Japan and the Philippines – then Yellowstone is the diamond. Anyway, because eruptions are mostly rare… I don't know… I hope we didn't offend."

Both Erin and Aubrey accept this explanation with a simple non-verbal exchange.

"We really are sorry," Rose reiterates, with a color that suggests sincere embarrassment.

In what seems to be an attempt to end the awkwardness, Erin asks, "What's Yellowstone? You mean the park, right?"

"The park sits on a giant cauldron. Yellowstone cauldron is a super-volcano. Her eruption could take the northern hemisphere into another ice age. And some say its sixty thousand years past due," Rose says triumphantly.

"Rose is really a connoisseur of disaster scenarios. She's even maintaining a blog about them."

"The Volcano's Virtues," Rose interrupts and then apologizes to her husband immediately. "I have to get readers, somehow." She almost takes the opportunity to mention her attempt at her own fables but squelches the impulse by recognizing that she still should be embarrassed by her last self-centered declaration.

Aris amusedly looks at his wife. "Anyway, Yellowstone is her favorite. She is even re-making a government, just in case,"

134

Aris says. "'Be Prepared' is her motto. And the Boy Scouts have nothing on her."

"That's not fair. I am sure that there are many old scouts better prepared than I am. For instance, I haven't built a bomb shelter yet. Although I have a few plans. It will definitely need a zen yoga room equipped with a small rock garden and a working fountain," Rose says with certainty.

"What's a bomb shelter without a yoga room?" Erik asks.

"Incomplete," Rose answers. "I suppose you would need growing lamps for your topiary works."

"I like the idea of a yoga room. I guess I would want a sauna and whirlpool bath," Aubrey admits enjoying the segue conversation.

"Good idea. Where are my blueprints?" Smiling, Rose checks her back pockets. "I'm going to update my 'underground' blog shelter with an added whirlpool. Oh yeah, and my charming and supportive husband also bought me a Ham radio as a wedding gift. He also built me an enormous antenna. I am a few steps deeper into my bomb shelter."

"To make those steps mean anything she needs to get her license," Aris says barely audibly, for her benefit and his amusement.

Rose squints and produces a mocking leer for her husband.

"What kind of yoga do you practice?" Aubrey asks. "We could take a class together."

"I guess flow yoga. I usually practice at home," Rose explains.

"Classes are fun. Let's go next week," Aubrey says insistently. "Erin and I go on Tuesdays and Thursdays."

"Okay," Rose says and then turns to look at Aris with her attempt at a meek smile.

"Wanna practice darts? There is a bar across the street from her yoga studio," Erik asks Aris with a tone of sarcasm.

"Sorry man, I am traveling next week. I am visiting Northeastern PA. The EPA is doing a presentation on their findings regarding the environmental impact of the Marcellus shale project for several counties' local governments and, ahem, concerned citizens," Aris comments. "I am not looking forward to it. Politics, I hate politics."

Rose tugs the basket to her and pulls out two Tupperware containers: one large and flat for the sandwiches, the other tall for the fried chicken bites. "Chicken bites and Sundried tomato and garlic cream cheese sandwiches with fresh tomato, cucumber and bean sprouts on twelve grain."

Aris stands and offers more wine to both Erik and Erin, whose glasses are near empty. "We have another bottle in the fridge, right?" Aris looks at Erik as he notes the empty bottle.

Erik nods. "We also have a bottle of apricot dessert wine. The wine lady told me to try it."

All fill their plates with smatterings of both finger sandwiches and fried chicken. "This is delicious, Rose. Thanks," Erik says sincerely.

"Was this last earthquake severe? High death count?" Rose asks quietly. "I was pretty busy today and have not even checked my email since yesterday morning. And just so I make a good impression, I hope you realize that I am not... I wouldn't wish disaster on people..."

"I understand. I find hurricanes fascinating. I am glued to the TV if there is a good hurricane," Aubrey says lightheartedly, sincerely appreciating the aside.

"So was the death count high?" Erin asks.

"I am afraid it was, not like Haiti, but many buildings were toppled mid-day. I do not know the official count. But, I do have a..." Aubrey reaches for her purse to pull out her IPhone. "Thirty-two thousand and counting," she reports a short while later.

136

Rose raises her glass. "To the family and friends of those who are no longer with us," she says. The party chinks their glasses. "Mother nature certainly has her own virtues," Rose adds pensively.

Aris reaches his hand to her cheek and pinches her chin. "Did you see the stars? The hunter now becomes the hunted." Aris points to the Orion constellation.

Rose lies back on her elbows and looks to the sky.

Aris watches her face for the predictable satisfied smile that always appears on her face when she remembers to look at the stars. "So many worlds," he says.

"It is so easy to forget that earthquakes and volcanos shaped our world. A lot of our visions of paradise, like Hawaii, were built upon fiery volcanos."

"Hey, and when it is your time, it is your time," Erik adds. "I am going to get another bottle of wine. Does anyone need anything from the house?"

"I need to use the ladies," Aubrey admits. "Erin?"

"Yeah. Good idea," Erin says.

The three walk to the house. Rose watches as Aubrey takes Erik's hand when they reach the stairs of the back porch. "Hey, did you see that?"

"He likes her. She likes him," Aris says. Looking at Rose, he adds, "And I love you. Thanks for doing this for him."

Rose rolls toward him and nuzzles her nose in his neck. "This is fun. I am glad you know Erik. Yet, I must admit that after spending the past couple of days with him, I am having a seriously hard time seeing him with Danika. How weird was that?"

"I think she hurt him quite a bit. I hate to admit it, but he was the better of the pair. Anyway, it was years and years ago. I think I'll always think of him as a brother," he says. He pauses in his speech to give her a kiss. "I'm glad you like him," he says as he kisses her again.

"I feel safe here," Rose declares. "Like all we really need to do is move back in time two hundred years."

"I think I know what you mean. Life seems more natural back here."

"Sometimes nature does seem to have a maternal, nurturing effect, doesn't it?"

"Sometimes, and sometimes not."

"Huh, Mother Nature. I think I could probably write an entire book about that phrase. I could spin it like that Backlash book. Did you ever read that book?"

"Don't make it like that, okay?"

"Of course not, I will make it hot, passionate and sexy. She'll probably end up with a couple of kids."

"A couple of kids? A boy and a girl?" Aris digs.

"Maybe. However, with Mother Nature acting so temperamentally – she'd probably decide that it's not a good idea to bring children into the world," Rose returns with the subtle wry grin at a shot well-played.

Aris reaches his hand and puts it under her shirt and starts gently squeezing her ribs as he works his way up. "We can certainly practice… Prepare ourselves for when it really counts, right?" Aris reaches one of her weak spots.

Rose sighs heavily. "Practice? Not in front of the children," Rose says as she points to the statues and then to the party returning from the house.

"I feel like I am going to explode," Aris whispers into her ear as he quickly stops his actions with a huff of frustration.

"Hot. Maybe, we should probably get out of here and find some shelter."

Δ15Δ

The aim of art is to represent not the outward appearance of things, but their inward significance. – Aristotle

I haven't had a black and tan for years. Good choice," says Erik as he and Aris find two empty barstools in the quiet pub, their pints in hand.

"I used to drink these all the time in college," Aris admits as he takes his first sip. "They are as good as I remember."

"It's cool to be hanging out like this. It's been a while. So your work trip was cancelled?" Erik asks.

"More like postponed; more politics," Aris answers. He takes a breath. With Rose and Aubrey away for their Yoga class, Aris hopes to confide in Erik. "I am happy that I don't have to travel. I've been worried about leaving Rose alone. She has been having these really nasty nightmares. Listen, I'm pretty sure she would not be happy with me talking to you about this, but I have to talk to someone."

Erik situates himself on the bar stool to connote his willingness to listen. "I get it. I like Rose. I really like her. So talk."

"Cool." Aris takes two long sips before continuing, "I love her, Man. I've loved her for years. Yet, she scares the hell out of me at times."

"What do you mean?" Erik asks. He leans back into his bar stool to allow space for his friend to talk.

"She's beautiful, gorgeous even. She's smart, funny, clever. She is also loyal and faithful," Aris answers.

"And you have a problem with which of those," Erik says with a small laugh, almost incensed.

139

"I am afraid she is too much. She has this way, but I guess I'd call it a *weight* about her," Aris says looking into his beer. "And the way she loves me. Jesus, Man, I can be who I am and I can also be more than I am. I can actually be Aristotle, if I want. It is like I don't have to change around her, but it's not like I can relax either. You know what I mean?"

"She is a bit intense. Jim calls her the hot little number," Erik admits. "I'm not sure what that means. I would warn you about Jim, but Rose can handle him, probably even better than his own mother."

Aris smiles upon hearing this. He looks at his friend for a long moment and wonders how far he can trust his confidence. "All right, so here's the thing… This is it… I believe in God. I do. I guess I always have. But she believes that he is in the room talking to her. I mean, she really believes."

"And you don't believe her?" Erik asks shrugging his shoulders with his palms open trying to stave off judgment.

"That's just it. The things she says. The conversations she says she is having. I don't know who else could be talking to her," Aris admits. "But it is scary, you know. She has been my best friend for years. She told me all the time that she was talking to God about this, or praying to God about that. I guess I didn't realize what she meant. I guess I was picturing her praying, closing her eyes and folding her hands, or something like that…"

Erik nods and finishes his beer. "Well, what *is* she doing?"

"The other night, at like three a.m., I woke up and she wasn't there. I walked down the stairs and she was outside pacing in our backyard actually talking to the sky. She was just walking around talking. Actually it sounded like she was having conversations with many different people. You know, like a schizophrenic."

Erik laughs uncomfortably. "I've caught her talking to herself a couple of times. Sure, most people talk to themselves using

140

their inside-their-head voices. She doesn't. That's not a big deal."

Aris sighs. "Yeah, I suppose you're right. How am I supposed to keep her in check? I mean, shouldn't I be worried. I know that I was worried enough that night that I just stayed in the shadows and watched. She was out there, talking, for an entire hour. And these nightmares… She takes them so seriously. " He realizes immediately that he crossed the line and said too much. He sits back further into his bar stool and contemplates how he should take back what he just said. "I hope you realize that I am out on a limb here."

Erik just nods and slides his empty glass around on the shellacked table. "I understand. Did you ask her about it the following morning?"

"I asked her about her dream," Aris says. "Presumably the reason why she wasn't still in bed."

"Did she tell you about it?" Erik asks.

"Yes. But she didn't tell me about walking around in the backyard. I think she is hiding that part. I wish she would just tell me about that part."

Erik is silent. He tries to consult his own conscience about what he has heard and what his role should be to his friend and to his employee, who is also quickly becoming a close friend. He asks, "What do you want me to do here? Do you want me to rationalize her behavior? I think I can. Or do you want me to give you permission to be worried? I think I can do that too."

Aris pointedly stands from his seat. "Two more beers?" he asks, raising his own empty pint.

"Absolutely," Erik answers. Erik stands as well, the two men departing their barstool confessional. "Nine ball?"

"Take quarters?" Aris asks the bartender, only now realizing that the slightly haughty, twenty-something hipster must have heard more than a small bit of his bleeding heart.

141

"Five," the bartender responds, giving no indication one way or the other. "There is a change machine in the corner next to the dart board."

"Good place for a change machine," Erik jokes.

"The last time I played pool was this past winter at my folk's house right before I proposed to Rose. Mina beat me eight to two. I guess I was a bit preoccupied then," Aris admits.

"Mina is pretty good," Erik says as he racks the balls. "Danika was awful. How you could have a pool table in your house and never play pool…"

Aris shrugs and then breaks. The nine ball nearly hits the left back corner pocket. "Almost," Aris says.

"Losing your touch, eh?" Erik laughs.

"I'm gonna blame Rose," Aris jokes, but his demeanor shows otherwise.

Erik tries to humor his friend, but allows the conversation to continue. "Excuses, excuses. I have to admit she's a good one to be preoccupied with. You've dated some doozies."

"What's a doozy?" Aris laughs.

"I think you know. Rose is the bomb," Erik jests and misses his bank on the two.

"That's what I am afraid of," Aris says hitting a two, three combo.

"So these nightmares, what are they about?" Erik asks as he watches Aris set up another combination.

He makes the shot before answering, "A lot of fire."

"Have you ever looked up dream interpretation on the web," Erik suggests sincerely.

Aris furrows his brow. "I haven't tried that. Somehow I get the impression that the internet, although it can be a good source of information… anyway, you cannot believe everything you read."

"I don't know. You've heard that losing your teeth in a dream means something, right? Maybe fire does too."

Aris pulls out his iPhone and looks up dream interpretation. "Get this. Fire in your dream can symbolize destruction, passion, desire, illumination, purification, transformation, enlightenment, or anger. It may suggest that something old is passing and something new is entering into your life. Your thoughts and views are changing."

"Well, that ought to help. It's all right there," Erik says and walks to take his turn. He knocks the five, six and seven.

"Remember that bar fight we almost got into years ago with that drunk who claimed that we had to call the pocket for the eight ball? And he wasn't even playing…"

Erik laughs. "The kind of guy you are supposed to put in front of the change machine late at night. Yeah, I remember that guy."

Aris gives up on his tangent. "Erik, I love her."

"I know. The good thing is she feels the same way. I don't know, Man, I think you may have a reason to be concerned, but… Well, the thing is, she is not a normal girl. You shouldn't expect her to be normal. But if it is really bothering you, then maybe you should ask her to speak to a professional," he advises.

"Yeah, I suppose I could apply a little pressure, just to cover our bases. I guess I can try to work a little of the ole magic and try to get her mind onto something else. She needs a hobby. She has started this blog thing and I am not exactly sure if it is helping. The radio, well…" he says as he picks up his stick and knocks in the eight and nine in succession. He reaches his hand over to Erik. "Good game."

"Another?" Erik asks.

"You rack 'em," Aris says grabbing his beer and taking three solid gulps. "I could also use another beer."

"Me too," Erik says lifting his empty pint to his friend with a look of suggestion. Erik deftly racks another game of nine-ball and then replaces his current cue with another.

Two minutes later, Aris returns with another two pints and two dollars in hand. "I think we have time for at least two more games. The ladies will be over here in about thirty minutes. I'm glad Rose is driving. I feel like drinking."

"This could be a weekly thing. The girls do yoga and we get drunk," Erik says, laughing.

"Sounds good to me. This is fun," Aris admits and then breaks. He sinks the nine. "You wanna just play to eight?"

Erik nods.

Aris decides that he has actually achieved a small piece of mind and realizes that sharing with Erik actually did help. He chalks his cue and thoughtfully asks, "How are things going with Aubrey?"

"Good. Well, I suppose there is a little bump in the road. The thing is, she is really close to Erin and so Erin is out with us almost half the time. I like Erin, but I would rather spend more time with Aubrey alone and not have to share. I am not sure if that makes me a good guy, or not. I am not sure if I have the right to ask for more time..."

Aris listens as he watches Erik run the next three balls. "You like her though. You really like her."

"I think she is awesome," Erik says. "And she doesn't wear tons of makeup or put hair goop in her hair. Her hair is soft. She shops, but her credit card bill is not the topic of conversation."

"I guess here is where I am supposed to say that it must have been you who has dated a few doozies?" Aris smiles as he realizes that Danika is pretty much the definition of a doozy.

"I like her. I think things are progressing, you know, getting serious. However, this is usually when I mess things up. Have you ever noticed that it is usually women who are afraid to commit? I don't know. I think I need to go to the gym or maybe stop drinking, or maybe go on a diet."

"Maybe we should take up yoga," Aris jokes.

"Yeah, good one," Erik says.

144

The two gentlemen joke with each other as they burn through two very quick games.

While racking for the next game, Erik astutely observes that Aris seems to be acting like himself rather than actually being himself. After chalking his own cue, he asks, "So these nightmares, do you think that maybe she is not being challenged enough? Her pharmaceutical job was pretty demanding, right? I guess I could give her more responsibility."

"I really don't think that's it," Aris says. "Maybe it's just all of the changes that have happened. The chocolate thing, the moving thing, the career thing…" Aris then fully considers his friend's mindset. "Anyway, Erik, I know she really enjoys her current job; she is challenged. She says that she's physically tired when she gets home, although you wouldn't notice," Aris says drifting to the nights they have spent together.

"She does seem to have boundless energy. What are you feeding her?"

Aris huffs a laugh through his nose and finishes the table.

Suzu

Suzu peers through her cobalt blue bangs at her inker, Ichiro, unsure of whether she should share her idea first or show him later. They have worked as a team for many years and their methods are tried and true, and quite successful. The pair has been referred to as the "wonder twins" amongst their small guild of anime artists working inside Tokyo. At first, they both hated the dubious distinction. Being compared to simple, crude American cartoon characters is easily considered an insult. Yet, they have since discovered that through their combined talents, they can create stunning worlds and epic story lines. They have also discovered new and interesting ways to hide their artistic trademarks of both animals and water in each and every cell. Therefore, they are now perfectly content being the wonder twins and have since marked their artistic union with shared locks of cobalt hair.

Ichiro sets down his two-hundred-year-old inkstick and cleans his fingers with his pale blue linen cloth. "Miki, we need a world for Miki, a beautiful chronicle," he says looking across his white draft table into the eyes of his partner. "We don't have a lot of time. The story board is due next week."

Suzu smooths her hands across the fine, wool fiber parchment in front of her, her primary working requirement. Every project starts with an inspirational drawing on this paper. She looks at the soft beige page for a few moments before setting her eyes upon Ichiro. "I had a dream about Krakatoa," she offers to her partner, "Krakatoa, the loudest sound in history."

"Krakatoa," Ichiro repeats.

"Munch's 'The Scream' was said to be inspired by the atmospheric influence of the eruption felt all the way in

146

Norway," Suzu says meekly, gently. She means to inspire rather than manipulate. "Miki's world?"

Ichiro's head falls to the right as he stares into the distance, his mind creating the foliage of Miki's world, the island of Krakatoa. "Thirteen thousand times the explosive power of Hiroshima's Little Boy bomb."

Suzu quietly nods to him, conveying a full comprehension of his reference. She looks down at her blank parchment and declares, "I have been dreaming and waking and dreaming about Krakatoa. I am dreaming about the sound of Krakatoa. I think I can draw from it."

"Does the story take place before the eruption, or after?" Ichiro asks putting a blue lock behind his ear.

Suzu looks to the right at her watercolors. She stretches out her right arm to reach them. The tips of her fingers glide over the tops of the tubes of color as she considers their use. She ever so slightly shakes her head. Her eyes return to the parchment and then move to the left to find her acrylics. "I do not know."

"I think we should start with the sound," Ichiro suggests. "How do you draw that kind of sound?"

Suzu smiles at her partner as she recognizes his headfirst method. "Munch did not really capture it, did he? He was too far away."

"There was not enough pain in the image. He did not show enough in the eyes," Ichiro says grabbing his own paper. He begins to pencil sketch the slanted eyes of his fair maiden Miki.

"Can you keep your eyes open?" she asks trying to relate the sound of her dreams. "The sound I dream about is darkness – it is complete blackness, like your mind cannot withstand the noise. Your mind cannot co-exist with any other sense."

Ichiro finally starts to hear her and lowers his pitch to inquire, "This dream. How long have you been having this dream?"

147

"It started four nights ago. It's been happening every night," Suzu discloses while pulling forward her tray of oils, the obvious choice. "I don't know why it has taken me so long to…"

"Miki and the Sound," Ichiro says.

"Krakatoa," Suzu firmly suggests.

"Miki Whispers," Ichiro adds trying to establish the balance between his vision and that of his partner.

"Anak Krakatau. It is the name of the island that is forming now due to the continuous eruptions that started back in the twenties. It means the Child of Krakatoa."

"The Child of Krakatoa," Ichira announces. "The Child of Krakatoa."

"Good," Suzu says. She makes the first mark on her paper.

Δ16Δ

The Farmer and the Cranes

SOME CRANES made their feeding grounds on some plow lands newly sown with wheat. For a long time the Farmer, brandishing an empty sling, chased them away by the terror he inspired; but when the birds found that the sling was only swung in the air, they ceased to take any notice of it and would not move. The Farmer, on seeing this, charged his sling with stones, and killed a great number. The remaining birds at once forsook his fields, crying to each other, "It is time for us to be off to Liliput: for this man is no longer content to scare us, but begins to show us in earnest what he can do."-Aesop

Aris looks at his wife, who is cleaning up in the kitchen after the meal he cooked. She spent the entirety of dinner discussing an article she read about Somalia. He smiles at her passion for things that she can do very little about. And as he watches her happily clear away the dishes, he decides to tell her about his day.

"I have good news to report. I heard from my boss today that I won't have to travel for two months. I'll be working in-house, heretofore referred to as the Potomac Project," Aris announces.

With childlike abandon, Rose jumps up and down in excitement. "I am going to be able to sleep with my husband every night! Awesome!"

"Sleep?" Aris says as he wraps his arms around her. "Is that what you think you have been doing… sleeping? It feels more like kicking and sounds more like screaming."

"Yeah, I guess I have been having a few nightmares…"

"A few nightmares… Geez." Aris takes on a tone of worry. "Do you mind if I offer a suggestion. How about you just focus

149

on radio for now – something purely technical? I think it would help ground you, and maybe lessen the nightmares."

Rose stares blankly at her husband. "Maybe you're right." She drops her chin into her chest and tries not to emotionally overreact. *He's supposed to understand me.*

"Writing about disaster scenarios is certainly not helping things. Maybe focusing on the technical aspects of radio will give your creative mind some much needed rest. I mean, there is nothing scary about transformers, right?" He teasingly adds, "Get it? Transformers? It's a joke. I'm funny, right?"

Rose winks. "You're right. There is nothing scary about a race of beings masquerading as can openers and coffee machines; it's just slightly twisted. Get it?" she jokes.

He smiles. "I love you."

Rose tries to find the next sentence to continue the light, easy conversation he desires, but, as per usual, she fails. Her very real nightmares are occurring with increasing frequency and she really needs her husband's help and support. She needs him to understand that her blog posts, her virtues, her stories contain a very sincere effort to stop the nightmares. She is trying to tell the truth; she is trying not to keep secrets. "I truly believe that as soon as I get these ideas out of my head, they will disappear from my dreams. I am afraid that if I ignore them – they'll just get worse."

"You told me that you used to have lots of nightmares when you were a child. Do you remember them?"

"I remember it took my mom hours to convince me to go back to sleep," Rose says not quite sure if she actually remembers those nights or whether she remembers her mother's retelling of those nights. She does remember what her mom said to her the last time she was home. *Secrets.* She recognizes the opening. It is time to tell him her secret. She starts, "My mom told me that I had nightmares as a child because I was keeping a secret."

150

"Are you keeping a secret?" Aris asks simply.

Rose nods once as if she is resolved. "These dreams feel so real, so vivid, and so scary... existing on a level I dare not admit. And, the truth is, I don't tell you all of them. But that is not the secret." Rose takes a deep breath as she realizes that she would rather not rehash her nightmares, and risk her relationship, while standing in her now tidy kitchen. She leads him to the couch and together they sit.

Aris puts his arm along the back of the couch to provide a place for her to curl up in his shoulder. "I really thought that having a physical job would help you sleep better."

"I am beginning to think that... well... never mind," she says with a tone that is both resigned and discomfited, nearly overcome with a sinister feeling of déjà vu.

"Tell me," Aris quietly pleads. "It might help to talk about it."

"As I have said before..." Rose briefly wonders at the sound of her broken record, yet continues, "I guess when I am working at Erik's I am spending a lot of time thinking about *the garden* – the original garden complete with the snake and the disallowed tree – the essence of unrecognizable evil. And I have recently arrived at the conclusion that the snake is probably not near as scary as God's next test."

"Okay," Aris says nervously. He lifts her chin with his index finger so he can see her eyes. "So you're waxing theological while at work, and..."

"The truth is, or my secret is..." Rose furrows her brow because, right now, she really does not know the difference. Right now she thinks that *the truth* is a secret. "I think God is trying to tell me something," Rose says quietly and ashamedly. She is quiet because she fears she may be offending God. She is ashamed because she fears that her thoughts are not based in reality. Rose looks down into her sweaty palms and speaks, "I am scared, Aris. I fear if I tell you my thoughts – you might

151

think I'm crazy." She pauses and prays for courage. She finds it. "But I think that God is trying to tell me something – something important."

"Oh Rose, I already know you are crazy," Aris jokes. "Crazy like a fox. What does that mean, anyway?"

"Foxes are reputed to be cunning." She smiles at the tease.

"Just checking to make sure you are still rational and reasonable," Aris says with a smile and a wink.

Rose tries to laugh at herself as she anxiously locates the floor, the couch and other tangible items in her surroundings. She reaches up to intertwine her right hand with his across the back of the couch. "Yep, that's me, rational and reasonable."

Aris has a secret of his own. He is secretly hoping that tonight's conversation will be different; that tonight's conversation will be about what she is hiding, not about what she is thinking. "Alright so God is talking to you. What is He saying?" he asks shifting his attention to her fingers and his. The scene of his wife in the backyard talking to the sky is still vivid in his mind.

"Don't eat yellow snow," Rose jokes and then swiftly shows she is serious. "I wish I had a simple answer. It's not simple. It's sorta like notes to a symphony given all at once. Like a zip file and I do not have the program to unzip it. No, it's more like a zip file of a symphony yet I only have the program to unzip the second chair oboe. It's very frustrating." Rose attempts to find her clearest voice before taking the next step. "Husband? Do you believe in prophets?"

"What do you mean? Dollar signs? Or Moses, Elijah, and that guy in the whale?" Aris inquires.

"Prophets and prophecy… like the stories are true?"

"You mean the stories aren't true?" Aris jokes. He pinches her chin and notices the golden flecks in her eyes. For a brief millisecond they appear even more radiant.

152

Rose leans forward to bury her nose into his shoulder as if this action alone will relieve a small portion of the burden she is trying to unload.

Aris looks down into the spirals of her hair before responding. "I guess I have always been comfortable with the notion that the stories about those guys were parable – expressing an idea, not a fact," he says as he moves her hair to reveal a portion of her face, "like fables, like your comic virtues." He finds her eyes and breathes deeply only to remind her to do the same. "Yet part of me accepts the sincere possibility that they are true. I was raised Catholic and received my entire education in a Catholic School – high school and college."

"I've been talking to God a lot lately. While you are sleeping, I'm talking." She averts her eyes and utters, "I think God is trying to tell me about that truth, warn me about that truth. A truth that time lost. A truth about prophecy."

"I see you sometimes, talking in the backyard," Aris says relieved by the admission.

"You have?" Rose says, frozen, holding her breath. Her face flushes.

Aris nods. "I have." Seeing her exposed vulnerability, Aris tries to stop her from shutting down. "So there is something lost – and you think this is the fire in your dreams?"

"I think…I think I love how you love me," Rose's says, her spirit lifting. "I've really wanted to talk to you about this stuff for a pretty long time now. I'm afraid…afraid of what you might think or how you might react."

"Rose, just talk to me. Not talking to me, keeping it to yourself, hurts me more."

Rose begins to hear the sweet echo of her mother's wisdom. "Keeping a secret," she whispers to herself to bolster her confidence.

"Is that your secret, your conversations in our backyard?" Aris asks with a very gentle voice. His voice then deepens. "I see you at night, out there. I've been hoping that you would tell me about it someday. I didn't mention it because I trust you, and understand that these conversations are private, but Rose, I am your husband." Aris grabs her hand and takes it to his lips. "We are married."

Rose tries to breathe. She is still afraid. She worries that he has no idea what he is asking; she worries that he will not understand. She deliberates for a few moments before returning, "Are you sure? Are you sure you want to know more? It might change how you see me."

"I'm sure," he says followed by an inaudible gulp.

"Okay, you asked for it..." Rose looks down at her lap and her hands to organize her thoughts. Her demeanor completely changes from scared and melancholy to something light and energetic as she says, "Let's start with the full reality of Ancient Egypt."

Surprised by the change and involuntarily bracing himself, he says, "I knew when I married you that you were high maintenance. I did, I swear I did." He lets out a nervous laugh.

"You just didn't know how high."

"Maybe I had some idea. So what's this about Ancient Egypt?" Aris asks trying to force a relaxed version of himself into the couch.

"Can you imagine walking through the city in its original grandeur? I heard that the outside pyramid walls were sanded to a polish and the sides of the pyramid reflected light, like a mirror, like the skin of Creativity. The essence of what I am trying to say is that...I mean...Well, the pyramids are still impressive today, but much, much more than their luster is lost."

"And you think in-between the perfect pyramids and Park Place – a divine truth is, or has been lost," Aris says astutely.

154

"Exactly. Some sort of truth that defies vocabulary," Rose says. She realizes that she may have just accidentally lied. She knows the word. "Maybe transcendent?"

"Transcendent. Good word."

Rose looks up at her husband and decides to sit up. She puts approximately two feet between them. She has thought about her argument over the past few weeks. She says, "You know that movie *Contact* starring Jodie Foster?"

He nods and re-offers her his hand. He then asks, "Wait? Are we still talking about Egypt?"

Rose laughs and winks. "Admit it, you love my banter."

Aris huffs and shakes his head.

"When she took the trip, 'They' said to her that they have been selecting a single traveler from a world to make the magnificent journey, always one, always alone." Rose looks at their hands and smiles. "That movie showed a plausible scenario of how an entire life and way of thinking can change in an instant."

"Or with eighteen hours of recorded static," Aris adds.

Rose chuckles at his summation. "Anyway, I guess I am afraid this 'transcendence' stuff, the nightmares, the virtues, all this stuff, is God testing my faith. Right now, I cannot prove what I think is going on. I don't have any proof; I only have coincidence. I guess that I am afraid that, in the end, I am going to be the Jodie Foster character trying to convince a room full of politicians what really happened and they will not believe me even if…" She looks down into her lap realizing that her argument was not worded as well as she wanted.

"Even if they have eighteen hours of recorded static?" Aris repeats.

"She had this profound life-altering experience and they weren't there," Rose says in an attempt to slow her mind and the conversation. Feeling both dizzy and disconnected, she repositions herself back into his arms.

155

Aris internally smiles and relaxes as he feels his wife return to where she belongs. He brushes her hair with his hand and kisses the top of her head until their breaths synchronize. He finally finds the courage to continue the conversation. "I like having you here."

"In your arms?"

He pauses for a beat to recognize how much he loves this amazing, odd being in his arms. "Transcendence," Aris says with a deep breath. "I have an idea. Why don't you tell me about the nightmare you had last night. The one that caused this scratch." Aris lifts his short sleeve to show her his left shoulder with a faint surface scratch. "I want to hear about that one. Do you remember it?"

"A bedtime story?" Rose laughs, as she shares her secret name for these events. She looks up into her husband's beautiful, dark brown eyes. "Scheherazade. Do *you* remember that night we watched that movie together? That night in my apartment? You made me dinner?" she says relaxing deeper with every word. "I feel like Scheherazade from Arabian Nights. I can almost see the pyramids in the background. You're not going to kill me after I finish the story, are you?"

"Depends how good it is," Aris says with a laugh. He continues his tease, "Did you see this scratch? I am afraid you are going to kill me." Happy for the moment, he pushes a few strands of hair from her face.

Rose looks up into his face, bats her eyelashes, and starts her telling. "I am walking in a university town. And I notice that there is this very beautiful and large white snake in a tree lining the sidewalk, smiling at me. I almost grab the snake, yet don't. I have that dream a lot. I am not afraid of the snake, just respectful, I guess."

Rose notices Aris's very handsome features as he listens. She wants to reach out to touch his ear lobe, but is content with the reminder of just how much she loves her husband's ears. "I go

156

down an alley just to the right of the snake tree and end up in a large room with marble walls and step into a line of people. There is a man, with a darkish Indian complexion at the top of the line directing people either to the right or the left. When I am at the front of the line, I turn into a giant baby cobra. The Indian man directs me to the left."

"How do you know you're a baby?" Aris asks.

"In my dream, I yawn like a baby," Rose answers simply without offering any further detail.

"Alrighty then, sounds pretty normal thus far," Aris says with the right corner of his mouth turned up.

"I follow his instructions and walk down a marble hall; I am no longer a snake at this point. The hall has shadows of flames dancing on them and I literally run into a stretcher with a ballerina in full tutu regalia asleep on it. She wakes up and walks past me into a series of cloth walls, sorta like curtains, only more like a tent..."

"I am not sure how this dream ends up with you clawing me."

"Patience, Shahryār. My normal, average nightmares are when I am college age making the same mistakes that I did when I was that age. Then there are the dreams where I learn something – something that I have no business knowing, like last night's dream. In last night's dream, I was aware of the fact that I could leave the place where I was. I knew exactly where the door was. I could leave but everyone else there couldn't. They didn't know it. You have that scratch because I was trying to stop the ballerina from blindly walking into the super-hot flames. I could feel the heat, but I couldn't save them. And the screams, they were so awful." Rose makes a face in an attempt to relate the sound.

Aris lifts Rose's chin to get her full attention. "Again, maybe just putting a little distance between yourself and these thoughts might stop the nightmares..."

157

Rose quietly accepts the fact that he either has not heard her, or simply does not believe her. Rather than taking issue, she decides to make an effort to believe him instead. She communicates this resolve with a gentle shrug of her shoulders, as if to say "it's possible."

"I looked up dream interpretation and fire the other night, out with Erik, and it said…"

Rose interrupts, "That I am happy or sad, confused or focused, too far in the future or stuck in the past… Yeah, I looked it up too." It is not difficult to notice that she is starting to get frustrated. She overcomes and retakes the rein of the conversation. "What I'm trying to say is…I think I can actually hear transcendence. In my backyard talks, I think I am hearing and feeling a fraction of His divinity. And believe me, you definitely don't want more than that. And these dreams of earthquakes and fires are a part of that tiny sliver of true reality. Because my experiences are merely dreams…"

"Hearing God's transcendence?" he asks, his eyebrows pierced together, his tone dismissive.

Rose reacts strongly, very much offended. "I am hearing God," she says raising her own voice. She angrily sits up and turns to him. "You are not listening to me," she yells. "And I am seriously getting tired of it. Hear me and stop trying to shut me up or shut me down. My blog stays, the virtues stay, and my fables, or tales, or whatever they are stay…" Still yelling, but at a quieter, more controlled decibel, she adds, "And husband, you're just going to have to get used to it because, my darling, you're staying, too. These nightmares will pass. I will get past them, as soon as I get them out. You're just going to have to deal with your scary little dream girl a little longer. Capisce?"

"No, it's not okay." Aris shakes his head. He picks up her fight, and stands his ground. "Let me get this straight. You think your dreams about fire and volcanoes, is you 'hearing' aspects

158

of God's transcendence? You realize that's arrogance – the kind that can get you in serious trouble. And not just here."

Rose quiets. She remembers a point of her rehearsed argument. "Arrogance? Is it? Maybe it's faithfulness. I mean, if these are signs, signs of the times, God would send a prophet to recognize them, right?"

"And what? You are his prophet?" Aris cannot even believe the turn this conversation is taking. "You are not a prophet. This is bullshit, Rose. Complete and total bullshit."

Rose hears his response and internally recognizes it as more than adequate; in fact, it is what she expected. She remains silent as she moves her gaze from his profile down to her hands. "Aris, I am just trying to…"

"You are trying to scare the hell out of me," he says. He is truly considering that his wife may very well be certifiably mad. After a few deep breaths, all the while fighting the urge to actually throw a reckoning of his own, he slowly starts to hear what she actually said. He starts to hear her voice. "You are just trying to…" he repeats her last words.

Rose watches his sanity return and effortlessly pokes at her husband. "I suppose now is a perfect time to remind you that Crazy married Logic."

Aris finds the courage to laugh at her joke. He remembers to breathe. "Ah, high-maintenance, indeed." He breathes again and looks over his complicated bride. "Listen, I really want to say you are being ridiculous. However, I know that you could argue with me, convincingly even…"

Rose laughs at his concession. "It's alright. Admit it; you think I'm bat raving mad."

Accepting her amusement, he returns a casual smile and an affected nod. He laughs at himself again and finds his breath with hers. "It's funny. I am finding myself thinking about your brother. I thought it was funny when Zeke told me that you were

159

'crazy enough to be interesting'… Maybe I should have heeded his remark as a warning."

"Maybe you should have," Rose says with a little derision. She takes a moment to relax and process the past few minutes. "My point is –my secret is – I think God is testing me with a twist of that old Aesop fable, The Farmer and the Cranes. He may be using an empty sling shot right now – and these dreams are not real; they are just strange coincidences. If I take it to the next level, the scarier level, maybe these earthquakes and volcanos are small pebbles – warning shots…And maybe He is telling me, because He has to tell someone. He has to tell someone who is listening…"

"Like Jodie Foster," Aris says. He gently shakes the hair of her pony tail as he tries to calmly accept her musings on a plane on which he is comfortable.

She wants to stop talking, but there is still more to her plan. *A sugar coated pill.* "The scientist in me wants to chock up these experiences to random life experience and these dreams as chemical triggers firing random thoughts and images. The theologian in me wants to temper the mystic-esque nature of these creative musings to a logical argument with a solid academic construction. Yet the believer in me is honestly anxious, seriously anxious. The truth is – is that I really do think that God is talking to me. My responsibility to that truth is that I continue to listen, and try to make sense. Please understand…" Rose pierces her eyebrows together and tries to subdue the plea emanating from her eyes.

"Personally, I think that you need to talk to someone, a professional," Aris says.

"Crazy married Logic," Rose says followed by a resigned huff. She tenses up as she internally reviews the past hour. She is fully aware that it is more than likely that she said too much. *He is never going to see me in the same way*, she thinks. Accepting this thought as a very real possibility, she angers and

160

fires, "Can you see, now, why it is I chose to keep my backyard talks to myself? Do I need to remind you that you asked for it?" She looks up into his eyes with a stern stare from her own hurt one. "You did. You asked for it. You said you wanted to know. Aris, I am not insane. And deep down you know it."

Silenced by this revelation, Aris swallows hard. "Rose, this is what I know. I know you are a theologian, first and foremost. What I think… I think you are trying to understand the history of prophecy by trying to understand how the prophets may have actually felt? Like method acting?" Aris says with his eyebrows tightly pierced together. "Right?"

"Sounds like me," Rose says smirking. She understands her husband's grasping interpretation. She has had months to get used to this idea; he has only had minutes. In hopes of soothing her husband's concern, she says simply, "An easier pill to swallow…I think dreams have changed the course of history many times – all because the dreamer took them seriously. Dreams are important. They always have been. And I am not the first dreamer." Rose looks up at her husband. "Think about it. There are tons of examples. MLK, Joan of Arc, Einstein…"

Aris looks down into his wife's face and sighs with a gentle nod of acceptance. "And history never gives you the entire back story," he says quoting his own wife.

"Never say never," she says gently patting his cheek. "Okay, Saint Aristotle, this conversation is done. Let's watch a movie. I'll make popcorn." She kisses his nose, jumps from the couch and makes a mad dash for the pantry.

"Crazy married Logic, but did Logic marry Crazy," he mutters to his own heart. "God help me. She is a handful."

Δ17Δ

The Ass and the Frogs

AN ASS, carrying a load of wood, passed through a pond. As he was crossing through the water he lost his footing, stumbled and fell, and not being able to rise on account of his load, groaned heavily. Some Frogs frequenting the pool heard his lamentation, and said, "What would you do if you had to live here always as we do, when you make such a fuss about a mere fall into the water?"- Aesop

The sound of a jet airplane wakes Rose from an afternoon nap. She looks out of the bright window flanked by lemon yellow sheers waving in the wind. She notices the corn stalks topped with their tan feathers and is fully aware that the feed farmers would soon be out in full force harvesting their crop. She shakes her head as if to dislodge the cobwebs and tries to retrace her steps as to how she arrived in this room with this view. She remembers that Aris brought her here to rest.

"Aris? Aris?" Rose calls. She soon realizes she is alone in the house. She hears a noise below her and quietly follows the sound down the wooden oak staircase into the kitchen. She discovers that it is merely the screen door battling the wind. Rose carefully grabs the slender metal hook and places it into its corresponding loop. She calls again for her husband.

The kitchen is very large with classic black and white tiles both on the floor and the backsplash. They highlight the equally classic butcher block countertops. The cabinets are white with simple hardware made of hammered iron. There is a silver percolator sitting on a '50s peach metal gas stove.

"Coffee," she says, relieved at the sight. Rose reaches for the pea green ceramic canister labeled "Coffee." She lifts the lid to discover sugar.

"Odd," she says. She then grabs the pea green ceramic canister labeled "Sugar" to discover flour. She giggles as she grabs the "Flour" container to finally uncover the coffee. Rose easily fills the antique machine that is exactly the same make and model as her grandmother's and turns the gas stove dial. "Coffee."

Rose notices a strange amount of tar on her hand. She walks over to the sink only to discover the same tar surrounding the faucet. She determines that she must have picked it up when she filled the percolator. She grabs the nail brush and starts scrubbing. The tar just smears. "What is this stuff?" She looks for the soap remembering that detergent breaks the polar bonds of oil – she thinks that is how it works. She finds none. "Who doesn't keep soap at their kitchen sink?" Rose squats to look in the cabinet under the sink convinced that there must be soap, but there is none. "Maybe salt will do the trick?"

Rose locates the familiar blue cardboard tube and lifts the metal tongue and tilts to pour the salt onto the oil smeared across her palms. "Ants? What the…?" She throws the cardboard tube into the sink and watches an army of ants escape their home. She shudders and pushes herself away from the sink. "What the hell is…"

An extremely loud noise shakes the house and knocks the percolator onto the floor. Startled and scared, Rose quickly reacts and tries to stop the spilling by picking up the percolator. She burns her hand on the metal urn just as she witnesses, through the lower half of the screen door, a gigantic jet plane crashing into the corn field across the street. The plane breaks in half as it hits the field and then bursts into flames. Rose feels the heat blow in through the screen as she remains in her squatted position, paralyzed. The heat is chased by loud explosions as if

163

there were sequentially planted bombs. Within seconds the entire field is aflame. Rose runs to the phone and stares at the numbers and tries to think. "Nine one one." Not noticing that there is no dial tone, she begins to press the first of the numbers just as another giant explosion shatters the glass of the kitchen window. Rose watches the shards of glass from the window enter her eyes. She screams.

"Rose!" Aris puts his arms around her.

"Oh my God... it was so real," she says hyperventilating in their bed.

"No, Rose. It was a dream. Just a dream," he says in a whisper. He covers up his annoyance by gently kissing the top of her ear and tightening his embrace. "Just a dream."

Rose tries to make her body go limp. "Just a dream."

Aris picks up his torso and leans on a straight arm and finds his humor. "That's it, no more peppers for you," he says smiling at his sweaty bride. "Wanna tell me about it? I'm getting a funny sense of déjà vu. I am beginning to think I should wear a t-shirt to bed with 'Wanna tell me about it?' written in bold letters to save me a bit of time. "

Flummoxed, Rose does what he asks. "It was a plane crash... I was in a house sorta like Erik's... oh my God, the sound... you would not believe the sound."

"You watched the plane crash?" Aris asks.

Rose proceeds to tell him the dream, as it happened from beginning to end. "I could actually see the shards of glass flying right into my eyes."

"Yikes," Aris says and kisses his wife's eyelids, first the right and then the left. "Thankfully, it was just a dream." He lowers his body back down and grabs the back of her head and kisses her mouth. Not quite satisfied with Rose's return, he kisses her again.

"It was so hot," Rose says trying to talk in between his kisses.

164

"Hot." He raises his body above hers and pushes her drenched bangs from her face. "I see." He starts to remove the covers between them. "We don't need these, do we?"

Rose complies with his request and helps remove the covers between them. "You shouldn't wear a T-shirt to bed."

The two find sleep in fifty-five minutes.

***

Three hours later the alarm sounds.

"Rose, I wish you could have these nightmares on the weekends," Aris says as he reaches over his bride to silence the alarm.

"I don't regret last night." She rises to meet his body on his return. She touches his face and then maneuvers her body on top of his just as he returns to his pillow.

"Again?" Aris smiles. "Remind me to get more peppers."

Rose laughs. "Apparently, near death experiences excite me."

Aris touches her right ear and cheek. "Ah, my beautiful bride…Unfortunately, we need to get going. I have water to sample and you have hemlocks to shape."

"Wanna call in and spend the day in bed with me?" Rose says amorously.

"I do. I can't. I have meetings all day." Aris pecks her nose as he rolls her back to her pillow. He kisses her mouth and then her sternum and then her belly button. "I gotta get in the shower."

"I'll join you?" Rose requests.

"Down girl. Want to make me coffee?" Aris smirks in an attempt to both tease her and distract her.

Rose pouts. "Aren't you attracted to me anymore?" A very fit Rose stands in a Betty Boop pose.

Aris laughs. "A cold shower it is." He quickly enters the bathroom and closes the door.

Rose smiles and yells through the door, "I love you and I took your bishop with my knight."

"You certainly did."

165

Rose huffs in delight as she wraps herself in her robe and listens to the sound of Aris entering the shower. With a luxurious smile on her face, she descends the stairs into the kitchen to make breakfast. Rose brews her first cup of coffee and has several sips prior to starting her task. She retrieves the eggs from the refrigerator and the rye bread from the metal green box labeled 'Bread Box.' "Ants."

She cracks two eggs into her small fryer and places three pieces of rye bread into the toaster. She brews Aris's cup with the Keurig and sets the island with two placemats. She walks over to the coffee table and turns on the TV with the remote. She turns to her favorite morning news program in an attempt to get hold of the day's headlines.

Aris enters the kitchen cleanly shaven, wearing dark brown linen pants and a light blue linen shirt. "It's going to be a scorcher today. Ninety-eight degrees, I heard, even hotter than yesterday. Oh, and I pulled out my rook."

Rose smiles at his move. She then looks to the news channel. "Weather will be on in a few minutes." She places a breakfast plate with two eggs, over easy, and three halves of rye bread on Aris's placemat. "Do you want orange juice, too?"

"I would love a glass, thanks," Aris says as he gently smiles at his plate. "Thanks for cooking breakfast." He grabs the salt and the pepper and adorns his eggs.

Noticing a scene of familiar smoke on TV, Rose rushes to turn up the volume. "Look at this."

The news anchor's voice fills the room. "A few minutes ago, non-stop Delta Flight 713, a 320 Airbus, carrying one hundred and ninety-nine passengers crashed into a corn field in rural Pennsylvania. The flight left LaGuardia at six twenty-nine and was scheduled to land in Detroit at eight twenty-four. News correspondent Natalie Bart from sister station WKPS is reporting live from the scene in Lucinda, Pennsylvania this morning."

166

Rose is filled with dread as the newsreel shows the reporter standing in front of a scene cut directly from her nightmare. "Thank you, Deanna. As you can see, the devastation here is unimaginable. The flames in the field behind me have already destroyed hundreds of acres of dairy corn in Lucinda, Pennsylvania, a populated town just off highway sixty-six. Although fire fighters were quick to respond, you can see they have their work cut out for them. The summer's drought has really taken a toll on the fields and the fire is spreading very quickly and burning hotly. Sources say that it may take several hours to control the spread of the fire. It is estimated that over one thousand acres could be destroyed by day's end. Rescue workers must surmount the fire to reach possible survivors. Helicopters will be dropping in Emergency Medics to search for survivors. All we can do now is pray for these brave rescuers and hope for the best. Back to you, Deanna."

"We will be following this story throughout the day..."

Rose mutes the TV. "I am kinda freaked out right now. The phrase 'be careful what you wish for' is flying and crashing in my mind. This is my dream. Like precisely – I dreamed this happened."

"Calm down, Rose. It's just a coincidence," Aris says, standing from his chair and walking toward her. He almost believes himself. "Although I can understand being freaked, it does seem eerily parallel."

"Eerily parallel? It's the same god damned field," Rose yells exasperatedly. "It's the same cornfield, it's the same plane. I have never dreamed about a cornfield in my life."

"Let me call work and tell them I will be an hour late," Aris says sensing what is to be done. "I do not want to leave you alone right now. You seem..."

Rose immediately tries to get ahold of herself, as she notices the all-too-familiar look of worry appear on her husband's face. "No, don't be silly. It's okay. I'm alright. I'm overreacting.

167

You're right. It's just a coincidence," she says. "A strange, eerie, freaky coincidence, but just a coincidence. If I repeat that word often enough…"

"You may start to believe it?" Aris asks.

"It's just a coincidence. See?" Rose smiles and rises to the balls of her feet to kiss her husband. "I'm alright. Go to work. Call me at lunch just to find out that I am fine. And that this is all just a coincidence."

"Are you sure?" Aris says arching his back to look into her eyes.

"I am sure," Rose says. "My dreams are not reality."

"Let's hope not, anyway," Aris says with a sigh of relief followed by a tense laugh. "Although I guess sleeping with an oracle might have its benefits."

"Ha ha," Rose says. "Sleeping… is that what I am doing?"

"Maybe we should have stayed in bed this morning and called in," Aris says looking at his Rose. "You're sure you are okay?"

"Actually, I kinda have this knot in my stomach…"

Aris puts his hand on her stomach, "You are okay, though, right?"

Rose looks at the TV showing the flames and the cornfield with the exact same farmhouse from her dream in the background. "I think I am going to thrrrrr…" She runs to the bathroom and vomits.

Aris stands outside of the partially closed door and listens. "I am sorry I cannot help… I am wearing linen and I swear I'll start vomiting." He laughs nervously. "Are you okay? Please answer."

Rose stops and wipes her mouth with the back of her hand. She walks toward the sink and washes her hands and then rinses her face and mouth. "Ugh." Reaching under the sink, she pulls out Listerine, fills the caps and swishes for another thirty seconds and spits. "Ugh." She opens the door. "I think I am going to call in sick. I guess I really am."

"You want me to do it? Do you want me to call Erik?" Aris asks.

"Yeah actually, would you? I would probably tell the whole story... like an idiot."

"Sure," he puts his arm around her waist and kisses her forehead. "I could call in too, if you need me to. Do you need me to?"

"Aris, I am fine. I'll go back to bed and hopefully sleep for a couple more hours. And I could use the extra time to study a bit for my radio license... you know, follow your advice, and take my mind off of this disaster stuff. I could even do some yoga. And I have that meeting with the Ionosphere..." Rose looks at her feet and wiggles her toes as she tries to force order upon her chaotic thoughts. "I'll be fine. Good even. On second thought, maybe I should just go to work."

"I'll bring home dinner so you will have one less thing to think about," Aris says with a relaxed concern. "If you are sure... I should really get going. I will call you at lunch and in between every meeting. Keep your cell phone close." He kisses her again on her forehead and then, with his whole body, he reaches over to grab the last piece of toast. "I love rye toast."

She leans on his shoulder and walks him to the door. "Drive safe. Precious cargo."

"Stay home today. Get some rest," Aris says commandingly before giving her a gentle kiss on top of her head. He steps out the door. "I'll call Erik and... and try to have a good day, my beautiful oracle."

"I love you," Rose says and closes the door. She takes a few deep breaths before locking.

A few moments later Aris knocks on the door and Rose quickly opens it. "Did you forget something?"

169

"I was wondering if you had any insight into the lottery. The jackpot is over two hundred million," Aris says smiling. He quickly kisses her lips before turning and running toward his car. He yells over his shoulder, "I love you, too."

Rose closes the door with a giggle and turns the lock. "An airbus," she says out loud. "One hundred ninety-nine people in an airbus. God – that is one strange coincidence. A prayer for the families... and thanks for all that You do. I love You and my husband and my family and... my luck…and, of course, rye toast And God? If You are trying to teach me a lesson, can You do it without killing one hundred ninety-nine people?"

Δ18Δ

The Lion and the Eagle

AN EAGLE stayed his flight and entreated a Lion to make an alliance with him to their mutual advantage. The Lion replied, "I have no objection, but you must excuse me for requiring you to find surety for your good faith, for how can I trust anyone as a friend who is able to fly away from his bargain whenever he pleases?"- Aesop

Rose and Abner enter into the neighborhood clubhouse fifteen minutes early for the meeting of the amateur radio club named 'Ionosphere.' She is more than a little nervous about the next step into her commitment to radio. Feeling honestly overwhelmed and worried about disappointing her sweet, stern, grandfatherly Elmer, she attempts to suppress the part of her that wants to run and hide. Yet she finds herself standing very near Abner, much like a child would cling to a parent on his first day of school. She quickly scans the room. Her eyes immediately appreciate the beautiful woodwork of the chamber that creates the feel of an old world English study complete with built-in book shelves and judges paneling. She also notices the framed newspaper clippings of its members' activities dating back to Vietnam and possibly earlier. There is a long cabinet in front of two large picture windows that displays various radio station set-ups including one that looks to be a homebrew system.

Abner looks down upon his pupil and asks, "Are you ready?"

"I know I wasn't exactly born ready, but I am pretty sure I can handle a room full of Hams," Rose says looking up to her teacher. She projects an affected confidence, sincere admiration and a little humor.

"Let me introduce you around. In this corner, we have George," Abner says. "George, come here. Let me introduce you to Rose Isope, my new student."

George walks over and immediately extends his hand to Abner's guest. He looks her over with an exaggerated look of approval, clearly meant to put her at ease. "I hope you realize just how unusual it is for our group to have someone as young and as pretty join it?"

Rose blushes. "Uh, thanks."

"Oh, stop making her uncomfortable. She really is interested in radio. And she is here to listen. Don't get her started talking... she'll never stop," Abner tells his fellow Ham.

"Amateur radio is a fascinating hobby for listeners but can be a bit frustrating for talkers."

"She's a talker," Abner says.

"I can listen too," Rose protests.

"She is a good listener considering she talks so much," Abner says teasingly.

Rose is silent as she scans the Amateur Radio club house of which Abner is president. There are seven members attending, however the roster states that the membership is close to seventy-five. The club meets twice a month on the second and third Tuesday. The second Tuesday of the month is set aside for license testing and classes. The third Tuesday is used for general business, including equipment maintenance. Abner decided it was time to introduce Rose to other amateur radio enthusiasts so that she can start to focus her interest. The regulars are serious enthusiasts with vast interests, who are also grateful to talk to anyone about their particular hobby. Abner starts with George.

"George, how long have you been doing this?" Abner asks on Rose's behalf.

"I was licensed in seventy-two," George replies. "I started in the Boy Scouts."

Rose nods. "And your interest? Are you a homebrewer?"

172

"No, I don't have the patience. My system is pretty much set up for VHF or UHF?"

"Very High Frequency," Rose says, looking to Abner. "Right?"

Abner huffs. "Now, don't play dumb here."

Rose looks puzzled. "I am just learning about antennas. How each Ham has their particular antenna? I was just wondering…"

"Antennas are a good place to start. I heard Abner set up a dipole for you," George replies. "Do you know what you are interested in?"

"My husband bought me the radio. I guess I am interested in the information carried on the wave."

"She's both evasive and honest," Abner reports.

"And pretty," George says.

"Always a Ham," a younger, stocky, but fit Ham interjects. "So this is the Rose you have been telling us about?"

Rose looks at Abner. "Have you been talking about me?"

"I think you surprised him. Your generation is happy with the cell phone, and here you are. This is Peter, by the way." George says.

Rose nods at Peter and then turns to George. "I am happy with the cell phone too, that is, when I remember to charge it," Rose comments.

Peter laughs. "My wife has to remind me every night."

"Have you ever noticed that when you actually need, and I mean *need,* the cell phone it either has a low battery or cannot find a tower?" Rose asks.

"Cell phones… Radio is pretty much always there when you need it."."

"Peter drives a truck and has a radio both in his house and in his cab," Abner says.

"I used CBs when I first started. Radio is much better," Peter says. "So when are you going to take your test?"

173

"I have been studying for the past three weeks. I think I will try to take my test next month. I am trying to get familiar with the FCC portion right now. I am a little more comfortable with the electronic stuff. Well, I have had a little school on it and…"

"It's not an easy test. Well, it's not a gimme test like your driver's license," Peter confirms.

"I kind of noticed," Rose says with a smile.

Peter starts up a conversation with Abner about his current radio woes.

"Excuse me, I see coffee." Rose leaves the two men to talk and walks toward the large metal urn to pour herself a cup. She also grabs a donut. "You guys don't fool around. Donuts and coffee," she says to the two men standing near the coffee urn.

"It's written in the by-laws that there must be coffee and donuts at every meeting," Daniel says.

"Really?" Rose replies.

"Really. You must be Rose." Daniel extends his hand. "We have heard quite a bit about you."

"So I heard. It kinda makes me uncomfortable," Rose says understatedly.

"Hams can be a bunch of gossips. These guys are worse than my wife and her friends," Daniel admits. "It's good things he's saying. He is happy that someone in your generation is interested in Radio. We are an aging breed."

"Aging breed?" Phil says biting on a chocolate glazed donut.

"Phil, here, thinks that I should go ahead and admit that we are a dying breed. I disagree."

"Do you think there is a hog heaven for Hams?" Rose asks hoping her humor is not too hammy.

"I like this one," Phil says putting his hand on her shoulder. "Hog heaven for Hams. I'll bet we can make a bumper sticker out of that."

Rose smiles. "A fund raiser to buy more donuts and coffee."

174

"Hey Abner, this little miss is a riot," Phil says to Abner as he steps near to fill his mug. "She already has a plan to pay for donuts and coffee."

"Rose, you are here to listen," Abner says sternly.

"Yes, sir."

"Gentlemen, we need to get to it. Everybody's got their coffee?" Abner asks.

The men take their seats as George reads the minutes of their last meeting that included plans to purchase five additional repeaters to be placed on radio towers. Peter provides an update of tower agreements. The motion to purchase is set and seconded.

"I'd like to introduce you to Rose Isope, Frank's grand daughter-in-law."

Rose waves. "Good evening. I am here to listen. And just so you know, I've been warned about you all." Rose returns the smiles she receives from the table.

"She thinks she is interested in DXing," George says. "Phil, you might want to help her with that."

"I'll put her on our group list," Abner says. "She may be emailing questions. Help her out. It's nice to have some new interest in radio, and we should do our best to keep her interested."

"DXing?" Rose looks very confused. "Wait…I am interested in DXing?"

"Seeing how far a signal can go?" Abner explains. "I told him that that was where you seem to have the most interest."

Rose nods. "DXing."

"It is pretty much the oldest form of amateur radio," Phil adds.

"I am a fan of the classics," Rose responds.

"DXing is the hobby of receiving and identifying distant radio or television signals," Phil says. "Or making two-

175

way radio contact with distant stations in amateur radio or citizens band radio."

"When I was a kid, I used to get post cards from people who I contacted. They're called 'veries.' DX is for distance or distant," George says. "I sent quite a few cards too."

"Veries are also called QSLs," Phil reports. "What he is saying is listeners would mail 'reception reports' to radio broadcasting stations in hopes of getting a written acknowledgement or a QSL card."

"Collecting these cards became popular with radio listeners in the 1920s and 1930s, and reception reports were often used by early broadcasters to gauge the effectiveness of their transmissions," Abner adds. "SINPO."

"SINPO. You told me this already. It's an acronym, right?" Rose says.

"Your transmission gets graded-slash-rated on Signal strength, Interference with other stations or broadcasters, Noise ratio in the received signal, Propagation or the ups and downs of the reception, and Overall merit," Phil says. "We have a pretty active DXing club among the members of this club. I will send you some information about it."

"Do you attach an email address in your transmission?" Rose asks, laughing at her joke.

"DXing is also good for people who are interested in disaster scenarios," Abner says directly to Rose.

"Disaster scenarios?" Phil asks.

"I am a fan of volcanos and stuff," Rose admits.

"Now is the time to be a fan," George says. His boisterous voice trails off as he catches a look from Abner.

Abner incisively retakes the reign of the conversation by simply looking around the table. "We're hosting a field trip next week from Jefferson, the new charter school. They are bringing their seventh grade class to teach them about early radio. Peter has agreed to do the section on Morse Code. I will be teaching

176

about homebrewing and giving a history of hams helping in the war effort, World War One, World War Two and Vietnam. I would like someone to demonstrate Moon Bouncing. Anyone?"

"I could do it, but I am not sure I can entertain a seventh grader," one Ham speaks up. "It's a little complicated for seventh graders."

"Just talk about bouncing. They do not have to understand the physics," another says. "They do not have to understand the changing of polarity or the three-second delay. They can just learn that you can use the moon to bounce a radio signal to another part of the world."

"So Larry, are you volunteering," Abner games.

"When is it?" Larry asks.

"Next Thursday," Abner replies. "No, I'm sorry, it's in two weeks, August the third."

"Let me think about it. I'll let you know in a couple of days."

George notes in his minutes of the exchange and then adds, "Maybe we should do something on these volcanoes?"

Rose sits straighter.

"What are you thinking?" Abner inquires.

"Like maybe we should get covers for our repeaters?" George says.

"For what?" Phil asks.

"For ash," George returns.

"There isn't any chance of ash here," says Phil.

"Actually, there is with Yellowstone," Rose says under her breath, barely audible.

Abner hears her and is slightly annoyed. "How much are covers? Want to look into it? Look into it," Abner says toward George, snorting in the direction of Rose.

Rose hugs herself, not quite sure what she has done to make him upset with her. "Sorry," she says.

177

"So these kids visiting. I think that's a good use of this club," Daniel says. He notices the discomfort of the young woman next to him.

"It is. I think it is a very good thing for our club. If any of you have any suggestions about how to make this field trip more interesting, please speak up." Abner looks over at Rose and issues an apologetic smile. "Maybe we should do something regarding protocol for disaster scenarios," he says looking to Daniel and then to George to ensure that notes are taken. "We need to make sure those who are not here know about it too. You might be able to reach them on the airwaves faster than you can reach them via group email. Any other business?"

"We have received reminders for license renewals for a few members. Phil, if you see Bobby, let him know," George adds.

Phil nods. "Will do."

"Well if there is nothing more to do. Feel free to finish the donuts and the coffee," Abner says, adjourning the meeting.

Phil stands and walks toward Rose. "The DXing group is a good one. We have a few crazies, totally into end-of-the-world-type stuff, but they are good guys. There are a few women, too."

Rose smiles. "Let me get my license first. I need to learn the basics before I go any further."

"She needs to listen," Abner says jokingly.

"Geesh. Transmission received," Rose teases back.

"She's a spitfire," Phil comments. "Good to meet you, Rose. Hey Ab, I will get you that book about amateur radio in Vietnam. I can probably run it by tomorrow."

"Good, Son, thanks." Abner shakes his hand.

Phil nods at both Abner and Rose before he leaves.

"Phil is a black belt," Abner comments.

"Hmm," Rose says watching him leave the building. "Who's in charge of clean-up?"

"Peter."

"Should I offer my help?" Rose asks.

"You could, but he will decline the offer," Abner insists. "We should get going. Aristotle is probably wondering where his wife is."

Rose nods in agreement. "You speak the truth, Sir."

"I am glad you came with me tonight. It's important to meet people. This is a good group. We are serious people, capable people. And heck, we may even be a group motivated by disaster scenarios."

Rose agrees. "Hams."

"You said your father is an electrical engineer," Abner says. "He isn't in radio?"

"No, but I think my grandfather was very interested. When I told my dad about potentially getting my license, he reminded me that my grandfather was a Ham. My dad tells me he used to receive cards from Poland. Veries, is it?"

"I am presuming he is no longer on the radio," Abner asks.

"He died about nine years ago," Rose says quietly focusing her attention on the ground.

"Maybe when we get your license the FCC can give you his call letters. It's possible."

Rose beams. "I would like that very much. And I am sure my grandfather would like that too."

"Well, you have to actually take the test. Should we go ahead and put you down for next month to apply a bit of pressure. You seem like the type that needs deadlines."

"Directness," Rose says. "Again, you speak the truth, Sir. I am a bit flighty, yet insanely punctual."

"Let's sign you up then – last week of August." Abner turns to George, Daniel and Peter who are still standing around the conference table. "Rose is going to take her test on the last Tuesday of August."

"The second Tuesday of August, or the second Tuesday of September," Daniel says reminding Abner that exam dates have changed.

179

"September, please," announces Rose.

Daniel nods directly at Abner. "Are you administering?"

"I could. Yes. Yes, I will be administering," Abner says. "Plenty of time."

"If you say so. I am a bit nervous," Rose admits. "I'd hate to let you down."

"Then don't."

"Yes, Sir."

Abner and Rose drive back to their neighborhood in his luxury Mercedes. He points out the buildings he and his company built on their return. "You have been very lucky, haven't you, Sir?"

"Luck? I've worked hard," Abner says strongly.

"Okay then, a little lucky."

"Yes. A little lucky. After all, I did marry Clara."

"I like you sir," Rose says.

Abner lifts his chin and remains stern for the rest of the drive until he pulls up outside her townhouse. "Have a good night Rose. Get moving on that workbook. Stop by on Saturday afternoon around two o'clock and I will give you a few practice exams. The last person I taught scored very well. I would like you to do even better."

"I will take that as a compliment, Sir."

"And Rose," Abner says and clears his throat. "This probably goes without saying, but I will say it nonetheless. Being prepared for disaster is a good thing; being obsessed is something altogether different. I have met a smattering of both kinds in radio. I have also met a few who were unclear in the distinction. Never be unclear."

Rose holds his eyes and offers a slight nod to inform Abner that she did, indeed, hear him. "Saturday at two o'clock. See you then. Give Clara my best." Rose jumps out of the passenger seat and lightly jogs to her front door. She waves to Abner and watches him drive down the street.

Rose stops to smell the roses outside her front door. This day has been particularly full. She thinks about the word "coincidence," a word that was so heavy earlier in the day. She notes that it seems much lighter now. She says a brief prayer of thanks and then opens her front door.

"Aris? Are you home? I think I am really going to like radio, but I do have a question. Why would you need covers?"

Δ19Δ

The Lamb and the Wolf

A WOLF pursued a Lamb, which fled for refuge to a certain Temple. The Wolf called out to him and said, "The Priest will slay you in sacrifice, if he should catch you." On which the Lamb replied, "It would be better for me to be sacrificed in the Temple than to be eaten by you."- Aesop

I guess that COBRA couldn't use the serpent. Too bad, it'd be funny, Rose thinks to herself as she completes the necessary medical history collection forms for her appointment. She places her temporary medical insurance card back into her wallet and walks to the reception window with the clipboard. The receptionist is not there. Rose returns to her seat and places the clipboard on her lap. There is one other person in the waiting room in the far corner furiously texting. Based upon the body language of the texter, Rose assumes the young woman is fighting with her significant other.

She returns her attention to the clip board with three pages of medical information obtained by check boxes. Having entered medical charts into computer databases in her past, Rose wonders why Scantron sheets are not being used. It would be a faster way to check for missed questions as well as a quick way to capture electronic data. It would also be harder to read for the casual on-looker. Rose shrugs her shoulders. *It is Elementary, not Junior High*, she thinks.

The door to the waiting room opens and in walks an enormous man. Rose cannot keep her eyes off of him. He has the most beautiful skin she has ever seen. He awkwardly sits down in a chair built for someone two feet smaller than he is. One chair separates them. Rose cannot help noticing the length

182

of his fingers, his femurs and his calves. She is dumbfounded at the size of his feet.

"Are you seven-four?" Rose precociously asks.

"Seven-seven," he quietly answers.

"I hope you don't mind me saying this, but you have the most beautiful skin I have ever seen. You've a deep blue glow. You are so black, you're blue," Rose says with a look of complete amazement.

The enormous man with sad eyes gently looks at her with an expression of kindness, yet remains silent.

Rose awkwardly flips the clip board in her hand wishing she could learn to not say what she is thinking every time. "I'm sorry I talk so much."

The man laughs.

"The receptionist is somewhere. I don't know where. She has been gone from her desk for at least five minutes," Rose says nervously.

"You here to see Doc Streets?" the man asks with a very deep, yet soothing tone.

"I don't know. It's my first time here," she says, her eyes still on the movement of the clip board in her hands. She looks over the questionnaire and shrugs. "They do not appear to have a check box for people who think God is talking to them."

The man leans forward and rests his forearms on his knees. "God talks to everyone if people just learn to listen. He lifts spirits, like you."

Rose just looks at the man from head to enormous foot. "Do you have to duck every place you go?"

He nods.

"Seriously, your skin is so pretty. I have never seen skin the color of midnight."

The receptionist returns, and Rose jumps up from her seat. She hands in her clipboard. Just as soon as the clipboard is received, a nurse arrives calling for her.

183

Rose turns to the man and waves. "Thanks for, I don't know, for being beautiful. Have a great day." She follows the nurse down the hall. "Did you see how beautiful that man's skin was?"

The nurse turns to look at Rose as she opens the door to an office and directs her to sit in the chair in front of the desk. "The doctor will be here momentarily."

Rose hovers over the chair while looking at the bookshelves and gewgaws. She returns to her feet to get a closer look at the certifications that hang over an end table decorated with a simple lamp. She attempts to turn on the lamp only to discover it is not plugged in. She begins to pull on the cord to complete the task just as the doctor enters.

"The lamp is not plugged in," Rose announces.

"It's just for show," Dr. Welsh answers.

"I don't understand," Rose replies before shaking his hand. "I'm Rose Aesop." She rubs at her nose trying to forgive herself for still not knowing her name.

"Dr. Welsh," the forty-year-old man of a medium height and weight answers. "Please sit. What brings you to my office today?"

"Nightmares," Rose answers. "My husband asked me to talk to someone about my nightmares. They are keeping him up at night." Rose looks for acknowledgment of her humor and finds none. She takes her seat.

"And you are sleeping through them?" the psychologist asks.

"I am waking up from them." Rose pauses to think. "Actually, I guess he usually wakes me up out of them. I'm screaming in my sleep."

"Is it the same nightmare?"

"No. Actually they are quite varied and also appear to be somewhat premonitory," Rose replies.

"What do you mean?" Dr. Welsh asks.

Rose crinkles her brow as she tries to figure out which word he did not understand. Her face relaxes and she does her best to

184

answer his question. "I mean that I had this terrible dream where a jet plane crashed into a corn field killing those on the plane as well as burning fields around it. I woke up with that dream at three o'clock and four hours later, it happened. Delta Flight 713."

"And you think you predicted this crash," Dr. Welsh asks.

"No, I don't think…well, yeah, I guess I do. I mean, I have never dreamed of an airplane or a cornfield in my life and then this happened. The similarities were really kind of disturbing." Rose sits back in her chair and easily recollects that morning in her mind's eye. She can see herself in the kitchen handing a plate of eggs and toast to her husband and the since oft-repeated scene on the television to her right. She remembers how she spent most the day in bed, restlessly bouncing between sleep and wake. She dreamed of a volcano called Medicine Lake. "Take your medicine," a voice had whispered to her. Yet by dinner time, she was pretty resolved on the matter. It was, after all, just a coincidence. Rose smiles as she remembers the strange turn of events that took place after that – the events that brought her to this office.

It was Aris who did not fare well on that day. In fact, he was quite beside himself with anxious concern that he was to "do something" about the situation. He initially suggested talking to a priest. His second suggestion was her parents. Rose can recall his exact sentence verbatim. He said, "Rose, I think I am out of my depth on this one." This amused her greatly. She spent the hours between dinner and bed convincing her husband that all was well. She explained that it is, of course, most likely a coincidence. If the dream was prophetic or premonitory then it was tame by historical standards. Personally, she thought maybe it was God telling a small joke, with a punch line to the effect of "be careful what you wish for." His response was, "One hundred and ninety-nine people dying isn't exactly a joke, Rose." Aris immediately demanded that she speak to a psychologist. Rose

185

readily agreed. She was supposed to "take her medicine," after all. An appointment was made the following morning.

"I see you suffer from depression," says the doctor, his voice bringing her back to the present. "Yet, you did not list your medications. Is there a reason?"

"I am not on any meds. I checked none, didn't I," Rose answers with a tone of slight frustration. She is there to talk about her dreams, not a diagnosis provided ten years ago after being date raped. Rather than providing the back story of the diagnosis, she simply offers, "I think depression is part of life."

"Interesting. You think you are supposed to be depressed," Dr. Welsh says.

"Well, no. I think that it is often something that can be overcome naturally, without medications. I try to eat right, exercise and well, face my demons," Rose replies.

"Your demons?" The doctor closes the medical file.

"Yes, my demons," Rose replies. "I've got spirit, Sir."

Dr. Welsh flips through the questionnaire a few more times. "What do you think these nightmares are about?" Dr. Welsh asks pretending to look at her.

"I think God is talking to me," Rose answers simply, almost challengingly.

"God is giving you premonitory dreams," Dr. Welsh responds.

"Yes." Rose answers, relatively impressed with his efficient style of conversation.

Without missing a beat, he replies, "Interesting. How does this make you feel?"

Rose is immediately forced to reassess her initial impression. "You're kidding right? Interesting. How does this make you feel? Seriously?" she sneers. "Might I suggest you change up those questions a bit. They sound scripted – by a ten-year-old."

186

"Duly noted," the man says with a blank expression, more than likely also scripted. Yet, he lifts the right corner of his mouth to hide his smile.

Rose notices the human behind the doctor façade and decides that she could at least try to cooperate. She sighs. "Anyway, the question being how does this make me feel? I have an answer. I feel lucky, I guess. Yet, at the same time, it is kind of difficult to process the feeling with the word *luck*."

"Tell me a bit more. How are you processing?" Dr. Welsh asks moving from disinterestedness to something that almost resembles interest.

"I talk to my husband. I've been doing a bit more yoga to help me sleep. And I have very recently joined an Amateur Radio Club," Rose replies. "The usual, I guess."

"You say your husband asked you to seek help," Dr. Welsh says meaningfully.

"I guess. He said I should talk to someone. We considered a priest, but I have issues with the Catholic Church. I considered psychiatry, but I am not interested in taking drugs. So, here I am."

The doctor settles back into his desk chair. He swivels slightly to the right and then the left, giving the impression that he wishes he could swivel a little more. "Will you reconsider your stance on anti-depressants."

"I won't," Rose says defiantly. She looks down at her ballerina flats and questions herself. She determines that she might reconsider if Aris asks her to.

"Well then, I am not exactly sure why you are here," the doctor says shuffling papers through her file, glancing a bit more intently upon her family history.

"I guess I am not either," Rose says, still looking down, this time at the swirls in the industrial carpet. *To talk?* she answers internally. "I guess maybe I'm just following some sort of ingrained due process. I guess that I am inclined to think that it

187

is just as likely that I am suffering some sort of mental, chemical imbalance as I am experiencing some transcendent spiritual enlightenment."

Dr. Welsh inadvertently nods in agreement. "You have a history of depression and a possible bi-polar diagnosis?" Dr. Welsh asks reviewing her medical history pages. "Do you not know whether you were given a bi-polar diagnosis?"

"No, I guess I don't. I did not like that particular doctor. He seemed to be… he seemed to be a, um, a rubber stamper. I saw him because my mom suggested it to me. I was going through …something."

"You don't trust his diagnosis?" Dr. Welsh asks.

Rose quickly rehashes the memories and emotions on that time in her life. She thinks about the rape and trying to crawl away. She responds, "No. I don't."

"And will you trust mine?" Dr. Welsh asks with a very direct tone.

"I will listen and make a decision based upon my own processing, my own judgment."

"Fair enough," Dr. Welsh says. "Yet, I am, as was Dr. Echolls, a trained professional."

"True, but I am the one who has to live with my decisions and it is my decision to not blindly accept a cursory diagnosis, even if it is from a graduate of a fine school like Johns Hopkins," Rose says defensively, nudging with her chin to his diploma. "What was the environment like there? Competitive?"

"We're not here to talk about me," Dr. Welsh states authoritatively.

"No. Sorry, I was just curious. I know that that is one of the best schools in the nation, and therefore the world." Rose quietly starts to pass judgment upon the doctor who, in her opinion, has an unnatural practice. She wonders how it is that he plans on establishing trust without being able to talk about something as

188

simple as his college experience depicted in a gilded frame right behind his chair.

"What do you want from here?" the doctor asks. He projects a subtle restlessness with the conversation. "What are you hoping to gain?"

"I guess I want permission to believe in God," Rose says matter-of-factly. *Scientific permission?* she asks herself.

Dr. Welsh acknowledges her request with an odd sort of stare. It is both questioning and cold. "Well, that is not up to me, is it?"

"No sir. It most certainly is not." Rose awkwardly looks around his office, silently wondering what she is doing in such a place. Dr. Welsh clicks his pen several times while simultaneously opening the patient screen on his computer. "How many of these dreams have you had?"

"Dreams or nightmares? I have them both," Rose responds trying to steal a glance at the terminal interface.

"The nightmares. The reason why you are here." Dr. Welsh looks from his computer with challenging eyes. "That is the reason why you are here, right?"

Although his voice could be interpreted as combative, Rose decides to hear it as an attempt to guide. "Probably five to six a week," she replies, "maybe more …of varying intensity. My husband tells me that I should cut back on the peppers." *Another joke, and no smile,* she thinks.

"Has anything changed in your life recently? A significant change?" Dr. Welsh asks. He is reading down a questionnaire that he personally designed for his own medical notes.

"I quit my job, moved and got married. All of these in just the past two months, maybe three," Rose says. "But I do not think these things have made that much of an impact. They all feel pretty natural. My mom says that maybe I am keeping a…"

Dr. Welsh interrupts, "You quit your job, got married and moved. These are very significant life occurrences. The fact that

189

you are not willing to recognize these momentous events seems incredibly problematic to me." He pushes back from his desk into his chair. "I can tell that you are an intelligent girl. You must understand how that sounds to me."

Rather than defending herself, she chooses to explain. She shifts in her chair to portray a calm easiness. "My husband and I have been best friends for a decade. I should have quit my job years ago. And moving? I moved a lot as a child. What did Buckaroo Bonzai say? 'Wherever you go, there you are.'"

Dr. Welsh throws his head back with an amused snort. "Well anyone who can quote Buckaroo Bonzai is good in my book," he says followed by a sincere laugh. The corner of his mouth twists as he asks, "Older brother?"

"Zeke. Yeah, he told me to watch it." Rose smiles and relaxes. "Ah, common ground feels good."

Dr. Welsh offers a slight relaxing in his body language, yet remains authoritative. He pushes further back from his desk and crosses his right ankle over his left knee. He is silent for a few moments, maybe thirty seconds, before he starts to just nod his head while maintaining eye contact with his patient. "Well Rose, I think I would recommend that you meet with a psychiatrist. I see you do not have one in the area. I could recommend one to you," he says reclosing the paper file. He reaches for the pad to write the name of the psychiatrist he has in mind.

"And your recommendation is based upon..?"

"Previous history, for starters… However, I think these nightmares are very likely due to deeper issues than you are prepared to discuss. And there could be some underlying medical issues that we should rule out. A psychiatrist would be able to order an MRI and…"

"Wait? Deeper than the idea that God is talking to me?" Rose says caught by his first seemingly dismissive statement. "Is there a deeper issue than that?" she honestly asks.

190

Dr. Welsh almost entirely ignores her interruption. "I think that if you received a diagnosis for bi-polar disorder, we should make sure that you are not creating a deeper imbalance."

"I see," Rose says with renewed ire, wishing that she never sought psychological help now or back then. It angers her further that she is still being labeled. "And the doctor you would like to recommend? Man or woman?"

"Would you prefer a woman?" Dr. Welsh asks.

Biting her tongue, Rose tries to just answer the question she was asked and not fall into what she perceives to be a baited trap. "I don't know. I guess I would prefer a psychiatrist that believes in God. Do you have *that* information handy?"

"I am not sure if faith should play a role here," Dr. Welsh says sincerely.

Rose grips the arms of her chair. The finely educated doctor has completely missed the entire point. *God, what am I doing here?* Pressing her back into her chair, she tries one more time to reach him. "I think faith is paramount to any discussion of the mind and its perceptions. I will take the name of a doctor if and only if they are comfortably able to say they believe in God. If you do not know of such a doctor, then save your recommendation for someone else..."

Dr. Welsh opens and closes her paper file as he processes his patient's request. He is actually unsure whether his physician network captures the question of faith of the medical practitioner. The question is also curiously absent on his own questionnaire. "I will look into it and my office will contact you with a referral."

"Fair enough," Rose replies. *I feel railroaded,* she thinks wishing she had the courage to say that aloud. She takes a breath and grips the arm rest. "Sir, do you believe in God?"

"I don't know," he answers honestly.

Rose calms upon hearing this simple, honest answer to her loaded question. Without thinking she utters, "Common ground can be reached from an uncommon ground."

"My office will contact you," Dr. Welsh responds.

"I'll be waiting," Rose says standing from her chair. "Thanks for your time." Rose feels light-headed as she turns toward the door. "The lamp is just for show? Really?" She huffs in amusement and quickly and quietly exits the office.

I wonder if he is still here, she asks herself as she walks down the hallway to the reception desk. She stops at the counter to pay her co-pay. She looks out into the waiting room. *He's not.* Rose pouts.

Δ20Δ

The Camel and the Arab

AN ARAB CAMEL-DRIVER, after completing the loading of his Camel, asked him which he would like best, to go up hill or down. The poor beast replied, not without a touch of reason: Why do you ask me? Is it that the level way through the desert is closed?" –Aesop

"Husband, I'm home," Rose calls from the foyer table as she places her keys into the basket.

"Hey Thorn, how'd it go?" Aris says descending the stairs. "Are you insane?"

Rose puts her hair behind her ears and cat arches her back. With a deep inhale, she responds, "Apparently there is hope. The doc said that anyone who can quote Buckaroo Bonzai is alright in his book."

"He said that, really?"

"Yep," she says as her hands find her hips as she relates her own spin. She decided on her ride home that she would not share the negative aspects of her meeting with the good doctor.

"Any psychologist that thinks of Buckaroo Bonzai as a standard for mental health is alright in my book," Aris says as he brushes the hair from his wife's shoulder. He places a kiss on the flesh exposed and openly admires her in her red halter tie cotton sun dress. "You look nice."

Rose smiles. "I am nice."

"So tell me more," Aris says as he hooks her elbow and leads her to the couch. "I suppose he wants you to take drugs? Are you considering it?"

"Yeah, he kinda mentioned it," Rose says. "He seemed nice – but not exceptional. He wants to run some tests. He suggested a psychiatrist and an MRI to rule out any physical

193

anomalies that might lead to nightmares. Get this, he also said he will look for a psychiatrist who also believes in God."

"Do you think there is such a man in psychiatry?" Aris asks.

"He's probably a woman," Rose jokes.

"An MRI?" Aris says concerned. "They think you have a tumor?"

"Well, isn't that just jumping the gun? I am sure it's pretty much standard procedure. And probably just a suggestion," Rose says with a bitter laugh.

"So tell me more about the doctor."

Rose tilts her head to the right and looks at her husband cock-eyed. "Actually, I think I met the true doctor in the waiting room, and the guy sitting behind the desk surrounded in diplomas – well, he was just a stand-in," she reports.

Aris focuses on the red cotton against her skin. "I don't understand."

"While waiting in the waiting room, this huge black man, he was actually seven-seven, came in and sat down near me. He was huge and so black he was blue. I had to say something…"

"You didn't," Aris probes fretfully.

"Of course I did. Anyway, we got to talking and I volunteered the information that I was there to speak to someone because I thought God was talking to me." Rose looks at her husband and is smugly amused as she observes the color draining from his face. Aris has consistently tried to warn her against her open nature. He feels as if she is often too trusting.

"I wish you wouldn't talk to strangers," Aris says gently shaking his head. "Someday you are really going to regret…"

"Anyway, do you know what he said?" Rose inquires.

"No, I'm sure I don't."

"He said God is talking to everyone if people would just learn to listen." Rose smiles and grabs the top of his ear. "I think he was the real doctor - the one that God sent."

194

Aris laughs at his wife. "Well, I see no reason for concern there…"

"I'm fine, Aristotle Milton Irwin. Really, I am."

"So, what else did the doctor say?" Aris asks. He considers verbally adding the Aesop to his name, but decides that now is not the time to mention her lapse.

"Which one?" Rose asks sincerely. "The one in the waiting room says I lift spirits."

"Did he? Well what did the one at the desk say? You know the one with the license?"

"Dr. Welsh? He said that all of this might be due to the major changes in my life. He thinks that quitting my job, moving and marrying you are all huge significant changes and that is why I am having these nightmares." Rose is proud of herself for just reporting the facts. She even manages to keep the skepticism in her voice to a bare minimum.

"Makes sense, right?"

"Maybe? But it doesn't sound right. Spending ten years apart from you was definitely more stressful than being with you. I hated my job and I am really enjoying the one I have now. And moving? Moving is fun. I have never had any problems with moving. I miss my parents and the coffee shop, but other than that…" Rose smooths her dress against her thighs as she internally questions herself. After a quick internal deliberation, she returns to the conversation absolutely sure that these nightmares are not a result of these mundane factors. "Aris, I'm really happy with my life right now. And these nightmares, they really aren't that bad. I am sure that the both of us would like more sleep, but in the grand scheme of things…"

"You are saying that, but…" Aris says. "I suppose there could be some sort of deep-seated thing. Something in your subconscious, perhaps? Maybe these doctors can help."

195

"Imago Dei?" Rose answers laughing. "I was wondering, is it deep-seated or deep-seeded? Seated, right? Do you think that maybe the original saying was just misheard?"

Aris shrugs and grabs her hand with his, leading her to the couch.

"This visit did teach me one thing. I think that there really are angels among us, perhaps disguised as seven feet, seven inch blue-black men," Rose says, unapologetically. She continues to entertain her more private thoughts, thoughts she has been scaling and balancing on her drive home. She thinks that maybe she actually met Efficiency in the waiting room. She knows that the thought could very easily be interpreted as insane; yet, she cannot stop thinking that the man she met, the being she met, was an angel, specifically there for her to *efficiently* tell her that God is talking to her and others.

Aris listens to her but does not quite hear her. He is more than struck by how good she looks. He speaks his own mind, "Have I ever told you how beautiful you look in red?"

"Every time I wear the color," Rose says nuzzling her head into his shoulder. "Hey, enough about me, how was your day?"

"Fine. Normal. Easy. Governmental," Aris responds. "I did not meet any angels. Please don't change the subject. I have been missing you all day. And have been kind of worried, too. I want to hear more about your visit."

"Ah, love." Rose swings her legs and straddles her husband on the couch. "My day was good and promises to get even better." She starts kissing her husband's neck and immediately notices his non-interest. Rose pouts. "Do I have to keep on talking or can I suggest we do something else? I'm feeling frisky."

"Rose," Aris says. "Come on, now..."

"Really?" Rose asks meekly. "Are you sure?" She pulls on his belt buckle.

196

"I'm sure," he says as he grabs her hand and brings it to his mouth.

"I don't know what else I can say. I didn't exactly learn anything today, well other than there are angels in the waiting room," Rose says with a giggle, really wanting to change the subject and the activity. She is tired of talking.

"What about the nightmares?" Aris asks.

"As I said, he thinks that they are a reaction to the major uprooting of my life."

"And you don't believe him?" Aris asks sternly.

"No, I don't. Well…Okay, so that is a bit harsh. It's not like he sounds crazy or anything," she says, laughing at her joke. "However, I do think that a fifth grader could make that observation. And I am confident that that is not what's happening here." Rose defensively swings her legs back around and chooses to sit on the other side of the couch. "Listen Sweetheart, you wanted me to talk to someone. And I did."

"Don't be a brat. This is serious," Aris insists. "Your nightmares are keeping me awake too, remember? Did you schedule a follow-up?"

"I'll say it again. He wants me to see a psychiatrist. He is going to give me a name and I will follow up when that happens," Rose says nearly yelling, a habit that she has. Rose has trouble controlling her volume when she feels she is not being heard. Taking a deep breath she says, "I don't want to fight… I want to…"

Aris extends his arm to suggest that she return to the position she held earlier. She begins to notice the beautiful color of his skin, like milk in an amber glass. She resists by catting from the far cushion onto the heavy arm rest, balancing in a tight squat.

"Am I supposed to come there?" Aris asks, somewhat confused by her body language.

197

Rose tucks her chin and leers. "It is strange. I am having these flash images of large cats fighting, blue-black jaguars. And I sort of want to bite your neck until you submit," Rose says. The vision of jaguars completely fills her mind; she cannot help but to immediately think of the blue-black angel. Unnerved by the passion rising in her body for her husband that is somehow tied to another man is too much. Not quite sure how to react to this emotional and physical onslaught, she chooses to run. "You know what? I think I am going to go for a run. I think I need to go for a run. I feel like I have been talking for hours and I am tired of it…"

Unsure of how to respond to her body language that is unusually sexually charged, he asks, "Do you want to run from me?"

"I don't know what I am feeling. Right now, it feels like my insides are on fire. I want to scratch your skin off and make love and babies…" Rose tries to steer her own mind. She turns to look at the door. "I gotta run."

Rose exhales heavily as she pounces from the couch onto the hard wood. She immediately runs up the stairs, two at a time, to find her well-worn Umbros and Asics. Aris enters the bedroom just as she finishes tying her first shoe.

"Babies?" Aris says suggestively. "You want to make babies?"

Rose furiously grabs her second sneaker and quickly ties it. She stands and throws her T-shirt on over her sports bra. "Babies and angels."

Aris steps toward her and puts his arms around her under her shirt, touching her skin. Rose arches away and digs her nails into his forearm and threatens to scratch. Her mind flooding with seemingly every image she has ever seen, she responds, "I gotta run. I gotta go. And Aris, you should definitely consider whether you want to breed with a crazy person."

198

Confused, Aris asks, "Rose, I don't understand. What is going on?"

Rose's eyes show her fire as she contradicts a deep and burning passion by gently pushing her husband away. "Oh my God." She grabs the Mp3 player from her dresser and turns to her husband. "I'll be back...later."

"Babies?" Aris yells down the stairs as his wife heads out the front door.

"And angels," Rose yells back and then slams the door behind her. She runs as fast as she can to the jogging trail that runs behind her subdivision. After passing the gates that flank the entrance to the trail, she slows her pace to a medium-fast jog. She tackles the hills while thinking about making love to her husband, coupled with images of both ice and steam. She laughs as she recognizes the calendar date and realizes that it is very likely that she is ovulating. *Biology.* As soon as she is able to recognize this, her deep belly breathing returns and she is able to hit her stride. *Aesop's The Babies and The Angels*, she concludes.

She passes several dog walkers on the path and attempts to acknowledge their presence without making eye contact. She stops briefly to catch her breath at the top of a small wooden bridge over the creek that separates the two subdivisions, both designed by Abner. After wiping her sweat with her T-shirt, she restarts her run back home, turning up both the volume and her pace. Red hot and sweating, she opens the front door.

"I am making falafel and cucumber salad," Aris says, bringing a glass of water to his wife at the door. "Dinner in fifteen."

"Thanks. All I need now is a cold shower." Rose drinks the entire glass of water and returns it to her husband who quietly stares at her. She kisses his nose and then runs up the stairs, strips and showers. She returns to the kitchen twelve

199

minutes later wearing the same sundress with her damp hair in a messy bun.

"You really do look beautiful in red," Aris says. "Feel better?"

"Yeah. Much. Thanks for making dinner." Rose kisses his cheek as he takes out the pita bread from a warm oven.

"Want to grab the feta?"

Following his instructions, she grabs the feta and the iced tea from the refrigerator and carries them both to the table. "Falafel and cucumber salad. Perfect."

"They sounded good to me, too," Aris says bringing dinner to the table.

Rose sits and hungrily eyes the food. "I'm starving."

"I figured you would be. You seemed hungry even before your run," Aris says suggestively. "Five miles?"

She nods. "There are some very dark clouds rolling in from the west. I think we are going to get a pretty serious thunderstorm."

"We can watch it from the patio," Aris says as he turns around to look out the patio doors.

"Summer thunderstorms are the best."

"I want to have two children," Aris responds with his own lightning.

She gulps. "I know."

"We need to get our marriage license soon. This week," Aris commands, returning to a conversation long neglected.

"Okay." Rose lifts her pita to her mouth, which seems unable to open.

"You know I love you, right?" Aris asks.

"I do." She sets the sandwich down on her plate and looks at her husband.

"I want to have two children," Aris restates with direct eye contact.

"I'm afraid," she says veering her eyes back down to her plate.

"Of what?" Aris asks sternly.

Rose wonders if she should remind him of the fact that her nightmares are coming true. Instead of pointing out the obvious she returns her attention to her dinner plate. "Of what?" she says quietly, under her breath.

"There are angels in the waiting room," Aris replies. "You see angels in the waiting room. How could you think that you're not safe?"

"For every one angel I meet, there seems to be hundreds of...of things that aren't angels," Rose says. "Can we wait until..."

Aris looks at his wife. His eyes are reflecting a deep love and a tempered annoyance.

Rose sighs. "Two?"

Aris replies, "Two."

Rose furrows her brow as she looks to her husband. "Aris?"

"I have one question. How can you say that you are happy with me and not happy with the world?" Aris says. "You are the one seeing angels in the waiting room. You are the one who has enough faith in humanity that you are actually trying to build a virtuous government. You are the one who believes the world can be a better place..."

"I'm waiting for the other shoe to drop," she explains, idiomatically.

"I want to make a joke here about you being barefoot and pregnant, but I can't find it. It is right here on the tip of my tongue," Aris says. He sticks out his tongue and points to its tip.

"I am pretty sure that I would not find it funny," she says unsympathetically. Rose laughs at herself as she recognizes an overwhelming urge to jump him from across the table.

201

"I'm sure you would," Aris says, laughing as well. He then takes on a self-satisfied look while biting into his pita.

"Aris, I'm serious..."

"No, Rose, you're ridiculous. Yellowstone is not going to explode," Aris says authoritatively.

"Aris, I don't want to talk about this anymore," Rose says. She finishes her water, stands and walks to retrieve more.

"Well, I do," Aris yells at her. "I am tired of this. You are worried about something that will never happen, well, not in our life time anyway. There is literally not a single sign or any rumblings of any kind. And there will be plenty of warning – probably years and years of warning. We will have enough warning to take ourselves and our two beautiful children somewhere safe. I will keep you safe."

"Every relatively wealthy person will have the same plan, where are we going to go?" Rose spits back.

"It's never going to happen," Aris says with an exhausted tone. "Rose, you are being ridiculous."

"I'm not!" Rose yells as frustrated tears start to form in her eyes. "It is not if, it is when!"

Aris starts to walk toward her. Rose steps back until she backs herself into the refrigerator door.

"Where are you going to go?" Aris asks with his chin to his chest and a hard stare into his wife's eyes. He puts his right hand on the door inches from her left ear. The movement is met with a very loud crack of lightening followed by an immediate crash of thunder.

"Well that kinda snuck up on us. Did you hear any warning?" Rose asks, starting to form a mystic argument.

Aris laughs. "Do you think it is God talking to you?"

"Ha. Maybe it's God talking to you. Maybe you would hear the both of us if you would just shut-up and listen." Rose slams down her glass and walks to the patio doors. She opens the door

202

and immediately feels wind from the storm. "It smells beautiful out here."

Aris approaches her and gently hooks his right arm across her clavicle and gently speaks into her left ear, "You really think you saw an angel in the waiting room?"

"I do." Rose forcibly breaks his hold and walks to the middle of the yard. She turns to watch her husband stand under the awning. She catches the first few heavy drops. "Want to join me?"

Aris shakes his head.

Rose reaches her arms up and begins to untie her halter dress. "Are you sure?" The sky opens, unleashing a downpour as if her movements called the rain.

Aris runs out to meet her and catches the straps of her dress just as she is letting go. "You are mine. And I will not share your exquisite form with the neighbors."

"Imagine the beauty we could conceive tonight in this rain storm," Rose yells over the hard rain as she tries to pull the straps from his grip. "You want two, now?"

"Oh, my God," Aris mutters as he swoops his arms around her to carry her back into the house. "Rose, you are really scaring me."

"Make love to me," Rose requests in a heavy whisper. She rests her head on his right shoulder. Her fingers dig into his chest. "Please."

"You are Love to me," Aris responds setting his bride down on her feet. He slowly and deliberately ties her halter and then with his index finger lifts her chin to look into her eyes. "I want two children and our marriage license." Aris looks to the ceiling. "God, she is more than a beautiful handful."

"Denied," Rose says with a pout, and the lightning cracks.

203

火山 21 火山

The Probability of survival is equal to the angle of arrival.

"The United States has approximately fifty-six active volcanoes; forty-four of those are located right here in Alaska," Dr. Frank Mancus says to his class. "The USGS is the main Federal agency with the responsibility for assessing and monitoring active volcanoes in the United Sates. However, this work is primarily done by the volcano observatories."

"I don't get it Dr. Mancus, how did we not know that Lassen Peak was going to erupt?" a young male student asks from the middle of the lecture hall.

In response, Dr. Mancus pulls up what is now termed as a "hypothetical model" of the Lassen Peak Volcano system to try to answer the student's question with his own theories. Dr. Mancus laughs through his nose as he provides the beginning of his answer, "Will you accept the only answer I can provide? We were wrong."

A couple of students in the front row enjoy the response and issue a small laugh in support of their favorite professor.

The professor acknowledges his pet students before continuing, "The vast majority of my work with the USGS was assisting and coordinating efforts to create integration protocols between USGS, NOAA and the FAA. Our goal was to detect and track volcanic ash clouds from eruptions as it pertains to air traffic safety. We, my team and myself, used Alaskan volcanos, specifically Redoubt and Mt. Spurr. I can say that these protocols really worked for Sacramento and I am happy to report that major air disasters were averted and contained due to these protocols. I am proud that these protocols worked, but I'm disappointed, I dare say embarrassed, in our efforts to predict the eruption."

"Are you going to answer the question, Professor?" the same student asks impatiently.

"As you know," the professor answers in a haughty tone, "it is our general belief as volcanologists that the preeminent sign of an impending eruption is the recordable and predictable seismic activity below the volcano. Volcanologists and Seismologists can successfully interpret these readings with respectable accuracy, readings such as ground deformation, increased release of volcanic gases and changes in the composition of those gases. These predictors are textbook and are employed all over the world. Although hindsight has provided information about Lassen Peak that chronicle a solid interpretation of an eminent eruption – these indicators were overlooked due to their banality."

"You mean the symptoms were not severe enough to raise flags," Jennifer says from the front row.

"Exactly. All indicators were within the normal range, albeit at the high range of normal. The truth of it is, they were all present – but they weren't yelling loud enough," Dr. Mancus adds with his narrative charm. "One possible reason for this is that our instrumentation may not have been tuned appropriately."

"Are people going to lose their jobs?" a female asks from the back of the class.

"I am sure of it, although I am not sure if they'd deserve it. I say that because the science itself is in its infancy in many ways. It's hard to collect good, solid, statistically significant data from volcanoes – not only are they virtually unapproachable, but are generally dormant for the life of a scientist. But I am sure that science will advance leaps and bounds because of these errors. If you do not mind me quoting my favorite movie, 'These little set-backs are just what we need to take a giant step forward.'"

Jennifer laughs from the front row. "All of my filth is arranged in alphabetical order. This, for instance is under 'H' for 'toy,'" she mutters for her professor.

Dr. Mancus smiles gently at his student and then looks out into the lecture hall. "Any more questions, observations, insights…"

"If we were wrong about this one, could we be wrong about others?" a male student asks from the far right.

"Sure," Dr. Mancus answers straightforwardly. "But as a scientist and a volcanologist, I can assure you that it is not as likely as it appears. We have been right ninety-nine times out of a hundred. Lassen Peak is an anomaly."

"Is it possible that the other volcanoes were?" a meek voice says from the second row.

"Were what – anomalies?" barks a student from the front row.

"Yeah," the meek female says with a subdued challenge.

Dr. Mancus looks at the shy, yet well-performing student. "It's hard not to feel a bit of anxiety about this situation. Volcanoes are serious events. They shape our worlds, our lands. When something like this happens, hits us in our blind spot, it is easy to doubt ourselves and our understandings," Dr. Mancus says directly to Samantha. "We have to learn from this and move forward."

"Sir, what about Yellowstone? It's not like other volcanoes. Its hotspot moves. What if we are wrong about that one? It's past due, right?" Samantha asks straining to maintain an audible volume. "What if the earth's core is feeding these volcanoes? Wouldn't that…I mean, couldn't that explain these things?"

"Then God help us," Dr. Mancus says. "That would cause an entire polar shift." The professor looks down into his desk, taking a moment to actually process what his student said. His eyes find hers and he offers a gentle nod. "To tell you the truth, that's a very interesting theory, Samantha." He turns his attention from her to the rest of the class. "However, I would like to remind you all that our instrumentations, our measurements, our understanding, our geologists, our seismologists, our volcanologists are all very good." He shifts his attention back to Samantha. "We are not flying blind here. I doubt a volcano the size of Yellowstone can take us off guard. I also seriously doubt that we could be missing a change in the earth's core," he says, taking on a fatherly tone. "Yet, I must admit it's a pretty good theory."

Samantha looks down at her note pad. "Thanks," she says modestly.

"Actually, that is more than a pretty good theory. Tell you what, I promise that I will look into it and discuss its possibility with some of my colleagues," Dr. Mancus says after quickly consulting his own deeper questions, themselves newly formed after Lassen Peak. "For tonight's assignment, I would like each of you to write your own interpretation of the events of Lassen Peak. How did it happen? Why did it happen? What could we have done differently? Where were our shortcomings? What did we do well? For instance, our first responders did an excellent job evacuating the site. I want you to visit the sites of NOAA, USGS, our observatory, the FAA, etcetera. If you are an aspiring geologist, approach this event as a geologist. If you are a seismologist, approach this event as a seismologist? Any questions?"

"How many pages?" a male from the third row asks.

"I am not sure if I care about that. I want you to think about it, seriously consider the facts of this event. If you must have a bit of structure – how about five outlined points," Dr. Mancus says and then looks at Jennifer. "I just want to know that you have thought about it. This is a major event in geological sciences. We should pay it its due – an homage, if you will."

"What's it worth?" another male student asks.

"What's it worth to you? You are seeking a degree in geology, you should care about it," Dr. Mancus says with a blending of irritation and disappointment.

"Sir! Sir!" a female student shouts from the back of the class. "They are saying that Medicine Lake is erupting."

"What?!" Dr. Mancus says with a tone of utter disbelief. "Medicine Lake? This almost proves it, we must have been wrong about the source."

"It was just announced," the student says waving her IPhone in the air.

Just as the sound waves meet Dr. Mancus's own ears, two of his graduate students burst through his classroom door. "Sir, Dr. Greene from the Cascades Volcano Observatory is on the phone. It's an emergency," the first says with a strong even tone. "Medicine Lake is erupting."

"Class? These are certainly exciting times. I, or Paul here, will send an email to you all to keep you posted on any information we get. These are indeed exciting times, especially for those of us in this profession, really exciting times," Dr. Mancus says as he rushes from the classroom.

Δ22Δ

All persons ought to endeavor to follow what is right, and not what is established. – Aristotle

Aris sets down his novel to watch his wife tap out on her computer. He is a little more than slightly concerned about her. She is not behaving abnormally. In fact, it is as though nothing has happened. He internally acknowledges that his bride has always been exceedingly good at compartmentalizing, but her current rigor is unsettling.

"What are you working on?" he asks in an attempt to make small talk, hoping it will lead to bigger things. He is hoping that she will say something about the sudden eruption of Medicine Lake.

"My fables?" she says as if she is unsure of the word. "I am putting together teams of virtues to attack the problems that are arising from the food shortage," she replies matter-of-factly. "Yet, I think I need a break. If you don't mind, I think I'm going to try to catch that power yoga class at seven-thirty with Aubrey. I feel kinda wired and I think yoga might help calm me down. I'd like to get some sleep tonight."

Aris just furrows his brow wishing that she would stop pretending she is fine and talk to him. He reassures himself that she will talk to him when she is ready. She always does. "I can imagine," he says and then quickly looks to his watch. "You don't have much time, then."

"Will you do me a favor?" she asks, tentatively. "Will you read what I have written? I think it makes sense and is also entertaining, but…"

"I'd love to. I'm actually curious to see what you have been working on."

209

"Really?" Rose asks somewhat meekly. "I thought that maybe you thought this whole thing was…"

"I really like the idea of a marriage of Aesop and Aristotle in a children's book," Aris says trying to be as delicate and supportive as possible.

Rose quickly saves the file and carries her laptop to him. She scrolls back quite a few pages before stopping. "Just let me know if they make sense to you. Let me know if they seem real to you." Rose kisses her husband on the top of his head, grabs her pre-packed gym bag and yoga mat and is out the door in under a minute.

The door reverberates slightly from its most recent use. The sound it makes bothers Aris; it sounds like he feels – shut out. His wife will not talk to him. He stares at the door for a moment, as if he is expecting her to return just as quickly as she left. He sighs as he shifts her laptop around on his thighs and tries to find a comfortable position. He hopes she is trying to reach out with this gesture. She told him when she started writing that these stories are to be a sort of wedding gift to him. He grabs the warming lager from his side table and takes several gulps before settling down for his read...

Understanding, a stern-faced, physically fit young man in his late 20's, takes three steps backward from the reception desk and tries to decide whether he should waste the minutes using the facilities or waste them pretending to be interested in the collated reading materials they have provided the interviewees. Before taking the fourth step, he decides that he should take advantage of the running water and flushing toilets – even if he is not in real need of them. He walks to his right and enters into the brightly lit bathroom of the governmental building.

"Warm water," he says under this breath. He tries to remember the last time he felt warm water. It has been close to ten days. "I'd probably take the job if they just promise me a daily warm shower." He looks at himself in the mirror as he

210

runs his hands under the tap. The stubble on both his head and his face appear to be growing at the exact same rate and this strikes him as odd. Normally, his facial hair grows twice as fast. He intellectually runs down the potential factors and decides that his last shave must have been done at the optimum time in the hair growth cycle. He towels his hands and checks his teeth before returning to the chilly reception room where he is to sit and wait...

A satisfied smile appears on Aris's face as he sees one of Rose's favorite action movie stars in Understanding, the one who is capable of maintaining Rose's "perfect amount of scruff." He moves his right hand to feel his own five-o'clock shadow before returning to the story...

Understanding steps into the hallway and encounters the unexpected. He hears a beautiful singing voice in the direction of the reception desk. He assumes it is the secretary that he met earlier, yet upon closer approach he sees that the voice belongs to someone else. Having an actual reason to walk in the direction of the voice, Understanding does not hesitate to follow it. He walks up to the source of the ethereal music, a petite Asian woman with hair the color of red chrysanthemums.

"You have a beautiful voice," he says earnestly.

Startled by the stranger, Value turns from the window and quickly wipes tears from both of her eyes. "Sorry, I thought I was alone," she says looking at the empty reception desk and then at the stranger. "You step quietly," she observes.

"Are you okay? You're crying," Understanding says, somewhat shocked by the sight of one of the most beautiful women he has ever seen. "I'm not exactly thrilled about this mandatory..." Understanding catches himself then sighs, as he recognizes that the situation does not call for a joke. He reaches into his pocket and retrieves an unopened pocket pack of Kleenex and gently offers the entire pack to the woman. "Where

211

are my manners? I'm Understanding. Is there anything I can do to help?"

Value docilely accepts his gift with a couple of gentle nods. "Thanks, this is very kind of you. And very gentlemanly..."

Understanding takes a step back to give the beauty more space and to expand upon his social graces taught to him by his mother, Knowledge. He takes this time to notice her hair, her stunning emerald eyes, and the adorable freckles that bespeckle her nose.

Value responds to his kindness and explains, "I lost someone very dear to me in the volcano's eruption. He always taught me to remember the things that many forget. I haven't heard music in more than a week. I remembered that I didn't remember," she says trying to explain her tears and her song. "I guess I just needed to hear music, so I started singing." She opens the pack of Kleenex and dabs under her eyes. "I must look a mess," she exclaims with a nervous laugh.

Understanding wants to say something of the way she looks to him - she looks like fall foliage at its peak, sunshine, and fresh air all rolled into one. He looks down to his feet and whispers, "I think you look beautiful."

Value modestly smiles at the compliment and makes a gentle attempt to move the conversation to something more meaningful. "So, you here to interview, too..."

Just as she gets the first sentence out of a less intimate conversation, doors simultaneously open on both sides of the waiting room. "Value?" says a woman standing in the doorway to the right. "Please come with me."

Value looks to the door and then returns her gaze to the very gentlemanly stranger. She tries to return the Kleenex. "My name is Value. I hope we get to talk again. Thank you for your kindness and your..." Value smiles as she remembers his name. "I really do hope..."

212

Understanding responds by gently gesturing with his hands that she is to keep the packet. He further offers his own gentle mimic of the nods she issued when they started their exchange. "We will," he says bowing a third time. He watches her walk to the woman who called before turning in the direction of the other door. "Are you looking for me?" he asks the interviewer.

Understanding and the interviewer enter into the office. After quickly running through the initial niceties, the interviewer asks, "Do you know why you are here?"

The gentleman responds with a simple affirmative nod. He ably answers all the interviewer's questions in few words while all the time peripherally wondering about the stunning woman he met minutes earlier. "Her name was Value," he mentions to the interviewer, looking at the door where they entered. He asks about her because there is something about her that he doesn't immediately understand. "She has the most beautiful voice I have ever heard."

"There are far more important things," the interviewer responds while shuffling forms. "I grant you, she is very attractive."

The statement from the interviewer singes his core. Understanding inherently knows that Value would find that utterance extremely disheartening. Recognizing both his mother and his father in this thought process, he passionately takes the initiative to defend his new friend. "You asked about my mother and my father. I wish you could have known them. Knowledge and Sensitivity would greatly enhance your trade. Value is infinitely more than attractive."

The interviewer smiles at this, providing Understanding with a glimmer of the intentions behind his questions. He further illustrates his total comprehension by adding, "It is good to see that Understanding has fire."

Understanding responds to the quip with an exaggerated nod accompanied by a laugh. "You're good." He laughs again,

213

slapping his leg and instantaneously lightening his mood. "So if I take this job, can I gain access to your showers? I have recently learned that my outlook on life is significantly dampened by a cold shower."

"I completely understand," the interviewer reports with a wry smile. "I think we can accommodate."

After completing the required paperwork, and setting up an appointment for the following day, the interviewer escorts Understanding to the door and thanks him for his time. Understanding exits back into the hallway just in time to see Value exiting through the stairwell. He steals a flower from a vase located on a side table and chases after her. "Value," he calls.

Already two flights down, Value stops and looks up to her caller. "Hi," she responds. "How did your interview go?"

"Very well," Understanding says with a bit too much volume for the acoustics of the stairwell. He adjusts his volume while descending one flight. "And yours?"

Value climbs up to meet him half-way, on the platform. She answers when he is a little more than two feet away. "My interview was yesterday. Today I found out that I will be working on the Econ task force – an international effort to help re-establish international currencies as well as their stock markets."

Understanding quickly tries to gauge the work involved in such an undertaking. "Sounds fascinating," is his short response. He pulls a rose from behind his back and offers it to the beauty in front of him. "I am not exactly sure how there are fresh flowers upstairs. Fresh flowers? I haven't had a warm shower in over a week and there are roses…" He hands the rose to her. "This is for you, for your friend, for your tears and for your song."

Value takes the rose and peculiarly presses her index finger into a thorn. The thorn pierces her skin. Value brings the blood

214

droplet to her mouth. "I'm on my way to the Red Cross to donate. Would you like to join me?"

Understanding drops two tears of his own as he thinks about his parents and how they told him that there was someone out there for him; someone who would understand. He inhales deeply enough that he can actually pick up the scent of the rose in the stairwell. "I can think of nothing else that I would rather do..."

"Even better than the comics," Aris says with a deep exhale. He takes in his own deep breath as he presses his head against the cushion of his reading chair that, in turn, responds with a deeper lounge position. "And look at that, she is still on topic," he says as he recognizes that she marries Value and Understanding just in time for school. Returning his attention to the computer screen, Aris scrolls down her story line and smiles as he reads the various names and scenarios of her virtues. He laughs as he notices that she wrote that Persistence is male.

As he compulsively re-saves the document and closes the file, he happens to notice another file that piques his interest named firedreams.doc. He questions his conscience before opening it.

He immediately notices that the file is a well-ordered documentation of her nightmares including dates, times and descriptions. Scrolling down, he discovers that there have been many more dreams than he ever realized. She has painstakingly kept the worst of them from him...

3:00 AM, April 9: A blonde, blue-eyed boy, age nine, puts a boat that he made out of newspaper onto a rain-made stream that is running along the shoulder of his road. He joyfully runs with the boat as it makes its way down the road. The small stream instantaneously transforms into a wider lava flow. The young boy, wishing to save his boat from catching fire, bends down to pick it up. In his hands the boat is fully consumed by the flames. The fire then leaps onto the boy. It was his unbearable screams that woke me from the dream...

215

4:18 AM, May 3: I am running on the jogging path and notice a small rabbit. Its fur is typical, white belly with a heather brown on its back and head. Its eyes, however, were green. That is what caught my attention. I stopped running to see if I could approach the rabbit to get a closer look. The rabbit remained still and then started to slowly, as if it were walking, hop into the woods. I followed it. The rabbit led me to a field with a very colorful play set in its center. There were children everywhere running, jumping, and climbing. Their laughs were infectious. I started to laugh too. I looked down at the rabbit to thank him for taking me to this wonderful place, but the rabbit had disappeared. Yet, it left footprints, multi-colored footprints. There were also snake imprints leading off in the same direction. Only slightly worried about the rabbit, I returned my sight to the playground. It had melted into countless colorful puddles. I was trying to make sense of the scene as I see a little girl approach me. She asks, "What happened to the monkey bars?" I told her I didn't know. The little girl starts sobbing uncontrollably and starts to hit me in her frustration. She says, "Everyone died. Why didn't you stop it?" I woke up trying to answer her question...

Of the fifty nightmares she has recorded, children die in twenty of them, she dies in five. And she never told him. A sick, gnawing feeling encroaches. He begins to recognize that his unwillingness to believe her has caused a breach in her trust of him. He immediately resolves to do something about it. "I've got to make it up to her. I've got to make sure that she knows that I am here for her, no matter what." He shuts down her computer and returns it to the coffee table.

"Understanding falls in love with Value," he says aloud. Aris just shakes his head and laughs as he picks up the couple's ice cream bowls from the evening's dessert and places them into the dishwasher. He is already resolved to let her tell him her secrets in her own time. But he wonders if he can push just a little.

216

Inspired, he walks over to the foyer table and grabs his keys, his mind on blue violets and chocolate covered cherries, some of Rose's favorite things. He envisions her reaction to the gifts and immediately looks at his watch. He still has some time left.

The door slams behind him.

Δ23Δ

**By myth I mean the arrangement of the incidents –
Aristotle**

Erik sits comfortably across from Rose at her dining
table. He is truly happy to have been invited for a small dinner
party. Before Aris returned to the area and brought his
captivating wife with him, Erik had been in desperate need of
change in his life. To him, it really is no coincidence that so
much has changed for him in such a short period of time. If Rose
did not want a job in landscaping, this night and these changes
might not have happened. He smiles at her as he finally reports
his news of a small promotion. "In short, you're going to be our
new rock girl," Erik says leaning over the glass bowl of clam
linguine to retrieve seconds. "And before you even ask, I have
talked to Julie and she will be more than happy to relinquish her
title."

"Rock girl?" Rose asks with both of her eyebrows.

Erik glances to the kitchen to find out whether Aris is
listening. He is amused by the sight of his scrupulous friend
wrestling with a wine bottle and cork screw. "Well, you said you
wanted to learn about the biz and I thought that Jay would not
mind some fresh blood. Also, I think a little more knowledge
and responsibility is due. You really are fitting in quite well in
my Palace."

Aris dons a large smile as he is finally able to pull the cork
from the bottle. Walking to the table, he says, "I am notoriously
bad at opening wine and she is completely unwilling. My
advice, Erik – take care to fall in love with someone who likes
opening wine."

"Any advice you can give…" Erik says to his friend. He
looks over at Rose and can tell that there is something a little off

218

about her. Her energy level is not quite the same. He also notices the circles under eyes and remembers Aris telling him of her sleep troubles. He almost inquires, but holds back – a trait that is natural, but cultivated by his profession. "Rose, this garlic bread is fantastic." He takes a huge bite for her benefit.

"Thanks," she says. She turns to Aris. "Did you hear? I'm getting a promotion. I'm the new Rock girl."

"I did hear. So, who's this Jay character?" Aris asks, retrieving a second helping of his own.

"Jay is our rock guy. He owns Bolder Landscaping. We have a pretty good exchange with him. For some reason, rich people like giant rocks," Erik says unapologetically. "They do. I don't know why."

"Bolder Landscaping?" Aris says pouring the prized bottle of Fumé Blanc into his friend's wine glass. "Seems like a good name for a rock landscaping business." He turns to Rose. "Are you sure? It's supposedly a very good pairing."

"No thanks, I'm sure," Rose says watching her husband as he wraps the bottle.

Erik takes another bite of his garlic bread. "Seriously, this garlic bread is fantastic."

"It's one of my talents. I make really good garlic bread and fantastic popcorn," Rose admits. "I was thinking of putting one or the other as an epitaph for my headstone. Does Jay do headstones?"

"No," Erik says firmly, almost laughing.

"She does make really good popcorn. Although I'm not sure if that belongs on her headstone. I think it should say something about her Danish."

Erik huffs in amusement. "I am sorry that Aubrey could not be here for this. Her sister-in-law is having some sort of baby shower or something or other. I wasn't invited to whatever it was."

219

"Babies are cute. It is just too bad that they typically grow up to be boring and ugly adults," Rose says conversationally.

Aris grimaces. "Tell her ours wouldn't be boring or ugly."

"Ours?" Erik jokes, gesturing at himself and then at Aris.

"He wants two," Rose says. She shrugs and points with the top of her head in the direction of her husband. "He wants to bring two beautiful beings into the world filled with wars, drugs, guns, violence, poverty, famine, inequality, earthquakes, volcanos, and … and national debt."

"Don't forget about yew bunnies," Aris says with a light chuckle.

"I want kids too," Erik admits. "They seem like a good distraction to me."

"A good distraction?" Rose larks. "I wouldn't even consider them except that his nose is just so incredibly perfect. It is the most perfectly formed nose in the entire world," Rose says looking at her husband. "Knowing my luck, he or she would get mine."

"What can I say, the luck of the Irish," Aris says trying to deflect the feminine compliment. "I am smart, successful, well-bred… and it's my nose she wants to carry to the next generation."

Erik takes a moment to appreciate the banter of the couple, both hoping and wishing that his current relationship can grow into something like that of his two dinner companions. "You do have a nice nose. I've never noticed. Huh. How's mine? Good breeding potential?" he asks Rose as he strokes his own nose.

"You have nice ears, exceptionally nice ears," Rose declares.

220

"I want to breed with her because I think she will make a tremendous mother," Aris says looking directly into his wife's eyes. "And have you seen her stems?"

"Aw, wanna go get naked?" Rose asks only half kidding.

"Uh, you have guests," Erik says laughing. He quickly shares his envy. "I am thinking of asking Aubrey. Do you think it's too soon?"

"You are the only one who can answer that," Aris says straightforwardly. "Yet, you have only known her for less than two months, so…"

"Is she in love?" Rose asks.

"I know I am," Erik admits. He looks between his friends several times as he asks himself whether he should ask for more details about their courtship. He knows from Aris that it was extremely lengthy. He is unsure of Rose's perspective. "I'm just of the opinion that when you know, you know. But I guess we need more time." He sighs and raises an empty glass in silent plea for a refill. "I will just have to wait until she knows."

"Timing is everything," Aris says. He capably refills Erik's glass.

"I don't know about that. I think it is more important to value the same things," Rose says and then grabs the last of the garlic bread. "Like garlic bread, for instance."

"And epitaphs on headstones," Erik says with a chuckle. "So, the funny thing about Jay is – is that he has a Sisyphus complex. You know – the guy who pushes the boulder in hell."

"You can take penicillin for Sisyphus," Aris jokes.

"I love that myth – poor guy. Actually wasn't there a philosopher also named Sisyphus? He and Socrates talked about deliberation…?" Rose asks looking between the two of them for her answer.

"Huh?" Erik asks.

"She gets like this," Aris says as he stands and moves behind her chair. "So Miss Smarty Pants, what's for dessert?"

"That's Mrs. Smarty Pants." She drops her head back to look at him. "I used tonight as an excuse to buy that copper fire pit. I was thinking we could toast marshmallows. We haven't done that in a while and it's a nice night," Rose says. "I also have graham crackers and Hershey bars, if so desired."

"Hershey Bars? Really? I thought we were still really mad at them," Aris says, somewhat surprised.

"We don't like them, yet," Rose answers her husband simply. "I heard from Nick yesterday. Apparently there are closed door negotiations going on about breaking grounds for the schools. I thought a little support was in order. I meant to tell you about it earlier. I guess I forgot. Abdul might get his school after all."

"Congratulations, Rose," Aris says sincerely. "I can't believe you forgot to tell me something like this…" he utters under his breath.

With his interest piqued because of the odd tension developing in the room Erik cannot help but to ask, "Abdul? Wait, who's Abdul and who's Nick?" He looks to Aris for the answer, but Aris's eyes are fixed on Rose.

With obvious intention the hostess stands and walks quickly to the study. She returns with a small framed picture of a young boy. She hands the frame to Erik. "Abdul," she announces. "And I think if we were truly being honest - he is pretty much the reason we are together today. I pretty much became obsessed with him and getting him a piece of chocolate. I think Aris noticed that he was taking my attentions from him… I think he was jealous. And interestingly enough, a few months later, he gave me this ring." Rose looks at her hand and then shows it to Erik. "What do you think, Aris? True? Did this boy give me chocolate and diamonds?"

Aris shrugs and nervously swallows. "I guess he was my first real competition," he says trying to laugh off the question. "Yet, I think I should probably mention that he is only eleven …"

"Nick wasn't eleven," Rose notes.

Erik's internal deliberations bounce between the two. There is something odd present– a tension that he has never noticed – a power struggle. Because both tend to joke, even about serious things, he is not quite sure how to take this information. Was Aris really jealous of an eleven year old boy? He begins to wonder if Aris, like his sister Danika, require attentions and affections that border on obsessive. He remembers that Danika only started to pay attention to him when someone else was interested. With this thought bearing, he looks at Aris with a new lens. He thinks about inquiring further about Nick, yet his cultivated patience reigns supreme. He knows when not to cut in.

Instead, he files his observations away, thinking that it might be nice to share these notes with Aubrey, who finds fault with his admiration of the couple. Aubrey thinks that the couple is equal parts self-absorbed and self-centered, yet fun to be around, if only to talk about later.

"I love Abdul," Rose says squeezing the portrait to her chest. "So yeah, we have Hershey Bars. And I think it's a beautiful night for a campfire."

"An evening sitting around a fire?" Aris says, with a clearly confused tone.

"We can huddle under the boom," Rose says with a light laugh. "I really like having a boom in my backyard. Fire and a boom – it's funny."

"You are so odd. Is she making sense?" Erik asks Aris. In an effort to distract himself from feeling as if he is moving from friendly to judgmental, he stands from the table and collects his own dish before offering to carry more. He jokes with Aris, "I don't think she is making sense."

Aris looks to his friend with eyes that suggest he agrees. "We have an antenna in our backyard. I am trying to get her to pick up a hobby – she needs strictly defined distractions. Amateur radio was my suggestion," Aris explains. He gives Erik

223

a meaningful look that Erik immediately understands as an unspoken request to play dumb.

Erik nods to convey his understanding. Slightly disillusioned, he realizes his friend possesses a little bit of Danika's qualities. He sighs as he picks up the bowl of parmesan and brings it to the kitchen.

"Anyway," Aris continues, "I guess she is only somewhat interested. So now we have this giant antenna in our backyard and she still has yet to get her license."

"In my defense, Erik," says Rose, as she eyes her husband, "I have a lot going on right now. It is kind of hard to focus on dialectics, capacitors and transformers. School is starting in two weeks and besides, this is supposed to be a hobby, not a sentence. And Aris, I already heard an earful from Abner for not completely acing the last practice test."

"Not completely acing... Honey, an A minus is still an A," Aris says with a complaining tone of his own. "I know Abner was just kidding. The truth is you're just dragging your feet on this."

Realizing that Aubrey may be at least half right, Erik decides to ask, "Is this your first fight? I was sure that you guys never fought. In fact, I recently told Aubrey something to that effect."

"Actually we have been fighting for weeks. I want to get married, license and everything, and make babies and she – she wants to prepare for the apocalypse."

"I think I am multi-tasking," Rose says light-heartedly with a shrug of her shoulders.

Erik watches her pick up the last of the dishes from the table. He muses to Aris, "What are you feeding her again?"

"Forbidden fruit, I fear," Aris says nonchalantly. "And she has been so touchy lately that she probably doesn't even think that's funny."

"Everything goes back to Adam and Eve with strings attached," Rose says. She leers at her husband before poking her tongue out at him. She grabs the chocolate, marshmallows and graham crackers. She leads the party out to her newly purchased fire pit surrounded by her patio chairs. She grabs the elongated lighter from her chair and hands it to her husband. "I've been warned not to play with fire."

Aris lights kindling under the three logs and takes his seat across from his friend. "Did I tell you how much Rose likes fires," he declares with a tone of sarcasm.

"Who doesn't?" Erik asks.

"Burn victims," Rose gracelessly blurts followed by a gawky shift in her chair. With a feigned effort to shield herself she posits, "So, Sisyphus, eh? Aris's favorite myth is Prometheus. The god who stole the fire from the gods and gave it to man. Did you know that Prometheus is also credited with creating men from clay?"

Erik snorts and says, "I guess it's true, then. Everything actually does go back to Adam and Eve."

"Yep. Speaking of…Did you guys know that Noah was the great, great, great grandson of Cain, the son of Adam and Eve, who killed his brother?"

"What *are* you feeding her?" Erik asks Aris, again.

"She's always like this, whether I feed her or not," Aris confesses.

"I actually just made that connection recently. As you may know being good Catholic boys, Cain killed his brother because God did not accept his sacrifice of grains and God did accept Abel's sacrifice of a calf, or lamb, or whatever. God never did give Cain a reason why his sacrifice was not accepted. Anyway, in a jealous rage, Cain killed his brother and was banished from the garden. Although God said he would still protect him."

225

Noticing the fire has a good roll to it, Rose puts a marshmallow on a skewer and passes it to Erik. She does the same for Aris and then for herself. "Anyway, Cain went off and met a couple of ladies and had a couple of babies, and so on and so on..."

"Those were the days – multiple wives..." Erik says light-heartedly.

"I don't understand the concept of two wives," Aris says earnestly.

"You better not," Rose says. "I am more than enough."

"Actually you're almost too much," Aris says pretending to focus on his marshmallow while contently smiling at his ridiculously complex wife.

"Almost? Are we still fighting?" Rose says leaning over for a kiss. Aris meets her and they lip lock for a few long seconds.

"Uh, guests," Erik interrupts again with enough amusement in his voice to show he does not really mind. He quietly wonders whether one could do without the other. "So Noah is a descendent of a murderer. I guess I missed that biblical lesson. Although, they don't tell you that kind of stuff in Sunday school, do they?" He lifts his burning marshmallow and blows it out. He returns the other side to the fire. He signals that he will very soon be ready for both the chocolate and the graham crackers.

Rose quickly hands him both. "What I find interesting is that I think this is a backstory of the olive branch. So Cain was a farmer in charge of crops. His sacrifice was, suitably, a portion of his crop. God did not accept the sacrifice then. But after the flood, after God killed just about everyone, he delivered a piece of a fruit tree to Noah. Interesting, right?"

"Maybe to you," Aris says deeply.

Rose shoots her husband a look. "Well, I think it is interesting. It's almost like a double apology. I think it's romantic." Rose looks down at her feet and feels the flames warm her forehead. "You love me like that," she mutters.

"Noah's illustrious patronage…" Aris says.

"I think you guys should breed. I think you'd make great parents."

Rose looks at Aris with both an obvious fear and an emotional longing. "The Sisyphus Deliberation?"

"Nerd." Aris shakes his head at her. He then looks to Erik. "She is waiting for the second olive branch to be delivered – in Greenland," Aris says sarcastically.

"Bringing children into the world *after* the flood makes more sense," Rose says for Erik's sake. Her eyes are staring at her husband's profile.

"Wow, you guys really are fighting, aren't you? It's both heavy and cute," Erik says astutely. "Should I leave?"

"No, Erik. I hope we're not making you uncomfortable. This little argument you are witnessing started a few days ago. We were supposed to get our marriage license on Friday. He's particularly moody because we did not get it done. Getting our license is important to him. And my opinion is… well, I think we need to have the major issues ironed out first. The biggest is children. I'm having a hard time making that promise when there is all this crap going on in the world," Rose says beseeching her husband for a small bit of mercy through Erik.

"She's not giving you the whole story," Aris says.

"He doesn't have to know the whole story. Need I remind you that although he is your friend, he is also my boss," Rose says angrily and then immediately adjusts her tone. "It's not that I don't think you are my friend… you understand, right? What I mean is… We are both really stubborn and…"

"I am not the one being stubborn." Aris stands from his chair and takes four paces away from the fire. He turns to Erik. "I'm definitely not the one who's being stubborn."

227

Erik gulps the last of his wine. "Need another glass. I think you guys need a minute or two." Not waiting for a response, Erik beelines for the patio door.

Erik enters the house and closes the screen leaving his two hosts to apparently stare at each other in their garden. He uses the facilities and tries to take a bit more time than he would under more normal circumstances. After a few moments of pacing in his friends' living room, he walks to the patio door and stealthily observes the couple in the firelight.

Aris motions to Erik and nearly yells, "It's safe. We have years to have this conversation." He adds the last words of his argument just as Erik makes it to ear shot. "The world is not perfect. And it's not supposed to be."

"I'm not asking for perfection. I'm asking for a world that wants to make a better version. I want a world that is more interested in the children mining the tungsten than the iPad, more interested in the children harvesting cocoa than the chocolate," Rose declares. "I don't think that's too much to ask."

"Your argument does not hold much water considering your schools are being built."

"Closed door negotiations? Come on now, Aris. This fire here blows less smoke. I bought the chocolate as a prayer to God, hoping that it's true. Not actually believing that it is true. You understand the difference, right? I think the world is still Falling. Either that or Hell is rising."

Erik notices that her energy is back to a normal level for her. He has observed enough of her work ethic over the past few weeks to know that she is unhappy when things are left undone, or unsaid. She must have said what she needed to say.

"Rose, maybe you are supposed to accept the snakes in your garden – they play a role, they have a purpose, even in a playground. Look at this fire. It's beautiful and it's not going to hurt anyone. And the truth is – it's really not for you to decide. The only real choice you have is that you are either going to be

228

thankful for the gifts of life, or not. The balance of nature is not a choice. Well – it's not your choice."

Rose is stunned into silence. To cover, she presses back into her chair.

Erik's initial reaction is to rescue Rose in that particular moment, but he is not sure why. Yet, there is definitely a part of him that thinks he should assert himself in this moment. He has more than a passing thought that they may have actually forgotten that he is there. He cuts in. "Rose, do you need anything to drink? Water, perhaps. Coffee?"

"I'm sorry. We did it again. We're being rude," she says almost ashamedly. She adds timidly, "But, I could use some ice water. That is, if you don't mind." She immediately looks into the shadows to find her husband.

Erik sets down his wine glass and immediately returns to the kitchen to pour a glass of water. He takes a moment to appreciate his own easier relationship with Aubrey. He returns to the fire with the resolve that this fight will be postponed, or he will be leaving. He says, "So, you guys alright now? The fight is over. If you need to smooch for a few moments, I can take it."

"Thanks Erik. We're alright. Love conquers all and stuff," Rose says. She turns her attention to watch Aris still collecting himself and logs for the fire.

Erik takes his seat and charmingly changes the subject back to something less personal and more social. "I like bible stories. Very cool. Noah descended from a murderer – that's one to remember." He notices the disposition of his hostess begins to lighten as she sees her husband making his return from the dark. She fixedly watches him stack three more logs at his feet, slowly and deliberately before extending his hand to her. Erik smiles as he watches Rose rejoice with a little self-contained dance in her chair.

"Sometimes fire is awesome, isn't it?" Rose says with a subdued jubilance.

"No garden is complete without one," Erik responds. "Jay will be teaching you all about the types of stones that you can use to make more substantial fire pits. Actually, I am thinking of hiring him to build up that section of the garden at my house. I think it's about time that I tried to make that yard my own."

"Aristotle and I want to know," Rose says, her hand still firmly in Aris's, "can you pay the rock man with rocks?"

Δ24Δ

The Eagle and the Arrow

AN EAGLE sat on a lofty rock, watching the movements of a Hare whom he sought to make his prey. An archer, who saw the Eagle from a place of concealment, took an accurate aim and wounded him mortally. The Eagle gave one look at the arrow that had entered his heart and saw in that single glance that its feathers had been furnished by himself. "It is a double grief to me," he exclaimed, "that I should perish by an arrow feathered from my own wings." –Aesop

Rose stares outside patio doors watching the falling snow trim her rose trellis in white. She takes both pleasure and delight in the first snow of the season to reach the southern state; the scene evokes the snow of her childhood. Following the wide flat flakes with her eyes, she is completely immersed in the moment as she rubs her hands up and down her firm, round belly. When she feels the first contraction, she says with a cool calmness, "Aris, it appears as though our baby wants to be born during a snow storm."

The couple arrives at the birthing center somewhat nervous, somewhat excited. But just like most soon-to-be-parents, they are mostly frightened. Aris takes in the rotunda of the birthing center that he has visited a few times before this moment, but it has never appeared as grand. "I cannot believe how quickly time has passed. I cannot believe it has already been nine months."

"Nine months ago – we were having dinner with Erik, remember? You told me to be thankful for life's gifts? Remember?" Rose says reaching up for her husband's hand that he has soothingly placed on her shoulder. She lowers herself into the wheel chair that was immediately presented upon her arrival.

"I remember we fought that night. And my, how we made up," Aris says amorously in her ear. "Do you realize we have not fought since?"

Rose looks down at her round belly and engorged breasts. "This body doesn't feel like mine. Will it ever again?" Her torso shoots up straight signaling her husband to do his due diligence. "Five minutes?" she asks.

"Yep, five minutes. I'm not scared," Aris says gulping air audibly.

"What do you have to be afraid of? I am the one that is going to push a ten pound…" Rose is distracted by the doctor who greets the couple in the hall.

"This is the big day. The day we have been waiting for. Your baby chose a good day to be born. There is only one other couple here. You might even have the entire staff available for this delivery," the beautiful, fresh-faced Indian woman explains. Her tone suggests she has said the same thing countless times before, but her eyes suggest complete sincerity.

Rose looks up to her husband in wonderment as she tries to take in the moment.

"Are you ready to push?"

Rose is immediately catapulted into the delivery room. The sights and sounds are shaded, muted in her periphery, as she tries to peer around the lab coats to see her baby that was just removed from her body. Her eyes change focus to her husband who is closer to the new life than she is. Yet, she can barely see him; he is a blur. Rose blinks a few times hoping to regain focus. She is anxious, but her body feels numb. She rests her head back onto the pillow and tries to both breathe and keep her eyes open. She feels so tired. Yet, she has been waiting nine months for this moment. She chants her mantra. *I will stay awake. I will not fall asleep.*

Enormous, broad shoulders draped in white carry the crying baby to her. Rose single-mindedly places her attention solely on

232

the form cradled in the arms that capably deliver the baby to her. Rose starts to emotionally swell as she lifts the sheet to see her baby's face. "She is beautiful. See, she is…"

Just as she looks to find her husband's reaction, flames erupt. They move down onto the sheets and then completely overtake the entire room, consuming everything. Rose tries to escape the flames as they find their way back to her bed and begin to crawl their way up. In sheer panic and terror she huddles the newborn into her chest. She looks again at the swaddling form in her arms. The sheet falls open and dull, grey ashes fall onto her lap.

Rose wakes herself with a profound heart ache, immediately followed by a deep, guttural single sob as she tries to catch her breath. *Why?* She rolls over to look at the face of her sleeping husband. His breath is deep and rhythmic; his face is light and stress-free. His eyebrows form the perfect arch. *I love you.*

She rolls onto her back and focuses on the ceiling. Rose lifts her head to verify that she is indeed not pregnant. She wipes the last full tear of her dream before looking at the clock - 5:20. *I should just get up*, she decides. Slowly and quietly she leaves her bed, stopping at the door to turn to look at her husband. "I love you," she whispers.

"Then don't leave," Aris responds. "Want to tell me about it?" he says mocking her as he pulls on his imaginary T-shirt. His eyes are still closed, but his irresistible wry smile is firmly in place.

"You're adorable. It's nothing, go back to sleep," she replies.

"I can hold you," Aris says disappointed in her response. "We don't have to talk."

Rose has no other choice than to return to him and climb into their bed. He is asleep upon her arrival. She just watches him for a full hour before the alarm sounds and the day starts.

***

233

As a result of a truly upset stomach, Rose has left work early and is currently sitting in her study trying to conquer her inconsolable mind and queasy stomach with a diverting game of solitaire. She knows that last night's dream was the most personally disturbing dream she has experienced to date. The sight, the sound, the feel and even the smell are still strikingly present in her mind. The heavy and hollow pain of her heartbreak still booms in her chest. It seems that even her go-to game of Solitaire cannot distract her. Yet, while listening to the fairylike sounds of her game's winning hand, it dawns on her that she cannot be alone in this. There must be other people also experiencing terrifying dreams – she just has to find them.

"Ahh, Solitaire." She immediately opens her search engine and adjusts her position in her chair. Her eyes shift their focus from the white screen to her hands seemingly frozen on the keyboard. She recognizes the stillness. It is almost as if she has forgotten how to type. *What are you afraid of, Rose?* she asks herself.

"Starting," she answers aloud.

After a few deep breaths, she finally finds the courage to type in three words: *Fire, dreams and prophecy.* Google returns with over seven million hits. *A start,* she thinks.

Rose spends close to an hour following various links. On the twenty-third link, she finds an amazing video trailer for an anime film, not yet released in America, called "The Child of Krakatoa." The three minute YouTube trailer features its main character, Miki, reacting to an eerily silent 1883 eruption of Krakatoa, the reputed "loudest sound" in the world. Rose reads an artist interview about the film that explains that the original idea was inspired by a recurring nightmare of one of the artists, Suzu Amano.

She reads that the film is being heralded as a supreme artistic achievement, for it portrays the aftermath of Krakatoa in absolute silence. One reviewer said that it was "as if silent film

234

itself was re-awakened by Krakatoa only to reveal itself in a brand new, spectacular Technicolor brilliance."

Rose sighs at the inspired concept. Suzu was able to find a purpose for her nightmares. Stirred by the realization, she immediately formulates an active plan that will hopefully pull her out of the firestorm heating up her inner self. She immediately logs onto her blog and gets to work. Within twenty minutes, she crafts a new web page featuring the anime short at the top of the page followed by a short paragraph explaining the purpose of the new site – to collect stories from dreamers. She uploads the narration of three of her own personal dreams to provide examples and includes a form to collect dreams from others.

Rose sits and waits nervously for what she hopes will be an influx of reassurances that she is not crazy. She knows that her website already carries a large readership – readers who are interested in disaster scenarios. If just a fraction of these catastrophe enthusiasts experience nightmares about disasters, she can use that information to soothe her haunted psyche. After two nail biting hours, Rose receives entries from three of her readers detailing their own harrowing dreams. By dinner, there are six.

***

After tossing and turning for two hours, Rose finally gives up on finding her much desired sleep. "Come on now, Rose, it was just a dream," she says to herself loudly enough that her next impulse is to make sure she did not wake her husband. She rolls from her back to her hip to look at him. *But it wasn't just a dream.*

Even after learning that there are many people out there experiencing nightmares, she still cannot find the strength to emotionally react to this morning's mind trick. She cannot dismiss it either. She wants the day to be over. She wants to go to sleep. She cannot – the day is not over for her.

"God?" she whispers. She waits for a response while lying in her marriage bed, completely still, without even breathing for a very full minute. Rose finally gasps and notes the clock – 2:00 AM. She quietly leaves her bed and her room. "You will talk to me," she says descending the stairs. *It was my baby.*

She reaches the kitchen and brews a cup of chamomile tea hoping to quiet her uneasy stomach, still upset from the morning's dream. "God? I can't marry him now, can I? I mean, if you are telling me that I can't have children, then I can't marry him, right?" She looks to the ceiling. "God?"

Rose lifts the tea to her lips and sips. "He should have stayed with Nora." She looks at the contents of her mug and thinks of spilling it on herself to feel something other than what she is feeling now. She giggles at the insanity of burning herself with tea. "The last temptation…"

Rose looks to the glass of the patio doors and her reflecting image. Tears start to form in her eyes, blurring the picture. She immediately wipes them and turns cold. "That dream was never meant to be mine. This dream…this dream is mine." She takes another few sips of tea in an attempt to steer her own mind. "How am I supposed to…God?"

Rose stands still and awaits an answer. Within seconds, she hears an audible voice speak into her ears. It says, "Parallel." Owing to the fact that it is rare for her to hear actual voices, Rose decides to acknowledge the voice. "Parallel? What is that supposed to mean? Parallel? Parallel tracks? Parallel Lines? Transversals? And by the way, don't try to fool me. You are not God." Rose regains control of her mind and attempts to coil around the full realization of the conversation she is having with herself, with God, and possibly, with the devil. "Why did I have to fall in love to find I cannot keep love?" Rose swallows a gulp of hot liquid.

She returns to her reflection. "Do I tell him, or do I just leave?" Quiet tears fall from her eyes accompanied by knowing

236

sighs and regretful breaths. "He won't believe you anyway. Just leave."

Rose begins to walk around the ground floor of her home. *There's not a lot of you here. Just a few pictures. He likes his job. He has friends.* She looks at her reflection again and, having moved away from the light of the kitchen, she can see more of the back yard. *You should take down the boom before you go.* These thoughts form larger tears. She sets down her mug and walks outside.

The night is dark and muggy. The temperature is seventy-two degrees according to the disk that hangs from the rose trellis. Rose takes the time to smell the roses in between her paces. "God, you know that I am beginning to think I am crazy. So help me make sense of this sacrifice, please."

She grips the grass with her toes and pulls up a few blades. "How am I supposed to do this? This government is never going to happen – it's stupid. These fire dreams aren't true –they're random; they're nothing. Aris is right. Yellowstone is never going to happen. He's always right. Why do I need to give him up? This heart is never going to get over his. You know I love you, but You are not the easiest relationship to maintain. Sometimes it feels one-sided…" Rose laughs at the causticness of this thought. She shakes her head as she thinks about the words she just uttered to God. "That must sound particularly funny to You. I would imagine that most of Your relationships feel one-sided." She walks to the edge of the lawn and places her hands on the pickets of the fence. "This is going to really hurt. It may even destroy… Are You sure?"

Rose pulls at more of the grass with her toes and while watching the action she discovers a very large white and brown feather resting under the gate's baseboard. She picks up the feather and smells it. She touches her cheek with it and then her lips. "Is this Yours or mine?" Rose starts to break. "I can't. I

237

love him too much. Leave him? I am going to miss him – like the Dickens."

She breathes a few more times before continuing her conversation. "Remember that cocoa thing? When Aris and I had that fight and he left? And I told You I would be better tomorrow. That I will dream a better dream? I thought this was the better dream. I thought that these moments of happiness with Aris was my reward for the work I did then. I thought..." Rose kicks the baseboard with her barefoot. "Ow!"

She stomps both of her feet several times and then jumps out a slight tantrum. "Great Expectations – rather than obtainable goals, You say? Was that You? Did You say that? I don't think so. So, I can't be a wife and a mother? I have to choose?"

Rose kicks the baseboard again. "Am I not listening?" Rose sits down on the dew covered grass and looks up at the stars. She sees the lights of planes and hears the sounds of cars. She rolls back onto her back and cradles her head in her arms. She straightens her legs and pushes against the wood planks. "I'm not listening. Probably because I talk so much. How am I supposed to do this?"

Rose puts her right ear to the ground. "I swear I can almost hear the grass grow. It sounds painful – like stretching on a rack." She turns her head to see whether her left ear can hear the same thing. She sees a rabbit duck under the shed. "My left ear hears it too."

Rose arches her back and balances on the top of her head to look at the trellis behind her and talks behind her stretched throat. "If I leave, he is going to be okay, right? He'll find someone who can give him the things I can't, right? His Mom is probably going to be happy. She really doesn't like me." She drops back onto her back.

Rose stares at the sky pondering, reflecting over the past ten years and the events that brought her to this garden. She sucks the dew off of a blade of grass. "God – I can't see when I am crying." Rose quiets and tries to focus on the sound of the grass, nearly falling asleep before her body jerks her awake.

Rose sits up and hugs her knees as she rocks on her sacrum on the soft, wet grass. She whispers aloud to her heart, "Patience? Impetuous? Am I being impatient?" She looks at her ring.

She tries to listen. She starts by considering her working definition of Patience. Her definition of Patience is not the first, or the second found in any dictionary. To Rose, patience means "quiet, steady perseverance." Her image of patience is Rosa Parks not yet sitting on the bus. It is a mother standing in line for gruel in famine stricken Somalia for her child. "I don't understand. Are you telling me to adopt?"

Rose performs a backwards somersault to standing. She walks back to the place where she found the feather and again, grips the fence. "Is this going to be my biggest mistake? Is this going to be my biggest sacrifice? How far am I going to fall? How hard am I going to hit? Will You take care of him? Will You please bring him someone even better? He is the best thing that has ever happened to me. You will take care of him, right?" Rose lets the tears fall. "Hear my prayer and judge my heart."

Rose sees the rabbit emerge from underneath the shed. She watches it watch her before it scampers under the fence and up the hill. Rose thinks of the first joke ever told to her by Aris. *How do you catch a unique rabbit? Unique up on it. How do you catch a tame rabbit? Tame way, unique up on it.*

"This is crazy, God. I love him. I am going to walk away from the only true happiness I have ever known – because of a dream. I am going to say it again – I am going to walk away from happiness because of a dream. No, that doesn't sound crazy at all." Rose kicks the fence and then looks at her toes. "Pain don't hurt. This God, this is going to kill me." She drops her head and closes her eyes. "Be patient, He says."

Rose laughs. "But you know I am much more like Impetuous." Rose turns as she hears Aris opening the sliding door.

"Thorn, what are you doing out here?" he says in a whispered yell.

Rose looks at him, confused. "I'm talking to..."

"Come back to bed. I miss you," Aris says.

"I can't. I can't sleep."

He follows her foot tracks in the dew on the grass. "Are you okay?"

Rose shakes her head. "I was thinking of the fable, The Eagle and the Arrow. The eagle is killed by an arrow feathered by one of its own feathers. I guess I would have assumed that the feather came from another eagle - kin. Then again, I guess you actually know when it is your own feather..." Rose chokes back tears in an attempt to feign composure.

Aris laughs at her. "Must be some conversation you are having...Come back to bed. We don't have to sleep."

"Ow," Rose mutters to her heart.

Aris watches her and her body language as she seems to grip the fence even tighter, as if she would rather hold on to the slabs of wood than to him. "You're not okay, are you?"

Rose closes her eyes and bows her head. "I need to be alone for now. We have the drive to my parents' house to talk. Okay?" She looks up at Aris. "It's just that I am not quite done here, okay? Just a few more minutes..."

"Rose?" Aris asks in a whisper as he peers through wounded eyes. "I'm worried."

"Make me breakfast?" Rose asks tentatively.

Aris sheepishly nods and leaves her alone in the garden.

"My feather? My priorities?" Rose says gripping the fence to complete her prayer. "God and my marriage." She bows her head for a nearly perfect minute of silence and then walks back into her home and into her marriage.

"Better?" Aris asks.

Rose looks across the room at his perfectly arched eyebrows and lies, "I think so. I'm hungry."

Δ25Δ

The Apes and the Two Travelers

TWO MEN, one who always spoke the truth and the other who told nothing but lies, were traveling together and by chance came to the land of Apes. One of the Apes, who had raised himself to be king, commanded them to be seized and brought before him, that he might know what was said of him among men. He ordered at the same time that all the Apes be arranged in a long row on his right hand and on his left, and that a throne be placed for him, as was the custom among men. After these preparations he signified that the two men should be brought before him, and greeted them with this salutation: "What sort of a king do I seem to you to be, O strangers?" The Lying Traveler replied, "You seem to me a most mighty king." "And what is your estimate of those you see around me?' "These," he made answer, "are worthy companions of yourself, fit at least to be ambassadors and leaders of armies." The Ape and all his court, gratified with the lie, commanded that a handsome present be given to the flatterer. On this the truthful Traveler thought to himself, "If so great a reward be given for a lie, with what gift may not I be rewarded, if, according to my custom, I tell the truth?" The Ape quickly turned to him. "And pray how do I and these my friends around me seem to you?" "Thou art," he said, "a most excellent Ape, and all these thy companions after thy example are excellent Apes too." The King of the Apes, enraged at hearing these truths, gave him over to the teeth and claws of his companions. ~ Aesop

Rose bounds down the stairs barefooted with her hair still wrapped in a towel. She is finishing the bow of her wrap-around cotton camouflage dress when she enters the kitchen. "Where's

242

Aris?" she asks her mother who is stirring a large metal pot of cooling blackberry preserves.

"He and your father are taking the boat out," Grace responds as she turns from the pot to look at her daughter. "We have preserves to can, you might want to change."

"Nah, this dress is like five years old – and it's camouflage. Blackberry stains would just add to it." She quickly towel dries her hair in the middle of the kitchen and then throws the towel down the hallway. She watches it land two feet from the door to the laundry. Rose returns to her mother with a shrug of her shoulders, as if she fully expected the towel to make the hard left turn and land in the washing machine.

"Rose, honey, would you please pick up that towel and while you're at it, grab the canning pot from the shelf in the mud room," Grace says with a restrained tone. This is immediately accompanied by a slight smile as she gently reminds herself that in spite of her present actions, her little girl is not fifteen anymore. The slight smile deepens as she recognizes and admires the woman that her daughter has become – a smart, successful young woman pretending to be fifteen for a moment as a sweet display of love for her mother.

Rose immediately leaves the kitchen to complete the task. She returns to find her mother lining up mason jars in rows of seven, her favorite number. The set-up is familiar. Grace has been making preserves for years. They are gifts for the holidays, gifts for extraordinarily obligatory dinner invitations, and gifts for her congregation members who are in dire need of a sweet treat. Her preserves are known throughout the community and are often placed in high demand by friends and relatives.

"We got a great batch of blackberries this year. That heat wave really helped," Grace says to Rose, who is standing at a peculiar distance holding the canning pot as if she is not sure what the next step is. Grace tips her head to the sink to provide her daughter with the next step.

243

Rose fills the pot with water and brings it to the stove. "So they're fishing?"

Grace leans the small of her back against the marble curve of her kitchen counter top and purposefully dries her fingers with a dish towel, pulling on each of them at least twice before speaking. "Listen, Honey, I have been chosen to be the one to talk to you. They have cleared out for a specified two hours, so that really does not give us much time." Grace then offers a smug smile to her daughter expressing the underlying humor of completely disclosing the covert family plan.

Rose moves to the other side of the stove to give the conversation more space. She slowly lifts herself onto the counter, balancing by her triceps, before finally lowering her seat onto the golden marble. She issues a knowing smile to her mother to cover her actions. Rose is fully aware that her mother does not approve of anyone sitting on the countertops.

"Get down," Grace says gently slapping her daughter's knee. She is only slightly annoyed by her daughter's adolescent tease; she is mostly amused.

"You were chosen to talk to me about what?" Rose asks straightforwardly, not budging from her current position. Her eyes suggest only a hint of challenge. She rocks her body from right to left and kicks out her dangling legs with enough control that neither her heels nor her calves touch the cabinets below.

Grace explains that while she was out for her run, Aris talked to the both of them. She describes his articulated concern about her nightmares and that he was looking for answers, possibly stemming from her childhood. "He was afraid of taking on a parental tone with you," Grace surmises.

Rose sighs and then hops down from the countertop. "So he tells on me to my parents. Isn't he cute? I mean, seriously, could he be any more adorable?"

"Oh, Honey, you should have seen him. He was nervous and tentative and…"

"And super cute I'll bet," Rose says.

"You don't know the half of it. Actually, Honey, he is much more handsome than I remember him being. I always thought he was good lookin' – but he really seems to have grown into a very handsome man. I really like him, Rose. And it is very obvious that he really loves you. And nothing could make me happier," Grace says while compulsively straightening the lines of the jars, again. "I think we are ready to start putting the preserves in the jars." She hands the canning spoon to her daughter with a motion reminiscent of a scalpel delivery system. "At any rate, he is worried about these nightmares of yours. He thinks you are obsessing, and that you might be making yourself sick - like you might spiral into another depression. Do you think he's right? Are you making yourself sick?" Grace asks these pointed questions without a hint of hesitation. She is confident that her daughter will be able to answer them.

Rose touches the base of her stomach and shrugs. She cocks her head to the right. "You know me, what do you think?"

"He knows you, too. Perhaps better than you realize," Grace says catching her daughter's eyes with her own.

"Yeah, he really does know me. Actually, more to the point, he understands me. I don't know what to tell you…" Rose pauses at this sentence as she thinks about the curious truth that drips from the offhanded phrase. She is not quite sure what she should say out loud versus what she should keep to herself. "Well, Mom, the truth is – is that these dreams are actually, I mean really, scaring the crap out of me, too. Seriously they really are *very* scary. Especially the one I had two nights ago."

She momentarily relives the harrowing feel of the ashes falling onto her lap, both soft like talc and oddly weighted. It is the remembrance of the peculiar weight of the ash that forces her mind to return to that moment again and again. "I dreamed we had a baby, a baby girl, and when she was brought to my arms in the hospital bed – she caught on fire. It was really awful. I could

245

feel the heat – it singed my nose," Rose says. She tries not to mention the ash. "I guess I almost know the feeling – of what it means to lose a child."

Grace immediately reacts to this statement with severe disapproval. "No, Rose, you don't."

"Sorry, Mom. You're right." Rose hangs her head for a few moments. "Well, it was a very bad dream. I woke up sobbing. But, at the same time, it felt like more. It felt like a warning." Rose tucks her chin and unconsciously grips the berry stained dish towel with white knuckled fists as she tries to force her mind away from the dream. "The dream - it really felt like a warning."

"Warning you about what?" Grace asks.

"About not having children. I think the dream told me that I should not have children," Rose says trying to forcibly maintain eye contact with her mother. She finds the simple action difficult due to the remaining unanswered questions spinning in the back of her mind. She wonders, not for the first time in the last forty-eight hours, whether she should be sharing these thoughts with anyone, for they could be lies. She knows she could be lying.

Rose restarts the conversation and spends the next twenty minutes filling mason jars and giving her mother the much needed back story – the truth of her night terrors. She starts with the one she had in her bedroom, in her room above this very kitchen, the morning before she quit her job. She explains that some of the nightmares border on premonitions. She tells her mom about the plane crash and Medicine Lake. "The truth is - I think God is talking to me. And that God is lifting a little bit of the curtain. And I am trying to be faithful and listen, but what's behind the curtain is really scary – too powerful to witness. The dream I had the other night upset me, it felt so real that my stomach is still tied up in knots."

246

"You still have that reaction? I could gauge how upset you were just by whether or not you can keep the contents of your stomach."

Rose nods, laughing at the odd personality trait. "I have been vomiting quite a bit lately. These dreams are really scaring the hell out of me. And Aris too, but for different reasons. He's scared because he thinks I am going insane. I'm scared because I think I'm telling the truth."

Grace opens the box of mason lids and starts to top the jars while she processes what she has just heard from her daughter. This is not exactly a new conversation for Grace. She has been through it herself. She was "called" into the ministry through a dream, a dream that could easily be called a nightmare. She knows the feeling that her daughter is trying to describe – a feeling of knowing, a feeling of understanding – a recognition of an impossible undertaking that cannot be denied. She finishes distributing the last lid of the box before speaking. "Do you think that this fire could be fire of the spirit – rather than the type of fire that burns?"

Rose clenches the fists of both her hands as if she is trying to hold on to something – something intangible. She finally starts to feel her vitamin enhanced nails digging into her palms, and this feeling alone allows her to relax her fists. "Maybe I am misinterpreting the fire. I hope I am. I've been talking to God about it, looking for another way out, but…" Rose momentarily leaves her mother's kitchen and relocates herself back in last night's garden smelling a feather.

"It's possible, right, Honey?" Grace asks gently. "Aris also told us about your blog – volcanoes and earthquakes. He thinks that your focus on these destructive forces – forces out of your control – are the reason you are having these dreams." Grace realigns the jars back into a straight line. "He also told us about your government of angels," she says with a smile of real interest in her daughter's art project and in her daughter's

247

academic theology. "You are making a government ruled by Virtues, the angelic rank?"

Rose smiles upon hearing this. "I think he thinks that I am taking it all too seriously. On the one hand, he could be right. Yet, his real fear is that I actually think that angels are going to descend after Yellowstone. And to him, that's just crazy..."

"So you don't?" Grace asks with a hint of skepticism. Rose's mother is prepared with ammunition given to her by Aris, who went into great detail about Rose's New World order as well as her experience at the psychologist.

"Well, it's not that simple. I do think, perhaps it is better to say that I *believe*, that we may see more manifestations of the divine after something like that. I mean, Yellowstone is a super volcano. It'll be a calendar changing event. I think the world will change. And that a greater sense of 'people' or 'person' can and will rise from the ashes. Anyway, the point of my government – did he tell you? I am in the process of writing a children's book, well I suppose it is more of a book for older children – it's a book about virtues. I am drawing a parallel between a governmental constitution and a person's personal constitution – like how a person becomes more patient, more understanding, and more faithful. I want the reader to really think about what these virtues mean. So yeah, it's a book that marries the virtues of the philosopher Aristotle with the anthropomorphic fables of Aesop. Instead of animals – I guess I am using angels. Either way – the book – the book is my wedding gift to him – the marriage of Aristotle and Aesop. It's romantic, right?"

Grace looks puzzled. "Does he know this? I got the distinct impression that he thinks..."

"I told him," Rose replies.

Grace continues her puzzled look. "The way he was talking, it was as if you weren't making sense. Or that you weren't grounded..."

Rose lifts her pointer finger as if to say, *one sec*. She quickly runs upstairs to retrieve the rough draft of the storybook complete with her amateur drawings of each story at the top of each chapter. "You remember my virtues, right? I started it years ago. Anyway, I found my old comic book while unpacking and well… I have decided to write my own collection of fables to teach children about virtues. I mean, I think most people stop with Patience and Chastity…" Rose flips to the front pages that introduce the colorful characters individually, like the Fashion Plates she played with in her church's nursery. She points to Patience in the shape of an hourglass and then to Chastity with a zipper body. "Do you think Chastity might be a bit too risqué?" she asks her mother with her humor clearly attached.

"I wonder why he is so bothered by this," Grace says flipping through her hand-made, hole-punched binder.

"To be perfectly fair, I have been waking him up nearly every night screaming in my sleep – blood curdling screams. I guess when I was a child I had really bad nightmares. You probably just thought it was the presence of an over-active imagination. Aris, well, I guess he is seeing things differently," Rose says. "Again, these dreams are really scary, much scarier than the ones of my youth. I wake him up – kicking and screaming. And there is this premonitory aspect to them. I don't know. I am sure that he just wants me to feel safe. And that because I am having these nightmares he feels he is somehow not doing his job…"

Grace obtains eye contact. "Have you figured out *exactly* what's bothering you?"

"Exactly?" Rose becomes silent as she realizes that she can answer her mother's question. Rose walks to the other side of the island to stand next to her. She grabs one of the jars and tries to twist it even tighter. "I think I do know," she says in a whisper to her mother.

Grace leans over to kiss the top of her daughter's bowing head. "Tell me."

249

Rose reels over in her mind the escape plan she began to develop last night in the garden, between the feather and the rabbit. The plan where she leaves the love of her life so that he can have the children he wants, the life he wants. She tries to picture her husband standing with Nora holding a beautiful baby. She closes her eyes with a hard squint as tears begin to swell. She tries to breathe in through her nose to stop the tears from making an appearance. She exhales. "I can't have children. I think all of this – breeding virtues coupled with the destruction of fire, volcanoes, and earthquakes – I think all of it is telling me I cannot have children. Aris really wants children – two of them. I don't know, but I think this is God's way of telling me that maybe me and Aris – maybe we aren't meant to be. Maybe if I leave now – we can still be friends. Maybe we were only ever supposed to be friends…"

"I can't believe that, Rose. You have been in love with him since the day you met. You can try to deny it. But you'd be lying. You love him," her mother says as she reaches her arm around her baby to motion to her that it is alright to cry. "I think you are just scared – love is scary. Love is supposed to be scary, scary and wonderful. I think you felt safer when you kept him at a distance. You weren't risking anything. Now, you have everything – and you fear you are going to lose it all. You are afraid that it will be taken from you as quickly as it came."

"Stop making sense, Mom," Rose says with a giggle as she wipes her snotty nose on her mother's shoulder.

"You found true love, Rose. Don't let the devil take it away," Grace says softly into her daughter's ear. "Marry him. Make babies with him. And Love him. I am sure God wants your happiness."

Rose hears her mother and wants to believe every single word. She wants her life and love to be easy. She wants her life and love to be happy. She wants the fire of her dreams to just be a fear of a real burning love. "But Mom, the dream, it felt like a

250

warning. Commanding me – 'Know!'" Rose looks down at her feet wishing that she could force this feeling upon someone else, so she would not have to explain it anymore. Her mind's eye returns to an earlier dream she had – the one where she tried to stop the ballerina from walking into the fire. "We've really only been together for five months or so…"

"You told Aris about this, didn't you?" Grace asks peeling from her embrace of her rarely submissive daughter. She begins to understand that the tentative Aris she met earlier might have been revealing a level of desperation, not solely about the nightmares.

"I did. Well, almost all of it. I didn't tell him about maybe leaving…"

Grace is able to see the entire situation much clearer now. "Don't. Don't you dare leave him. If you do, you would be crazy," Grace says in no uncertain terms. She looks down the length of her island counter top. "Rose, he knows. Whether you told him or not, he knows. He can feel it. I guess I'm beginning to understand his side of this conversation. He's afraid he is losing you. He told me you won't talk to a psychiatrist. Is that true?"

"Mom, you know how I feel about drugs," Rose says. Feeling restless with the conversation, she grabs another jar of preserves to twist the lid a little tighter. "We really should get these into that boiling pot."

"But you have spoken to a psychologist?" Grace asks.

"Yes, Mom. Aris asked and I obliged," Rose says quietly tightening the last of the row and then carrying it to the pot. She lifts the lid of the boiling cauldron and slowly lowers the jar, nearly burning her fingertips.

"Be careful," Grace warns. "Use the tongs."

Rose steps aside so that her mother can demonstrate. After a brief demonstration, Rose just collects the remaining jars and brings them to her mother. Her mother methodically lowers them, one by one, into the enormous pot.

"Mom, I am trying. I'm trying to be the best version of myself I can be. I want to make you and Dad proud. I want Aris to be happy. But, in the end, there is God. There is always and only God. If I really am talking to God, like I think I am, I cannot deny what I think he is asking of me. I cannot deny what I think he is telling me. You understand what I am saying, right?" Rose looks down at the ground and whispers, "I don't really think that this is my decision."

Grace sighs. "I know you believe what you are saying. If you think that you are being called, you have to listen. You're right in that you really don't have a choice. I do know what that feels like…" Grace takes a step closer to her daughter and gently grabs both of her hands. "But realize that the passion involved in the call that can tear you apart in one instance is the same that can put you back together. I'm sure that God put Aris in your life for a reason. The virtues of Aristotle and the fables of Aesop, seriously Honey, how beautiful is that? I think you two may very well be a match made in heaven. And it stands to reason that a little fire must go along with that. Okay, Sweetheart?"

Rose lets her tears fall as she reflects on what her mother said. "Hey Mom, did you know that Grace is a virtue?" She looks up from the ground and into her mother's eyes. "I love you, Mom. You always give the best advice."

"I love you, too." Grace leans in and kisses the hair of her daughter and takes in the sweet smell of her shampoo. "You used the baby shampoo."

"I like washing my hair with baby shampoo every once in a while," Rose says with a childlike voice. "I like being home even more. Thanks, Mom. I feel much better."

"Let's get these out of the water and call in the boys," Grace says, feeling better herself. "I think we should go out for ice cream at The Barrel. They have this new banana ice cream jam packed with dark chocolate chunks, candied pineapple, and honey coated macadamia nuts. It's called Crazy Ape. You've got to try it. We can get Texas wieners too. And the gravy fries you like so much."

"Yummy. Sounds great, perfect even," Rose says quietly wondering whether her stomach will allow any of those things. Rose looks down at her camouflage dress that picked up only a few spatters of blackberry. She completely bows her head. She wants to believe her mother; she wants to believe in the fire of spirit. *God, I want my mom to be right.*

"I'll finish up here. You go tell your husband you love him."

Queenie Mae

"Mommy, wake up. You're dreaming," Sweet says to her mother who has fallen asleep on the couch during their afternoon cartoons.

Her body judders awake as she hears the voice of her summoning child. She opens her eyes and laughs for the benefit of her three-year old daughter. "You are right, Mommy was dreaming." *Thank God, it was just a dream*, she thinks.

Sweet looks into her mother's eyes with a peculiar sensitivity before redirecting her attention back to her favorite cat and mouse. She clings to her beloved stuffed bear as she returns to sit Indian style in her place on the floor, in front of the coffee table, two and a half feet from the enormous television cabinet that holds a comically small television.

Queenie Mae sits up from her reclining position and instinctually fixes her hair. *You are a dreamer, Queenie Mae.* The pendulum clock on her mantle proves that what seemed like hours was, in reality, only a little more than thirty minutes. She inhales deeply and readjusts her position to an even more upright position. She tastes the inside of her mouth before asking her daughter, "You thirsty, Baby?"

Sweet turns her head and lifts her caramel colored bear in the air and speaks in his voice. "Please, thank you, Mommy."

Queenie Mae smiles at her daughter's manners which are so very unlike her own. Her daughter is kind, sweet, as her name would imply, and is very self-contained in her interests and mannerisms. Her daughter is like her own mother. Queenie Mae, on the other hand, is loud with a booming voice that can scarcely fit into her very petite frame. Queenie Mae wants a bigger life and a bigger television, but is too insecure to act on, or rely on, her natural motivations. She has learned time and time again that each of her rebellions will be indubitably met with both familial and social stumbling blocks. She has resorted to actively try to stop trying.

She stands and walks her tiny living room into her kitchen to get two glasses of orange juice. She takes a moment to appreciate her new favorite juice glasses. They are a classic peach amber glass that belonged to her grandmother as part of her everyday china. Her grandmother brought them by last week with no explanation. She begins to pour the juice just as her husband returns home from the call center where they both work in self-publishing.

"My Queen," Isko says hanging his coat and immediately leaning in to kiss his wife. "You're sweating," he observes. "Do I need to call about the radiator again? He said it was fixed."

Queenie Mae jumps her petite seat onto the kitchen counter. "It's nothing like that. I just had this dream. A bad one. A really bad one. Mayon erupted," she states concisely. "We were driving and singing and an earthquake swallowed our car. Sweet just now woke me up."

Isko lifts his eyebrows inquisitively. "You are having nightmares, again?" He looks over his beautiful wife, flush with color and asks, "Remember when we were first married and I took that job on the cruise ship?"

"How could I forget? It was the Titanic over and over again," Queenie Mae remembers. "I was Rose in those dreams. And you were Jack." She looks down to her bare feet and cannot help notice that she needs to touch up her paint. She grabs onto her ring toe to scratch off the remnant color and in the process decides that the red will be replaced with black cherry. "Maybe we need change again. You have to admit leaving that ship has been great for us."

Isko looks into his wife's face and asks with a particularly clinical tone, "Are you working on a book about volcanoes?" He

255

turns his attention to his daughter who is entirely charmed by the colorful movement captured by the box in front of her. "Hi, Sweet. I'm home."

Sweet hears her beloved father's voice and immediately responds to the call. She runs into the kitchen to throw her arms around her father's legs with an impressive display of strength. "Tatay." She takes a step back reaching her arms into the air adroitly asking for a helicopter twirl.

Isko obliges his daughter and lifts her into the air and spins. After two complete rotations, she lands comfortably on his hip. "Did you have a good day today?" he asks her.

"Mommy had a bad dream," Sweet reports.

Isko looks at his wife before responding to his daughter. "She told me. Maybe she needs to sleep with Taglay tonight?"

Sweet looks down at her bear and lifts him to her mother. "You can sleep with Taglay tonight. But, you will have to give him back to me, tomorrow. Okay?"

Queenie Mae walks toward her family and kisses her daughter on the cheek and grabs the paw of her daughter's favorite thing in the world as if to shake his hand. "Thank you, Sweet. I think I'll be fine. I have my Taglay to sleep with tonight. Your father is my Taglay."

Isko looks at his wife and asks, "I'm happy. Do things really need to change?"

Queenie Mae responds with a gentle kiss placed on the cheek of her daughter and then on lips of her husband before answering, "Maybe just a small shift?"

256

Δ26Δ

Choice, not chance determines your destiny. – Aristotle

Aris looks over to his Rose who has fallen asleep in the passenger seat, the top of her head leaning against the window. He huffs. He knows that he could never fall asleep lying like that. Yet he quietly rejoices in her ability. He was counting on this. He learned a decade ago that unless she is driving, she will always fall asleep about an hour into a long car ride. He does notice that her sleep is not a deep one. She is still performing smaller movements that indicate a level of lucidness. Knowing that she could very easily be awoken, he drives with extra care. All he needs to do, at this strategic point, is make it to the next highway exit before she wakes – the exit that will take the couple to Elkton, Maryland.

Thirty minutes outside of the Elkton, a sleepy Rose awakes. "Did I snore?" she asks, wiping the small bit of drool from the corner of her mouth.

"Maybe a little," Aris says. "Did you have a nice nap?"

"I did," she answers simply. Rose looks out her window in an attempt to get her bearings. It is immediately obvious that they are no longer on the highway. "Where are we?"

"Rose, we need to talk." Aris says with a very serious tone.

"We do?" Rose says looking at his profile, which is glowing in the light of the dashboard. "You're not locking me up, are you?" she says with a slightly nervous laugh. She has heard horror stories about such actions being taken. And over the past forty-eight hours, she has considered doing it herself.

"The past few days you've been acting distant. No, you've been distant. It started on Thursday morning and kind of progressed from there. On Friday morning, I found you outside

257

having one of your conversations – and you completely shut me out. And when I asked about it, you lied."

"Don't worry about that," Rose says. "I guess I was being a bit melodramatic. That particular nightmare was really awful." Rose looks down into her hands and then into the shadow of the wheel well. She brings her knees up and muscularly hugs them into her chest. Recognizing an opportunity, and in spite of what her mother suggested, she decides to start laying her groundwork. "Do you think that maybe we are rushing things? I mean, we did just start dating seven months ago, and there was a period in there when we were kinda broken up."

Aris looks to the balled-up form in his passenger seat. He returns his eyes to the darkened and deserted road. In an effort to be the master of his own heart, he tries to retrieve it from his stomach. It's not budging. The only thing he can lift is his turn signal; he changes lanes. "Rose, I was very serious when I moved that ring from your right to your left. God was my witness. So whatever scaredy-cat move you are trying to make right now – you're not going anywhere. You are my wife."

"Maybe that was the two of us getting caught up in the moment..." Rose says with a very weak voice. "And besides, that was before...before the nightmares...before the crazy."

Aris does not take this speech very well. "Caught up in the moment?" he spits in a forceful whisper. "You really are a terrible liar. Before the nightmares...Give me a break. Whatever this is – this has been going on for a lot longer. I know your process, my love. I can tell when something is rehearsed. I can tell when you are lying to me. These nightmares didn't just start five months ago or whatever. Seriously, how long have you been having these nightmares?" Aris turns to look at his bride. His eyes are strong and commanding. "And remember, don't lie to me. I deserve the truth."

"The truth?" Rose asks. She is quiet for a few long seconds. "I guess it started years ago. When I learned what evil was..."

258

Rose says quietly digging her nails into her palms. "When I learned what God sounded like…" She swallows hard.

"The rape?" he asks.

"The Fall," she replies. "The rape, the drugs, the denial, the loss…I can't tell you how lost I was. I started to hear God right before that. I ignored it and boy, did it cost me. But then he sent me you. You saved me from all of that." Rose starts to shake, like she is cold, like she is scared.

"Wait? So you've been having these nightmares for over a decade?" he asks.

"Yeah. But, they've just gotten worse since…since our engagement," Rose admits. "In the beginning, when these fire-slash-volcano dreams started, I guess I thought it was an independence thing, like I was afraid I was going to lose my independence. Stupid, I know. Now, I guess I'm just ridiculously afraid I'm going to lose you. I'm afraid that because I can't give you what you want…"

"You are never going to lose me, Rose," Aris says. He considers pulling over, just to put his arms around her. But he knows her. He knows that she will stop talking the moment she feels safe. He needs her to talk.

"You want children," Rose says with an unexpectedly simple tone.

"I do," Aris simply agrees. He remains silent for a moment, concentrating on the road ahead before saying, "I do want children. I think having children is a good part of life. Watching them grow. Teaching them things you learned. I also think parenthood teaches you something meaningful, that you can learn in no other way. And I really want to have children with you. I want to see your eyes and my ears discover things for the first time. Can you imagine?"

Rose starts to choke on her emotion. "I can. But I can also imagine…"

"Abdul in school," Aris says, catching her.

259

Choked with emotion, Rose tries to smile, laugh and breathe, all at the same time. She finally settles on the smile. "Yeah, Abdul in school." She stares into her husband's profile for a long second and then returns her attention to the passing scenery.

"I love you, Rose. I really do. I hope you know that if you want, we can adopt."

Her entire body tenses and relaxes in that moment, like a heartbeat. It was all she needed to hear. She looks at her husband to capture the moment, the perfect moment. *After all this,* she thinks. "Really? You mean it?"

"Really," Aris says evenly, with complete sincerity. "Of course, I still hope you will change your mind, but I understand. You are more than worth the compromise. And before you ask, I have given this quite a bit of thought. I know you're right. I know that there are plenty of children, already here, that need a home. And we can be a home for them."

Rose leans over and places the softest, gentlest kiss on his cheek. "You're perfect." She cannot stop the tears from filling her eyes. She tries to breathe; she tries to explain. "My mom thinks that I am having these dreams because I have everything I ever wanted because I have you. And because of that, I am afraid that I will lose everything – as quickly as it came." She reaches out her left hand in a request for his right. "She said that maybe I felt safer loving you from afar because I wasn't risking anything…"

"Your mother is an exceptionally smart woman, isn't she," Aris says.

Rose smiles upon hearing her mother complimented. "She's pretty awesome. My dad is too." Rose looks out the window at a green highway sign. "Elkton?" she says completely befuddled. "Where's Elkton?"

"Rose, we are getting married tonight at midnight," Aris states.

"What?" she asks sitting up straighter in her seat, caught naturally between both fight and flight. "Tonight? You're kidding me, right?"

"Desperate means call for desperate measures," Aris replies. "I have our license and our birth certificates and I'm seriously tired of waiting. I know that you say that our ceremony in the tree was enough for you, but your actions over the past few weeks are telling me otherwise. So, we are doing this for real this time."

"Wait? Tonight?" Rose asks, looking at the clock, slightly overwhelmed, but mostly intimidated.

"At midnight," Aris says. "A Tuesday. I have always liked Tuesday's. Tuesday is the best day of the week." He looks over his nervous bundle and produces a slight shrug and a kind smile. His eyes are kind and strong.

Rose looks into him. "You could try to be more romantic," she says wryly.

"We used to meet every Tuesday as friends," Aris says. "Then we fell in love. I proposed on a Tuesday. Remember?"

"Let's see… Do I remember?" she jests.

"We should get married on a Tuesday. It just makes sense," he says.

Rose cannot refute his logic. "Tuesday, the most romantic day of the week."

"We are going to marry at a bed and breakfast place, one that specializes in elopements. With the help of your mother and father, I learned that Elkton has a long history of conducting marriages on the fly."

"Are you sure you want to marry me?" she responds thinking about the morning he proposed, the last time she remembers seeing this side of him. She then processes what he just said. "Wait? My parents know about this?"

261

"I've been working on this for a while," Aris says. "We are getting married tonight, in front of God and witnesses. For better or for worse," he says, "and I have never been happier."

The happy couple pulls into the parking lot of a beautiful bed and breakfast that maintains an exquisite wedding venue. They pull up next to a Camry Rose immediately recognizes as belonging to her mother.

"My mom is here?" Rose asks, energetically looking around for other cars she recognizes.

"Your parents, my parents, and my sister, Mina. She insisted. Something about it meaning the world to her, or some other such nonsense. It's still a very small wedding..." he says, a little choked.

Rose starts to cry, both touched and ultimately relieved that this surprise wedding is still her wedding.

Happy to see the desired emotion, Aris continues, "Everyone cries at weddings. And Rose, we're ready." He grabs her hands and brings them both to his mouth. He captures her eyes before saying, "We are."

Rose shrugs her shoulders then hurriedly dashes out of the car to meet her mother who is excitedly hopping in the parking lot. "Mom, can you believe this?" Rose says running to her.

"Oh Rose, I am so happy for you," Grace says putting her arms around her daughter. "Come on now, we don't have much time to get you ready. Guess what? You're going to be wearing my dress."

"Mom?" Rose says. *A dress?* she thinks. She tries to squelch the millions of thoughts she has running through her mind – thoughts about family, duty, tradition and customs.

"Don't be scared. Be brave," Grace says gently. She turns around to Aris, waves and yells, "We will take good care of her for the next hour or so, and then it's your turn."

The couple exchange classic vows in front of God and family at 12:22 AM, August 28, a Tuesday. The bride wore a red cotton dress.

Δ27Δ

The Miser

A MISER sold all that he had and bought a lump of gold, which he buried in a hole in the ground by the side of an old wall and went to look at daily. One of his workmen observed his frequent visits to the spot and decided to watch his movements. He soon discovered the secret of the hidden treasure, and digging down, came to the lump of gold, and stole it. The Miser, on his next visit, found the hole empty and began to tear his hair and to make loud lamentations. A neighbor, seeing him overcome with grief and learning the cause, said, "Pray do not grieve so; but go and take a stone, and place it in the hole, and fancy that the gold is still lying there. It will do you quite the same service; for when the gold was there, you had it not, as you did not make the slightest use of it." ~ Aesop

"So the nightmares have stopped," Dr. Welsh says. "What has changed?"

Rose looks into the psychologist's grey-blue eyes, matching them alongside the thin checkered stripes of his dress shirt that are coincidentally both grey and blue. A smile appears on her face as she recognizes his very real attempt to treat her psychologically. She is content to answer his question with an explanation that is not exactly true, but it is also definitely not a lie. "Thinking that Yellowstone is really going to erupt and thinking that I had to do something about it... Well, suffice it to say, I was taking myself way too seriously. I guess another reason for the turnaround is that I also let Aris and my mother convince me that the fire in my dreams was not a warning, but a blessing. A spirited fire for my belly, so to speak."

264

"I see," Dr. Welsh says.

"I'm pretty sure you can't. Not yet, anyway," Rose says touching her belly. She announces, "I'm pregnant. Two months, almost three."

"You're pregnant, that's great," Dr. Welsh says with a genuine smile. "Good for you. How do you feel?"

"Happy. I'm happy, particularly now that my morning sickness is subsiding," Rose says. She lowers her head to look at her married hand on her belly as her mind reminisces.

She remembers, in full detail, the day she found out she was pregnant. It will forever be etched in her mind as one of the most remarkable days of her life. After weeks of her stomach being tied in knots, she finally gained the courage to take the test, knowing full well what the result would be. She was upstairs watching the pee stick's predictable sign when her husband came home, yelling for her. After putting the positive pee stick in the back pocket of her favorite Levis, she answered his call. As soon as she reached the stairway, she could see what the fuss was about. Aris brought home a puppy, a pure white Akita, six-weeks old. He explained that although she was not quite ready for children, she was ready for a parenthood of sorts. She was ready for a dog.

On that day, her two-week anniversary, her husband gave her one of the best gifts she had ever received. She accepted the gift with opened arms and immediately named the adorable white fur ball Cat. With Cat squirming in her arms, it only seemed fitting for her to give him his gift. Rose handed over the pee-stick accompanied by an enormous smile. "Are *you* ready?"

She was very happy that day, and has pretty much remained so ever since, taking care to let her husband know just how much. Nevertheless, because of the "a-bun-dance" in her oven, her mind continues its diurnal visits to the burning hospital bed and the heavy, swaddled ashes. This she takes care to keep from her husband, for better or for worse.

"Yeah, good for me, I'm pregnant despite my supposedly ninety-nine percent effective birth control," she tells the doctor. "I guess it's as it should be. I mean, I used to be very afraid of having children – bringing them into the world – the way it is. But now..." The mother-to-be shores up the belief in her own words by thinking about her overjoyed husband. "Aris is over the moon, although that's probably an understatement. He's probably even higher than that. He's over the ..." She tries to fill-in-the-blank but cannot find an acceptable replacement. Picturing her husband jumping over the moon atop a cow makes her smile evermore genuine. She returns to her original answer, "I'm happy."

"You have a very good reason *to* be happy," Dr. Welsh says and then genuinely adds, "Congratulations."

"Thanks," she replies. While inspecting a few of the pictures on top of the psychologist's desk, she recaps, "Yeah, good for me. I'm going to be a mother and my nightmares have stopped. I guess you were right." She looks directly at him. "Remember? You said the uprooting in my life was causing the nightmares – getting married, quitting my job, moving... I disagreed, but now that things are more settled, the nightmares have stopped." She swallows hard. *The remembrance of them, not so much.*

"So I see you have started school," Dr. Welsh says as he notices her employment status has been changed to student. "Why don't you tell me about that?"

"I am working on a Master's in Economics at Georgetown," Rose gloats, happy to change the subject to something more upfront. "It is an evening program for professionals. I've met a couple of really cool people. I am still working, too. A bit more than fifteen hours a week."

266

"Good. Good. Good. So, are you finding the classes difficult, interesting, satisfying?" Dr. Welsh asks.

"School is going very well. Apparently, I'm a natural, well according to my Macro professor. He likes me," Rose exclaims. "And because school is actually kind of easy right now, I have time to work on another new interest. I don't know if I told you about this on my last visit, but I am writing a children's book, and I'm making very good Progress."

"A children's book?" Dr. Welsh asks, boosting his patient.

"Yeah, the book is the proverbial phoenix that arose from the ashes of my nightmares," Rose says with an overt poetic pride. She tells Dr. Welsh of the headway she has made on her fictitious mythological epic. Thinking that he might find the pairing somewhat interesting, she relates the story of how Logic and Crazy met, fell in love and got married. "The couple will be having twins – Baby Sense and Baby Mania," she tells him. "I think they will likely play out in a Cain-and-Able-like narrative. One might kill the other…"

"Interesting," the doctor says.

Rose looks at the man behind the desk trying to decipher whether he *is* actually interested. Based upon his side of the conversation, she decides he is probably not. In the same moment, she also decides that she does not care either way. "It's a pretty charming tale so far, and I am very proud of it. I feel a sense of accomplishment – like I'm becoming an active part of my exponentially great grandfather's legacy."

The doctor nods. His eyes move from her to his notes that contain the minutes of their last meeting. "And what of your interests in radio? At our last visit, you mentioned that you were getting your amateur radio license…"

"Ah, radio – the reason for the boom," she replies.

Dr. Welsh cannot help but notice that the mere mention of the topic causes his patient to fidget even more than is typical

267

for her. "Have you made any progress there?" Based upon his notes, he is fully expecting a string of apologies why it has not been accomplished.

"Curious that you mention the radio… My husband and I had a pretty serious kerfuffle over the whole radio thing a few weeks ago, and I'm still *crazy* mad about it. I guess this might be something that you can help me process. It's all one big lump of stuff."

Dr. Welsh adjusts his seated position and issues his patient a look that efficiently requests more information.

Rose attempts to describe her mixed bag of emotions regarding the radio. She starts by telling the doctor a bit of the back story in that it was initially given to her as a thoughtful wedding gift by Aris to remind her of the many styles of communication. She informs the doctor that she was initially thrilled by the gift, but soon after it started to feel almost like a sentence. "I knew at the start that I was sort of being man-handled. You see, my husband loves to dangle new things in front of me to keep me what he likes to call grounded. He thinks he's subtle, but…" Rose issues a look that imparts a layer of categorical understanding. She sighs, "Anyway, I knew I was being 'handled' but I didn't know to what extent."

"Interesting. Go on," the doctor says while swiveling ever so slightly in his chair.

Interesting. He meant it this time, she thinks. She proceeds to tell the story she now calls The Twist and the Transformer. "After dragging my feet for the entire summer, I finally took the test. Not for myself, but for Aris and Abner. I did very well, not perfect, but I only missed one. Abner was very pleased, almost proud," Rose recounts with a sweet, respectful roll of her eyes. "Anyway, to celebrate, both Aris and Abner took me out to dinner. While at dinner, Aris announces to me that he has *his* license. He tells me that he's been a Ham since he was twelve years old. Can you believe it? Why would he keep

268

this from me? I mean, why didn't he tell me about his license as a reason for me to get mine? Why wasn't he my Elmer? And if he kept something as silly as this a secret, then…The shortwave of it is –I feel like I was carelessly manipulated."

"Have you shared these feelings with him?" Dr. Welsh asks.

"I did. I was actually *really* angry when I first found out. So yeah, I shared, loudly and in public," Rose says with a cutting smirk.

"Did he give you a reason for the wind-up?"

"He said he had two reasons. The first was that it was to be 'a story for our children,'" Rose says huffing through a restrained smile. "The second was that it was a good use of the idiom 'everything old is new again.' You see, on our first date, I told him about my love of idioms. He used that idiom about us. We are Aesop and Aristotle." She sighs deeply at the simple memory. "I suppose it's a little more than sorta romantic, letting me in on a little part I didn't know, and reminding me about something I nearly forgot, but I … I still feel manipulated. I know he's never going to apologize. He's quite proud of himself. The thing is – I worked so hard on not keeping secrets and his wedding gift to me was, apparently, the start of a pretty serious manipulative machination."

"Manipulative machination?" Dr. Welsh repeats and lets a small laugh slip.

Rose just nods. She is fully content with the phrase. "Not only that, but he knew I was struggling and he just kept on applying pressure. He was man-handling me. And I let him do it. What does that say about me?"

"I am not quite sure what you're asking," Dr. Welsh says with concern.

Rose exhales loudly and completely. She knows exactly what she is asking. It is a question about keeping secrets and not telling the truth, of giving in and not fighting back. Yet she does

269

not want to talk about ignoring the very clear directive to not have children as an example of giving in. She does not want to talk about how she let her husband and her mother reign supreme over what she "knows" to be the truth of her dreams as an example of not fighting back. She does not want to explain these things –not to him. She wants to keep it a secret. She does not want to tell the truth. *What does that say about me?*

"I think you are adding weight to a relatively light situation," Dr. Welsh says. "A couple of years ago, my wife was keeping secrets and I actually witnessed her having conversations in the kitchen that seemed almost cryptic. I knew something was up, but I chose to trust her. And I am glad I did. It turned out that she was throwing me a surprise party for the tenth anniversary of my practice. My wife may have lied to me and handled me, but her motivation was to give me a surprise gift. Although your situation is different, there are certainly parallels."

"Parallels," she says with a huff. She lowers her eyes to the swirled carpet and attempts to forcibly push out the creeping memories of that night she spent in the garden making plans to leave. She clearly remembers her rationale that night. She distinctly feels her hypocrisy now. With that balance ruling she successfully steers her mind back into the office where she is able to recognize that her taciturn doctor just shared something about himself with her. She responds in kind, "Were you surprised?"

"Very. But it was a good surprise."

Rose smiles at him. "I guess I can easily say that I was surprised, too. Very surprised." Rose looks off into the distance as she remembers her feelings and behavior at the restaurant. "Maybe it should have been a good surprise. I don't know. I almost want to blame my reaction on pregnancy hormones…It really isn't like me. I mean, I yelled in public. I yelled at him."

"Hormones at the beginning of a pregnancy can be pretty intense," Dr. Welsh says simply, coupled with a gentle movement in his chair. "Answer this, are you more bothered by his ruse, or your reaction to it?"

"Ah, the proverbial twist of the transformer. Am I stepping up or stepping down? The truth is – I don't know. Again, it's like one big lump of stuff." Rose looks at her feet and grabs her right ankle. She ponders for a few seconds, shaking her head at the majority of thoughts running through her mind – mostly of that night in her garden. *My vow and my priorities*, she thinks. She almost decides to share these permeating thoughts with the doctor – her thoughts about the priorities she set and the priorities she lost. Instead, she shrugs her shoulders once and lies, "I don't know. I really don't."

Dr. Welsh looks kindly at his patient. "Something tells me that you will probably choose to appreciate his effort. That is, if you haven't already." Satisfied with his own handling, the doctor closes his notes. "Well Rose, I am sure that I don't need to tell you that you have a heightened intellect and a heightened emotional state. This combination can be very difficult to balance and may pose many interpersonal problems. I'm sure you have faced problems being understood as well as problems being misunderstood. And you must know by now that dealing with these understandings can lead to both mania and depression. I am honestly glad to hear that your nightmares have stopped, but…"

"But I should beware?" Rose interjects.

Dr. Welsh nods. "We need to find a way to keep you on the even path. Although I still believe that anti-depressants could really help you, I fully recognize that now is not the right time to discuss them. But I am glad you are taking appropriate steps during this time. Seeing me is an appropriate step."

Rose graciously accepts his observations for what they are – dutiful. "You might be right," she says. As she holds on to

271

her right ankle, she reflects upon what she heard. She decides to impart her own method of managing. "My book is also an appropriate step." Rose returns to an upright position. "I think it is *interesting* that months ago the book was driven primarily by desperation, desperation coupled with a teensy bit of inspiration. Yet, now, it is running much deeper, much richer than that. It really is my phoenix – overflowing with tears of healing and color and flight. I mean, out of the ashes of all of those nightmares… this entire book just sorta fell into my lap," she says. Expecting it, Rose allows herself to experience the wash of the ill-omened weight in her lap of that bygone dream. Yet, after months of practice she can swiftly substitute the nightmarish image with one of herself, in a stenciled rocking chair, reading her book to her baby. Aris is nearby, watching from the doorway. It is her perfect picture. She exhales deeply and smiles. "It's like a divine gift, you know. Like God is on my side. Like everything I have experienced over the past few months means something. It meant something."

Dr. Welsh astutely detects the struggle taking place behind her eyes. He knows that she is not quite telling the truth, but he is not sure of whether she is aware of it. Nonetheless, he begins to understand why she received a diagnosis of bi-polar mood disorder.

Rose notices his deciphering eyes and reacts by bowing her head. "I'm doing well, aren't I? I'm not sure if I could be doing better."

Dr. Welsh lifts the corner of his mouth to reveal an implied agreement. "I'm going to schedule another meet in a little less than two months, around the second week of December," Dr. Welsh says flipping through his calendar. "In the meantime, enjoy school, work and your book. But if you want my advice as a parent – take advantage of good quality alone time with your husband – that and sleep. A baby changes everything."

272

"So I have heard," Rose reports. Rose gives him an earnest smile before standing and extending her hand over the desk. She nods her closing, turns and playfully skips to the door. "I am going to be a parent. What do you think? Am I ready?" She does not await an answer. She gently closes the door behind her.

Δ28Δ

The Swallow and the Other Birds

IT HAPPENED that a Countryman was sowing some hemp seeds in a field where a Swallow and some other birds were hopping about picking up their food. "Beware of that man," quoth the Swallow. "Why, what is he doing?" said the others. "That is hemp seed he is sowing; be careful to pick up every one of the seeds, or else you will repent it." The birds paid no heed to the Swallow's words, and by and by the hemp grew up and was made into cord, and of the cords nets were made, and many a bird that had despised the Swallow's advice was caught in nets made out of that very hemp. "What did I tell you?" said the Swallow. - Aesop

"Twins?" Rose says looking at Chandra, then her husband and finally her mother. She mouths the word, again. "Twins."

"Yep, twins," Chandra enthusiastically reports. "You can see that there are two distinct babies in here." She moves the transducer between the two forms several times and waits for the news to sink in.

"Twins?" Aris says. "Two babies?" He gulps.

"Twins. Two babies," Chandra says with an amused giggle. "You'd be surprised how often I have to explain what twins are in this office. Your response is normal. Although in a few minutes you might feel pretty stupid about asking those kinds of questions."

Aris hears her full meaning and produces a laugh in response to her joke. He stares back at the screen in an effort to force his mind to remember the definition of twins.

"Twins run like wild fire in my family," Rose reports as if she is not at all surprised by the announcement. She is actually

274

somewhat relieved to know that there will be two babies rather than one delivered into her arms. Unbidden, the images from her dream erupts in her mind. Wanting to push the nightmarish shadow out of her mind, she keeps talking. "Like wild fire. Right, Mom?" she says, looking to her stabilizing mother, who stands near the foot of the table. "There are lots of twins in our family. It's not a big deal, right? They are going to be smaller than a single baby, right?" Rose hopes that her preoccupation with the delivery is not obvious to her husband and mother.

Chandra issues a look that amuses both Aris and Grace, but instills out-and-out fright into Rose. The look speaks volumes but she adds, "Each one tends to be a bit tinier than average."

"Every generation has had at least two sets on my side of the family, both sides of my family, healthy and happy, and not all that small either," Grace says with a light laugh as she tries to lightly mock her daughter's understandable fear. "I will tell you though, that every single one of those mothers would probably list the birth of their babies on the top of their list of the happiest days of their lives. I'm so happy for you, Honey, and proud of you, too. I am going to have twin grandbabies."

"Do you want to know the sex?" Chandra asks scanning the room. She decides quickly that they are the type that will want to know.

Rose looks at her husband with raised eyebrows. They have been debating the question, but were leaning toward knowing. "I am pretty sure we do, right? Last chance to change our minds..."

"I think the fact that we are having twins is enough surprise. Let's find out," Aris provides their answer to the technician with a tone of resolute authority.

"Well, let's see..." Chandra starts pushing the transducer. "Girls have three lines denoting their sex. Boys, well, they are a bit more obvious. However I would say about half of the babies I look at are modest, so we might not be able to find out the sex today. You may have to wait, okay?"

"Modesty is a good virtue. I would not mind if our children are modest," Rose admits. "Our children..."

"Well, I hate to inform you, but apparently neither of your children is modest. See here, three lines," Chandra says with a gentle smile.

"Girls," Grace says. "I was hoping for a granddaughter. I mean granddaughters."

Chandra lifts her index finger to inform the room that there is more. "There she is. And look, here he is. A brother and sister."

Aris starts to feel a bit lightheaded. He cracks the knuckles of his right hand as he tries to regain his focus. "Two. I wanted a boy and a girl. And of course, she gave them to me," he says in a whisper as if in a prayer.

Rose grabs her husband's hand. "Two babies. A boy and a girl. Mom, look at Aris. I think he is going to pass out. Mark the date on the calendar, November twenty-fifth – the day Aris exhibits human behavior."

Grace walks to the other side of Aris. She pushes him gently aside to lean in to kiss her daughter's forehead. "This is so very exciting. Fraternal twins. Boy and girl twins are pretty rare, right?" Grace says to Chandra without breaking eye contact with her daughter.

Chandra pushes her transducer to again show the sex organs of both babies. "I don't see them very often. But I actually don't know whether they are common for twins, or uncommon. I do know that both of these babies seem to be developing well. Now I just have to take a few more measurements of their heads and necks. I will need a few moments of silence. I know I am asking a lot right now. You must be very excited, but I really need to concentrate," Chandra says with a calm smile and awaits nods from all three present.

One minute passes. "Sorry I cannot be quiet anymore – twins!" Rose exclaims.

276

The technician laughs. "Try to be quiet for a few more seconds please. I am almost done."

Aris bends to whisper to Rose, "I love you."

"I love you, too," she whispers back.

"Alright, I am done. The measurements look good. I will walk these to Dr. Patel and she'll be in with you shortly."

Rose starts to jump on the table and rejoices in her ability to break the silence. "Twins. A boy and a girl."

"Hey, I almost forgot. Congratulations to the both of you, all of you," Chandra says as she exits the room.

"Congratulations, Aris," Grace says hugging her son-in-law.

"Congratulations, Grandma," Aris replies.

"Nana. I think I want to be Nana."

"Mom, I'm going to have two babies. A girl and a boy," Rose exclaims. "What do you think? Baby A and Baby Z?"

"Your father is going to have a field day with coming up with names for twins," Grace says kissing her daughter again. "I am so happy for you."

Dr. Patel enters the room and greets the three beaming adults. She informs the future parents that the babies do appear to be developing normally. She also takes the time to go over warning symptoms and diet recommendations to accommodate two babies. She finishes her visit by informing the couple of their next milestone appointment before offering her own congratulatory remarks.

Rose, Aris and Grace leave the hospital, each exhibiting their own satisfied smile.

"Lunch?" Rose says. "I'm hungry."

"Wherever you want to go," Aris says lifting her hand in his and kissing it.

"Mexican," Rose says. "Guacamole, guacamole, guacamole."

Aris walks up behind her and puts his arms around her neck. Looking at Grace he says, "Her baby, I mean her babies, pretty much like guacamole and nothing else."

277

"Our babies...They -- you realize that they are a they now. They like cheese, too," Rose says. "Just like their grandmother."

"Who doesn't like cheese," Grace says. "How are we going to get to the restaurant? We have three cars right now. I wish I didn't have to go home. I want to stay here with you – and make plans and shop and... But, I have charge conference at the church tonight."

"I have to head back to work, too. Not like I will be able to get any work done," Aris admits.

"We can all drive to the restaurant and then part company from there," Rose suggests. "I think I'm going shopping for twofer deals this afternoon. Do you think they have twofer deals? Although it's a Monday," Rose says divulging a morsel of her excited internal thought process. "I cannot believe that I am having twins! Two, two, two – two of everything."

Aris, still trying to process the news, decides to steer the conversation away from the parking lot. "Grace, the restaurant is on Lexington, just two exits up," Aris says pointing to the highway. "Going North, of course. Although you can follow either one of us."

The three separate to find their respective cars with a plan to meet at the restaurant.

***

Upon their arrival at Rose's second favorite Mexican restaurant in the area, the closest, the three are immediately greeted and seated in a booth with a great view of an obviously stubborn birch tree still clinging on to its colorful leaves. The mom-to-be issues her drink order and politely excuses herself.

Grace watches her daughter walk to the restrooms toward the back of the restaurant, quietly noticing that her gait is changing. She immediately seizes the opportunity for straight talk with her son-in-law. "Tell me the truth, Aris. How is she doing? She tells me the nightmares have stopped. True?"

Aris smiles at his mother-in-law's question. He is happy that she knows her daughter well enough to assume she may not be telling her everything. He stretches his arms on the table before responding. "You must know that you have a very complicated daughter," Aris starts with a light shining from his eyes. "Well, it's true that the nightmares have stopped, but she hasn't. She is still preparing for the end of the world, just in a more subdued, academic manner. Her latest obsession is with Erikson, the child psychologist. You know the guy with the stages. She thinks she is supposed to be in the adult stage of Generativity and therefore she must make her mark for herself and her baby. It's mostly adorable, but also a bit disturbing. It is not exactly her style to rush in to adulthood, of all things," Aris says looking into the corner of their booth. "A-dolt-hood, is what she called it when we first met."

Grace just smiles at his observation, taking note of just how attractive he has become.

"But, I know she is hiding something from me," he continues. "I know she is, but I don't know what. For now, I am chalking it up to it all just being a part of the nesting, or whatever. She'll tell me when she is ready. I do have to tell you that she's been blasting this song from Kate Bush called 'This Woman's Work.'" Aris forces light laugh. "It's driving me crazy."

"She loved that song when she was in high school. She played it all the time. I guess I could easily say that I know what you are going through. Has she tried singing along?" Grace asks laughing at the memory.

"No, I haven't had that pleasure," Aris says, chuckling. He smiles because of the moment he is sharing with his new mom. He thinks about calling her Mom, but hesitates because he fears it will sound forced. "Anyway, Grace, to answer your question. I think she is doing alright. I am pretty sure that the nightmares have stopped. She is sleeping better and so am I. But now we have these twins… I can't imagine what the thought of twins

279

will do to her. I was wondering...I thought it was normal for women to be tired in their pregnancy? It seems they are giving her even more energy, if you can imagine."

Just as Aris is finishing his update to his mother-in-law, his wife appears at the corner of the booth. "You guys done talking about me? If not, I could probably just go pee again. And I'm not kidding. Do all pregnant women have to pee this much?"

The three sit down to a colorful lunch of Mexican fare with extra portions of guacamole all-around for the expectant mother. The conversation is fun and easy as they discuss baby showers and diaper disposal. All want to remain in the moment, celebrating this amazing news, but appointments must be kept.

After paying the bill, the party walks out of the restaurant together. While forming an easy, social triangle on the side walk outside the restaurant and exchanging departure pleasantries an odd occurrence takes place beneath their feet – a barely detectable tremor. An earthquake.

"Did you feel that?" Rose asks.

"I did. I'm pretty sure we just had an earthquake," Grace says with a surprised tone. She off-handedly rushes an explanation to her son-in law. "We used to have them all the time when we lived in California, small tremors. I guess we had a couple 'seisable' ones too," she says lightly elbowing her daughter with pride in her pun.

"What? We just had an earthquake?" Aris asks, a little dazed. "In Maryland? Are you sure? I don't believe you."

Grace looks at her son-in-law with a calm look, as if she is completely unfazed by the disturbance beneath their feet. "I'm pretty sure we did. I'm sure they will say something on the news. It was just a tremor, though. It probably wasn't much more than a two point five. It's nothing to worry about."

"My mom has her own personal, internal Richter scale," Rose jokes, also seemingly nonplussed by the incident.

Aris looks between the two thinking that both should be having a greater reaction to the fact that there was just an earthquake in Maryland. He decides that if they can be nonchalant, he can too. "But this is Maryland?" he mutters.

"You do get the feel for these things," Grace says. "A two point five is my guess.

"A two point five, huh," Rose says. She wraps her arm around her mother's waist and leans her head on her shoulder. "I love you, Mom. You and your internal Richter scale."

"I love you, too," Grace says, returning her daughter's hug. "Aris, continue taking such great care of my daughter. I really have never seen her this happy."

"There's nothing I would rather do," Aris says replacing Rose's disengaged embrace with his own. He then demonstrably follows her orders and immediately puts his arms around her daughter. The three quickly discuss their Thanksgiving plans. Aris promises Grace that both he and Rose will be there for Thanksgiving, arriving late Wednesday evening.

Aris kisses Rose gently as she walks him to his BMW. "I love you, Thorn," he says. "Thank you for giving me everything I ever wanted. And have fun shopping. I'll call you from work. I think I can use this as an excuse to get out early. Keep your cell phone close, okay?" Aris gets in his car, starts the engine and looks through the windshield at his bride and her mother, who is standing nearby.

Rose uses her thumb, index and pinky fingers to sign her response as she steps away from his car and closer to her mother. She then hugs her mom and says her good-byes before stepping toward her own blue Mazda, parked immediately next to her mother's red Camry. Rose watches both Aris and her mother leave the parking lot before starting her own car.

"God, twins?" She smiles as she looks up and out her windshield and talks to the sky. "Twins. I think this means I can eat and eat and eat. I want chocolate. I want popcorn. I want ice cream. I also want to let You know just how thankful I am. It's like a dream – one of those good ones."

***

With the sounds of stopped traffic to her left and rescue workers to her right, the upstart News 4 reporter occupies herself with fixing her pumpkin colored cashmere scarf that, in her opinion, beautifully offsets her tailored cyan woolen coat. She does this in an attempt to subdue her frustrations with her camera crew. To her, it is essential that she does this spot before rescue workers remove the boulders decorating the highway, but for some reason, her camera crew is not exactly cooperating. She finally receives the long awaited signal from her well-seasoned camera man. She puts on her game face. "This is Brianna Walters, reporting live from the 495 beltway on site of a fatal accident, near Tacoma Park, Maryland. The accident involves several passenger cars and a tractor trailer transporting new Lexus vehicles to a dealership in Baltimore. According to police reports, the driver of the tractor trailer, a Steven Russell from Raleigh, North Carolina, who was life-flighted from the scene, lost control as a result of his efforts to avoid an enormous boulder that fell from this mountain cliff onto the beltway."

Brianna steps to her right to allow for better camera access to the scene behind her. "From these fragments, you can easily see that the boulder was indeed, gigantic. Crime scene specialists are piecing together that the boulder must have been shaken loose by a deep-set earthquake, now being reported by the USGS to be a significant, seismic four point eight."

The attractive brunette reporter points down the highway. "According to the eye witness accounts, the driver was initially able to avoid the majority of the boulder but lost control after hitting one of these two fragments," Briana says capably leading the camera man. "This collision apparently resulted in the transporter truck fish-tailing for several hundred feet, hitting several cars before slamming into this blue Mazda." The camera shows the charred remains of the vehicle. "It is being reported that the impact detached the trunk of the Mazda severing the gas line leading to an immediate and intense fiery explosion. Although police and fire rescue arrived only a few minutes after the initial collision, it was too late for the driver of this vehicle. It is not known, at this time, the identity of the driver in the Mazda. Traffic will be backed-up for several hours. It has also been reported that there have been smaller tremors in this area, tremors that are now being called after shocks. Drivers are warned that these tremors could result in more falling rock. Extra caution should be practiced. This is Brianna Walters, reporting live for News 4, Tacoma Park, Maryland. Back to you, Doreen.

火山 29 火山

What did the dad volcano say to the mom volcano?

Do you lava me like I lava you?

Seven hours later, across two time-zones…

Horse steps out onto his apartment balcony to enjoy the spectacular skies. The Northern Lights are stretching much further south than normal and Horse is completely enchanted by their presence. He is accompanied by his faithful companion and best friend, Joke, a Border Collie–wolf mix. With his scientific mind also processing their special presence, he cannot help but feel the heightened electricity in the air. He looks down upon the hairs on his arm to verify that this *feeling* is factual. The difference in the air's electricity is subtle, virtually undetectable, but it is definitely there, as evidenced by the hair on his arm. His spine chills and he shakes his shoulders in response. "There is something in the air tonight, Joke – something charged, something spiritual, and something extraordinarily sad."

Joke barks once as if in agreement.

Horse looks down upon his companion. "Beautiful, isn't?" He laughs to himself as he recalls the Indian myth about the Northern Lights that he heard a few months ago from Cheyenne. "Do you know what land this is?" He pauses to wait and see if Joke wants to take part in this conversation as well. "You are in the Land of the Northern Lights." Horse then recites the only remaining lines from the story he can remember, "And the chief said, 'I came here many years ago from the lower country. I walked along the Milky Way, which is the same trail over which you came.'" He looks at his companion and then looks up at the sky. "So you see, now *this* is land of the Northern Lights."

Benjamin joins his friend on the balcony and hands over a Corona. He is peculiarly quiet for a moment, as if the sight of the Lights has a stunning affect upon him; yet, it is only for a moment. "This is the land of the Northern Lights?" he says with a mocking tone. "Dude, with every day you spend with this Indian girl you are getting goofier and goofier."

Horse lifts the right side of his mouth and almost responds defensively. He catches himself. "Are these the last two?" he asks. He looks to his friend as he lifts the bottle to his lips. He returns the mock, "So, when are you leaving?"

"Right after I convince you to come with. Come on, Kemosabe, it's like a holiday. We should be celebrating," Benjamin replies. Always looking for a reason to drink, Benjamin arranged a pre-Thanksgiving get-together for the gang at work. He is hoping that, with the help of lubrication and his fellow colleagues, the night will convince the new girl, Loni, to give him a chance. "Come out, Dude.".

"Nah, not tonight. I think I will spend the evening enjoying the light show with Joke." He pets his dog. "It's gorgeous out tonight. There is something special in the air – something deeply sad and beautiful. Don't you feel it? Like something is out-of-place, lost; like the skies are crying and rejoicing at the same time. I guess what I am saying is that I just don't feel like dulling my senses – not tonight. Definitely, not tonight."

Benjamin sighs. "Indian jibber jabber. So what you are saying is … Are you gonna come out, or what?"

"Duuuude!" Horse makes an attempt to speak his friend's language. He immediately reverts to his own. "Nah, Man. I have to pack and Cheyenne's gonna call in just a few," he explains.

"It's too bad that Apache goddess lives in Canada. But it's cool that you guys are seeing each other this weekend. So, she's gonna meet the 'rent."

"Actually Cally, she's Cree, Cree and Cherokee, not that that matters. Well, not to her, anyway." Horse takes a swig of his beer as he thinks about the beautiful treasure he recently discovered at his favorite watering hole – a graduate student

285

visiting from Canada. A Cherokee-Cree Indian who cares enough to fly south to meet his mother. Horse takes another sip. "My mom is going to love her," he reports.

Benjamin bounces his fist off the wooden railing and then knocks. "Last time, Dude. You're coming out, right? What do you think cell phones are for? You don't have to stay home and wait for a call. And you can pack tomorrow," Benjamin, being Benjamin, unrelentingly implores his friend. "Did I mention that Loni is going, and she's a local?"

"Loni? Cally, when you are you going to admit that you are the one interested in Loni," Horse asks.

"The moment she stops being interested in you," Benjamin says with a deliberate shortness. "Hey, why don't you come out and tell *us* all about Cheyenne. How pretty she is, how nice she is, how smart she is…"

Horse laughs at his plan. "Sorry, Friend, you're on your own tonight. I really do want to try to catch up with these guys from the other side of the Milky Way. And Cheyenne is gonna call in like a minute," he says looking at his cell phone clock that is inching toward their pre-arranged phone date.

"Visitors from the other side of the Milky Way? Say no more, Kemosabe. Enjoy communing with Mother Nature, the Great Spirit and all that Indian stuff. We'll be at Red Rocks if you change your mind."

"Have a good time and don't forget we have an early shift tomorrow – a really early shift."

Benjamin nods and pets Joke. "Stay cool, Dog." He returns to the apartment, grabs his keys from the counter and pounds the remaining liquid in his bottle before throwing it into the recycling bin. "See ya, bright and early," he calls before leaving.

"No Joke, that guy drinks way too much," Horse says scratching behind his dog's ear. Horse looks up into the Northern Lights and is immediately taken in by their gentle patterns. He remains still, entranced until the phone rings.

286

Horse answers. "Hey Cheyenne. You won't believe who's visiting me right now," he says smiling, just anticipating the sound of her voice.

"Hey," Cheyenne responds.

"They're visiting from the other side of the Milky Way," Horse provides an easy clue.

"Heaven's DNA," Cheyenne responds with a picture of how she sees the Northern Lights.

Horse immediately jumps into the conversation he wants to have. "I am excited to have you meet my mom. I think you are really going to like her. I am sure that she's gonna like you," Horse says. "So what time are you arriving in Sioux City?"

"If all goes well, and there is not too much snow, seven fifteen," Cheyenne informs. "But they are predicting a bit of a squall. It's only like seven inches, nothing too bad. And it might not start until after my plane takes off."

"What's seven inches in Canada?" Horse asks.

"About eighteen centimeters," she says laughing.

"The sacrifices you are prepared to make for a stupid American. Thanks for dumbing things down for me."

Cheyenne's smile comes through the telephone. "I wish you could bring Joke."

Horse squats down to look into the eyes of his best friend. He scratches him behind his ears and then under his chin. "Did you hear that Joke? My girl likes you," he says. Horse grabs the mouse chew toy from the Adirondack chair and offers it to his friend. Joke accepts the gift with puppy-like fervor. "There is always a Joke with me. No worries, he'll be there."

Joke mews.

ABOUT THE AUTHOR

She wrote this novel as a sequel to *White Lies and Dark Chocolate*. She was told by a good family friend that in order to sell book one, you must write book two. Because the message of book one is so very dear to her, she wrote this novel in an attempt to capture a larger audience. The author does have Bachelor's degree in Biology and a Master's degree in Theological Studies. All the same, she is pretty certain that these things really don't matter to the reader. She does hope that you, the reader, enjoyed this novel enough to recommend it to a friend as well as pick up a copy of *White Lies and Dark Chocolate*.

www.ingramcontent.com/pod-product-compliance
Lightning Source LLC
Chambersburg PA
CBHW022146170626
46807CB00005B/2094